PRAISE FOR *BLACK NOWHERE*

"Reece Hirsch serves up the perfect blend of science and story in *Black Nowhere* . . . This is truly eye-opening stuff. *Black Nowhere* is so cutting edge you almost need gloves to turn the pages. A relentless ride with as many dips as a roller coaster and as many darts as NASCAR."

—*Providence Journal*

"A brisk and provocative series launch."

—*Publishers Weekly*

"*Black Nowhere* showcases author Reece Hirsch's mastery of the suspense thriller genre with this FBI procedural novel that will hold the reader's rapt attention from cover to cover."

—Midwest Book Review

"Hirsch adapts the realities of our brave new high-tech world into an entertaining nail-biter . . . Hirsch's protagonist, FBI special agent Lisa Tanchik, an online chameleon who infiltrates the criminal network, is an exciting heroine for these digitally defined times."

—*Diablo Magazine*

"There's something great about being embroiled in a book series from the start. This fantastic series launch will form part of the Lisa Tanchik series . . . We're expecting good things."

—Yahoo Style UK

"*Black Nowhere* is a next-gen thriller that will leave your fingertips blistered from scrolling pages so fast. Prepare to lose sleep!"
—Blake Crouch, *New York Times* bestselling author of *Recursion*

"*Black Nowhere* is an extremely unsettling thriller that haunted me for weeks. It's a shrewd critique of Silicon Valley start-up culture, a brisk FBI procedural, and a chilling look at a very modern form of amorality."
—Dave Eggers, author of *The Circle* and Pulitzer Prize and National Book Award finalist

"*Black Nowhere* is a blast. A gripping thriller with wonderfully nuanced characters. If you haven't been reading Reece Hirsch, it's time to start."
—Lisa Lutz, *New York Times* bestselling author of *The Passenger*

"*Black Nowhere* is a Dark Web *Scarface* for the twenty-first century! Hirsch hits all the right notes in this fast, smart, and timely cat and mouse page-turner that exposes the false utopia promised by the modern internet. I hope there is much more to come from Special Agent Lisa Tanchik."
—Matthew FitzSimmons, *Wall Street Journal* bestselling author

"Special Agent Lisa Tanchik is a terrific lead character, passionate about her work as she journeys into the Dark Web where cybercriminals lurk and nothing is what it seems. A must-read!"
—T. R. Ragan, *New York Times* bestselling author

"Smart, intense, and frighteningly real—I loved this book! Readers who enjoy thrillers with a heavy dose of high-tech computer wizardry will devour Reece Hirsch's gripping new novel. When two of the smartest people on the planet face off in a cat and mouse game that might be the end for them both, the outcome is anything but certain."
—Karen Dionne, international bestselling author of *The Marsh King's Daughter*

"A sleek and suspenseful state-of-the-art thriller with crisp writing and engaging characters that has something to say about the way we live now."
—Peter Blauner, *New York Times* bestselling author of *Sunrise Highway*

DARK
TOMORROW

OTHER TITLES BY REECE HIRSCH

The Insider

CHRIS BRUEN NOVELS

The Adversary
Intrusion
Surveillance

LISA TANCHIK NOVELS

Black Nowhere

DARK TOMORROW

REECE HIRSCH

THOMAS & MERCER

Text copyright © 2020 by Reece Hirsch
All rights reserved.

Published by Thomas & Mercer, Seattle
www.apub.com

Amazon, the Amazon logo, and Thomas & Mercer are trademarks of Amazon.com, Inc., or its affiliates.

ISBN-13: 9781542093262
ISBN-10: 1542093260

Cover design by Rex Bonomelli

Printed in the United States of America

To those who defend the United States against cyber threats

Frankly, the United States is under attack.
—Dan Coats, director of national intelligence,
speaking to the Senate Intelligence Committee about
foreign cybersecurity threats
February 12, 2018

1

Day One

Traffic was light in the late evening, so DC's national landmarks flashed past in rapid succession on Constitution Avenue: the Lincoln Memorial, the World War II Memorial, the Washington Monument, the Capitol. Under a fluorescent moon on a cold, cloudless January night, all that white marble looked downright funereal. Or maybe it just seemed that way because FBI special agent Lisa Tanchik was on her way to a crime scene.

As she drove north into Maryland with few cars on the highway, her thoughts replayed the day's events, which had started with the class on cybercrime investigation that she had taught that morning at Quantico and concluded with a couple of bureaucratic skirmishes over her pursuit of a phishing ring. Today had been one of her dark days, when she watched life happening to her like a patient under anesthesia. Her depression was so constant a nemesis that she had given it a nickname, the Black Dog, a phrase borrowed from Winston Churchill. She imagined Black Dog curled in the passenger seat now, rising to sniff the air occasionally when the car jostled him.

She lifted her coffee from the cup holder and took a couple of strong sips. When she'd received the call to this scene, she'd been at her Dupont Circle home with her boyfriend, midway through her third glass of wine. Jon had questioned whether she was in any shape to take the call, but Lisa would not be dissuaded.

This was her first lead in months on a hacker whom she had been pursuing.

And now the hacker had graduated to murder.

On dark days like these, it helped to have a problem to work, so she thought about what she knew so far about the crime (next to nothing) and the likely perpetrator (quite a lot). She reviewed everything that she knew about the MO and characteristics of the hacker she had been pursuing for nearly a year. She wanted the details to be fresh in her mind when she reached the scene.

At 11:35 p.m., she parked in front of a faux-colonial apartment complex in Columbia, Maryland. Columbia was a bedroom community south of Baltimore and about thirteen miles from Fort Meade, the head-quarters of the National Security Agency. A lucky break had brought her there. Lisa had issued a law enforcement alert for a very distinctive MO, and an officer with the Howard County Police Department had been diligent enough to read it and generous enough to alert her while the scene was still fresh.

Lisa downed the rest of her coffee, popped three breath mints, and stepped out of the car and into the cold.

The lights were all on in the apartment complex's lobby. A young uniformed officer was questioning the manager. The officer looked up at the frigid blast of wind as Lisa pushed through the door.

"You're FBI?" He sounded a little disappointed, like she didn't live up to his expectation of what someone from the bureau should look like.

"Special Agent Lisa Tanchik. They're expecting me."

"I'll walk you over." Then, to the apartment manager: "Could you wait here for a minute? We're almost done."

The manager jerked his head, a tense nod. Lisa couldn't tell if he was nervous about being in proximity to death or law enforcement. It was often difficult to distinguish the difference.

"So you've seen this sort of thing before?" the officer asked.

"Maybe. I'll know better once I get a look. The voice mail I got from your boss didn't provide many details."

"Well, I've never seen anything like it," he murmured.

There was another uniformed officer standing in front of the entrance to a two-story redbrick town house apartment. The door to unit C16 was closed, and there was already a strip of yellow crime scene tape across the doorway.

"She's from the FBI," the young officer said. "Special Agent—Tanchik?" He glanced at her for confirmation.

Lisa nodded.

When the door opened, the first thing she noticed was the lurid lighting. The small otherwise-dim living room pulsed with the bright white of a strobe. It had an immediate and disorienting effect.

The source of the flashing was the large computer monitor on a desk in the left corner of the room. A middle-aged man was splayed on the carpet nearby, his body twisted and back arched like a parenthesis, fists clenched. Lisa shielded her eyes. Murder scenes were always grim, but the harsh light, flashing at high frequency, added a particularly nightmarish quality. Along the rear wall, a large window looked down on a heated swimming pool from which spectral steam rose.

A man in a suit and overcoat who'd been standing near the window approached. He had a gray-flecked, close-shaved beard. The suit indicated that he was the homicide detective in charge of the scene.

He extended his hand. "Glad you could get here so quickly. I'm Detective Dexter Smalls." He nodded to the flashing computer. "This look familiar to you?"

"It does."

"This is some fucked-up shit."

3

"Yes it is."

"I didn't want to touch it until you'd had a chance to take a look."

"Thanks." Lisa approached the monitor.

She pulled a yellow Post-it note from a pad on the desk and stuck it over the computer's webcam.

"Why did you do that?" asked Smalls.

"Because for all we know the attacker has control of the webcam and is watching us right now. I'm also going to turn off the microphone."

"Crap," Smalls said. "You think that's a real possibility?"

"I'd say it's more likely than not."

Although there was a dead body on the carpet only a few feet away, for Lisa the circuit board and other components encased in brushed chrome were the true crime scene. The killer would not have left any fibers or latent prints in the apartment, but that didn't mean that there weren't any clues to her identity.

After disabling the computer's mic, Lisa turned her attention to the email attachment that was the source of the strobing light. She only glanced at it for a second, but it was enough to momentarily blind her, leaving an afterimage of green splotches swelling in her vision.

This was the same type of weaponized GIF that had been used in half a dozen other attacks that she had investigated, all of them aimed at victims who had been diagnosed with epilepsy. The victims had been tricked into clicking on the attachment, activating the strobe, and possibly inducing an epileptic seizure.

Her investigation, which was supervised by Special Agent in Charge Pam Gilbertson in the San Francisco field office, had begun nearly a year ago when the first strobe attachment had been sent to a journalist who had written several investigative pieces on white nationalist movements. There were no apparent links between the victims, except that they had all been journalists or strident political voices, whether from the Left or the Right. That told Lisa that the attacker was not an ideologue, but rather someone intent on deepening the divisions within the nation—and willing to kill to advance that objective.

In half of those cases, the strobe had failed to cause the desired effect. In three other cases, nonfatal seizures had been induced. It had been three months since the last attack, and this was the first fatality.

John Rosenthal had been very unlucky.

The strobe was designed to be difficult to deactivate, but Lisa had enough experience with the exploit to know how to turn it off. With a few keystrokes, she returned the room to its original dimly lit state.

"That's a relief," Smalls said. "That damn thing was giving me a migraine, but I didn't want to screw up your forensics."

With the GIF deactivated, Lisa could see the email that was open in the victim's in-box. It read:

> Honey, Sally sent us another cute photo from Henry's drama recital. Check it out.

The email address appeared to belong to the victim's wife, but Lisa already knew that there would be a telltale glitch, at least one wrong character, which the victim had failed to notice in his haste to view a family photo.

Lisa studied the sender's email address: laney.rosenthals@zapmail.com.

She leaned in close to the monitor, looking for another email from the same person, which she found soon enough. The address was laney.rosenthal@zapmail.com. Minus the extra *s*.

"The attacker was spoofing the email of, I'm guessing, his wife."

Smalls stepped up next to her to see for himself. "That one letter makes all the difference, doesn't it?" He shot Lisa a look, and she worried for a moment that he could smell alcohol on her breath.

"We can contact the email provider," she said, "get the account information for that address, but I'm not expecting much. Okay if the FBI handles that?"

"Sure. They'll probably respond faster to a request from the feds."

"Has the family been notified yet?"

"Yeah. The wife wasn't able to reach Rosenthal by phone or text, so she called the apartment manager, who opened up the unit and found the body. The wife lives in Charlottesville and is driving up here as we speak."

Detective Smalls crouched down to get another look at the body and added, "You'd think someone who works at US Cyber Command would know how to spot a phishing scheme."

"The victim worked at CyberCom?" CyberCom was the unit within the Department of Defense charged with conducting cyberwarfare and cyber defense.

"Cybersecurity analyst at Fort Meade. High-security clearance, apparently. When I saw that, I knew the feds were going to want in on this."

Lisa stepped around the body, which was lying faceup on the beige carpeting.

"Is this how you found him?"

"We turned him over."

The victim was in his late forties, with thinning brown hair graying at the temples and bushy sideburns. There was a cut on his right cheek, which appeared to have been caused by his glasses mashing against his face when he collapsed face-first into the carpet. The mangled glasses were beside him.

The victim's lips were flecked with white matter, most likely dried spittle from the seizure. Lisa touched his cold hand.

"Do you have an estimate on the time of death?"

Smalls peered at the monitor screen. "Well, the email with the strobe came in at 7:35 p.m. Based on lividity, I'd ballpark it at close to that time. We'll have something more precise for you when we get him to the ME."

"What's he doing up here away from his family?"

"The family lives in Charlottesville, but he stays in this apartment when he's at Fort Meade for extended assignments."

"So the lease is held by the DOD?"

"It would appear so. The apartment manager says government-employee types rotate through the unit. Most of them probably CyberCom spooks."

Lisa joined Smalls at the computer to reexamine the email.

"It doesn't look like he was handling any sensitive data at the time of death. Just checking his personal email account," she said. "And, to your earlier comment, just about anyone could have fallen for this. The attacker did her homework. She'd clearly hacked the victim's account, knew that his wife had sent him other emails that looked a lot like this one."

"The person who did this also knew that Rosenthal had epilepsy," Smalls said. "It can't be easy to get at that information. You think his medical records were hacked?"

"Not necessarily. The information could have come from his email. And you'd be surprised what people will share on social media."

"No I wouldn't. I have a sixteen-year-old daughter."

"But," Lisa added, "not everyone with epilepsy would respond this way to the attachment. It's called photosensitive epilepsy, and only one in twenty people with epilepsy have it." Including all the victims so far.

During her investigation into the other attacks, Lisa had learned that a light flashing at between five and thirty times per second, combined with rapid movement and heavy contrasts between light and dark, could overstimulate the primary visual cortex and then spread to other parts of the brain, creating a potentially deadly seizure. The illness had come to the attention of the medical community in the 1990s when an episode of the animated TV series *Pokémon* caused a wave of seizures among children in Japan.

Smalls rubbed his stubble. "So I guess the question is whether sending that sort of email attachment is considered murder."

"Sending that GIF to Rosenthal was the same as sending him a package of anthrax or a bomb through the mail."

"You get no argument from me," Smalls said. "So I noticed that you keep referring to the attacker as *she*. Does that mean you know who did this?"

"I don't have a name, but I'm pretty sure I'll be able to link this to six other similar attacks. It has all the earmarks of someone that I've been pursuing for nearly a year."

"After all that time, I hope you know something about her."

There was no harm in telling him what she knew. "I'm pretty sure she's operating out of eastern Europe, probably Russia but possibly Ukraine, and I know some message boards that she frequents. I also have a name that she uses online sometimes—NatalyaX."

"So what's the motive for these attacks? Any idea why this Rosenthal was a target?"

"I've seen this tactic used against Ukrainian activists and politicians promoting separation from Russia. It's also been employed by some ultra-right-wing groups here in the US against their enemies."

"You think Rosenthal made himself an enemy of one of those groups?"

"No, but I don't know much about him yet."

There was a pause; then Smalls said, "So this sort of work is your specialty?"

"Yeah, I focus exclusively on cybercrime. That's why I'm going to want to take that computer back to our forensic lab at Quantico." She clicked on an icon to start shutting the computer down.

Smalls shook his head and smiled slowly. "Nah, that's ours. We have a cybercrime unit, too, you know. You think we don't know how to do a forensic exam? But we're happy to collaborate with your guys."

Lisa wasn't surprised that Smalls was marking his territory. But if he became entrenched in his position in front of his team, it would become a matter of pride. She suddenly became aware that three uniformed police officers were following their exchange—and that she was the only woman in the room.

"Have you informed his bosses at CyberCom yet?" she asked, with a smile of her own.

He cocked his head. "Yeah, we made that call. So?"

"They're going to want the computer too. I'll bet they told you to stand down and wait for them to process the crime scene."

Detective Smalls's mouth twisted in a grimace. "Words to that effect."

"So you really think you're going to win a fight with two federal agencies? Someone from CyberCom will probably be here any minute. You're going to have to give it up to one of us. It might as well be me." Lisa broadened her smile. "I'll bet I'm asking more nicely than they did. And I know this attacker."

Smalls grunted. "I'll have to answer to my chief if I allow this."

"Look at it this way," Lisa said, talking fast, sensing that she was about to close the deal. "It's easy to muck up this sort of forensic investigation. And we're talking about a federal employee with security clearance. Anything that you do here, the FBI, CyberCom, and probably NSA, too, will all be looking over your shoulder and telling you and your bosses that they could have done it better. Stepping out of the line of fire is the smartest move you can make."

Smalls ran a hand over his face, massaging his stubble again. "Maybe I should just wait for CyberCom to get here and let you two sort it out. That would be entertaining. He *is* their guy."

"True. But I've been tracking NatalyaX for a year. If you hadn't seen the bulletin I put out, you wouldn't even know what you were dealing with." Lisa played her trump card. "I'll owe you one."

"All right. You can have it. It gets us all home sooner. But I'm sending CyberCom directly to you when they arrive. Do you have a card?"

Lisa fished a business card out of her wallet and handed it over. "You won't regret this."

"I probably will, but I'm prepared to live with it."

Lisa donned blue latex gloves, bagged the desktop computer and monitor, and loaded them into the trunk of her rental car.

Rosenthal's computer would need to be logged into evidence in the computer forensic lab at Quantico. Leaving it sitting in the trunk of her car overnight would spoil the chain of custody.

After that, she was going to need some sleep. The spooks from CyberCom would be paying her a visit, and she would need her wits about her to defend herself.

2

Day Two

Lisa awoke to the jangle of car keys lifting off the nightstand. As her eyelids fluttered, Jon Amis came into view, hair still damp and tucking his shirt. There was a dab of shaving cream under his jaw.

Seeing that she was awake, he leaned down and kissed her forehead. "You got in late. You should get more sleep."

"Mmm. Yeah." Then she remembered the garish strobe light illuminating Rosenthal's dead body. "But no."

"Why's that?"

She wiped the speck of shaving cream from his face. "I've got to get down to the forensic lab about a computer I brought in last night."

"Same perp with the strobe GIF?"

"Yeah, but this time she killed someone with it."

"Jesus."

"Yeah."

"I'd go in with you, but I've got a class to get to." Jon taught a counterterrorism class for second-years at Quantico. It was his first year of teaching, and he was a natural. Lisa liked to tease that all those years of mansplaining had prepared him well.

They had met two years ago when they were both field agents in the FBI's San Francisco office. Lisa had been in the middle of pursuing a Dark Web drug kingpin called Captain Mal when he had first asked her out, so it had taken a while for the relationship to develop. They had been living together for three months in San Francisco when Jon had been offered the position at Quantico. Lisa had decided to follow suit, landing a job teaching cyber investigative techniques, while continuing to report to the SAC in San Francisco. She'd accepted the opportunity partly to share her knowledge with a new generation of recruits but also to give her relationship with Jon a genuine chance. She hadn't thought of herself as the type to uproot her life and career for a man, but realized that if she wanted to have a fuller life, one that wasn't entirely dominated by her job, she had to remain open to these sorts of opportunities when they came along.

Lisa didn't regret the decision, but she missed San Francisco. She missed the city's cool summers, the hills that constantly revealed new vistas of the bay like a gem displaying its facets. She missed North Beach and browsing City Lights Booksellers. She missed the carnitas burrito at La Taqueria in the Mission, and the shrimp dumplings at Yank Sing. She missed watching the Giants fans in kayaks fishing home run balls out of McCovey Cove. She missed the perpetual (and sometimes misguided) optimism of the tech industry with its young coders and entrepreneurs, which she preferred to the jaded realpolitik of DC's politicians, bureaucrats, and staffers.

She sat up in bed, stretched, and reached for the glass of water at her bedside.

"What do you think about dogs?" Jon asked.

"I think dogs are great. As a concept."

"I think we should get a puppy."

Lisa nearly choked on her water. "Do you think this is a good time for that? With both of us working and this smallish apartment?"

"We could get a small dog. One that doesn't shed. And there's a nice doggy-day-care place around the corner. I've actually done a little research on breeds." Jon pulled out his phone. "I'd like to show you something."

Lisa lay back and pulled the pillow over her face. "No, get that away from me," she said. "Some things can't be unseen. And a really cute puppy is one of them."

Jon was undeterred. "They're called Brussels griffons. They look like Ewoks. In fact, George Lucas actually owned one and instructed his creature designers to use it as a model. Don't you want to see?" He waggled the phone at her.

The pillow lowered to reveal Lisa's grudging smile. "Show me."

Jon held the phone out so that she could see photos of a solemn little gentleman of a dog named Alfred, who had a pug nose, black beard, a tufted brown-red coat, and a frowny expression.

"I can't look away," Lisa said. "It's like staring at an eclipse. Where is this Alfred? He must be mine."

"Alfred already has a good home. But they all look like that. He—or she—could be our starter baby."

"Don't you ever combine those two words again."

Jon had learned from experience when to back away. "All right, all right. Just wanted to plant a seed." He sat next to her on the bed.

"Oh, it's been planted."

Then came the innocuous question that she always dreaded. "How are you feeling?" He always tried to underplay it, glancing away when he said it. She wasn't sure if that made it better or worse.

"I'm good. It helps to have a case."

The previous weekend had been medium bad. She had thrown gasoline on the fire of her depression by drinking too much, never leaving the apartment, and bingeing BBC police procedurals on Netflix, most of them set in rugged, rural corners of the UK. In the too-fast, hyperconnected world of cybercrime, there was never an opportunity to stare moodily out at a roiling ocean or walk rugged cliffs while unraveling a case.

Jon said that he didn't mind her weekend flare-ups, but of course he minded. She had managed to regroup and make it in to work on Monday, shaky but functioning. But she could tell that he was watching her the way one watches a bomb with a timer that's stopped seconds short of detonation. The countdown could resume at any time.

"There's a downside to that too," Jon said. "What if you're in the field and you're impaired?"

"I'm rarely in the field. Most of my work is behind a monitor."

"Yes, but that's not always true. What if you've been drinking one morning, and you're called in on a field operation? What if you have to draw your weapon?"

She shook her head. "If it ever came to that, I'd take myself out. I'd disclose my condition to my supervisor."

"Okay," Jon said, nodding cautiously. "I believe you would. But depending on when you did it, *that* could compromise an operation."

Lisa was not ready to have this conversation first thing in the morning—and it wasn't like this was the first time they'd had this talk. Sometimes she felt that her depression was just another form of system vulnerability, like the ones exploited by the hackers that she pursued. When she was in a particularly uncharitable mood, she suspected that Jon might be using her vulnerability for emotional leverage in their relationship. In long-term relationships, as in hacking, all vulnerabilities were discovered and exploited sooner or later.

But she also knew that he had a valid point, that it would be wrong to just bluster and deflect.

Lisa was relieved when Jon preempted further discussion by saying, "Well, I'm glad you've got a case. That always helps."

She went with the change in subject and said, "Got any lunch plans?"

"No, I'll just be in my office preparing a lesson plan."

"I'll try to stop by."

"Text me if you think you can make it."

14

"I will."

"But you know you're going to be totally immersed in your strobe hacker case."

"I might not be."

Jon raised a single eyebrow.

"Okay, you're right," Lisa conceded. "I'll see you tonight. Now get to class. Because if you're late—"

He leaned in and kissed her. "I know; the terrorists win."

———

The computer forensic lab was located in a three-story brown-brick structure on the edge of the Quantico campus. Lisa had to be badged in three times before reaching the clean room where the real work was done—the domain of computer forensic laboratory director Rhett Rawlings.

Rawlings was sitting hunched over a hard drive connected to an appliance on his desk. The counters of his work space were solid wood to eliminate conductivity. The slightest electric charge could compromise an output.

His back was to Lisa, so she was staring at the man bun that he wore in the lab.

"Wouldn't a hairnet be more effective?" she asked.

"Hairnets are for cafeteria workers." Rawlings's elocution was as soft and sticky as Georgia asphalt in August. "I suppose you're here about that computer from last night."

"What have you got for me?"

Rawlings leaned back in his chair and pushed his black-rimmed glasses onto the bridge of his nose. "Special Agent Tanchik, I like to think that our relationship is not purely transactional."

Lisa leveled an impassive stare at him, trying to keep from smiling. "So how is your day going, Rhett?"

"Very well, Lisa. Thank you. Still basking in the glow from a lovely weekend at a B&B in Chestertown."

"I'm so glad to hear that. Now would you like to tell me what you found on the computer?"

"I would, yes." He waved a hand toward where Rosenthal's PC sat on a desk in a corner. "Someone did indeed hack into the computer before sending the email. They used an obfuscated code to mask their keystrokes, so I'll need to write new software to decrypt the commands and see what files they accessed. It'll take some time."

Lisa removed a flash drive from a pocket of her laptop bag. "No need. I've been pursuing this attacker since San Francisco. I've already written that software myself." This was the first time she had investigated this hacker with Rawlings since moving from San Francisco to DC.

"Don't look so pleased with yourself," Rawlings said as she handed him the flash drive. "I mirrored the victim's hard drive," he added as he popped it into a port on the desktop and booted up the software. He studied the outputs.

"Okay," he said, nodding. "This is not uninteresting."

"Russian, right?" Lisa said.

Rawlings glanced at her. "That's right. The attacker was using a keyboard with Cyrillic lettering. Probably a Russian."

"What else?" Lisa asked, moving in close so that she could peer over his shoulder.

"Well, there weren't a lot of wasted moves here. The attacker clearly knew what he wanted."

"The attacker is a woman."

Rawlings raised an eyebrow. "Really? Cybercrime tends to be a male-dominated field, but I was wrong to assume. It's great to see sisters shattering that glass ceiling." His voice trailed off. "You go, girl."

In response to Lisa's deadpan gaze, Rawlings changed the subject. "As I said, not a lot of random snooping. Went straight to Rosenthal's email account, found an email from his wife, and repurposed it."

"Does it look like Rosenthal was keeping any classified materials on his computer? You know he was with CyberCom."

"So I heard. But, no, it looks like he was following protocol. I don't see any documents marked for security clearance."

"Any exfiltration of data?"

"Well, now that I can view the keystrokes, let's see." Rawlings perused Rosenthal's audit logs, looking for any large packets of data in outgoing emails. "I don't think so, but I'm going to need to spend some more time with this."

"You're going to need to work quickly."

"Everything is urgent; I understand. But this work takes time—"

"I mean you're going to need to work quickly because I'm not sure how long you're going to have Rosenthal's computer. CyberCom and the NSA are probably talking to our bosses right now trying to get custody."

"Even if that happens, at least we'll still have the mirrored hard drive to work with," Rawlings said. "And CyberCom isn't any better at computer forensics than we are."

"Doesn't mean they won't start an interagency pissing contest." Lisa definitely didn't want to get Rawlings started on the subject of whose forensic team was better. "And they may demand that we turn over all copies. What do you know about the strobe?"

"It's an identical match to the ones you showed me that were used in the previous attacks. Just one click of the attachment and—boom— high-intensity strobe. It's almost like having a flash-bang grenade go off in your face."

"Does the email used in the attack lead anywhere?" she asked, even though she already knew the answer.

"Nah, it's totally anonymous. The email originated from a proxy server in Ukraine, but then the trail goes cold."

"Just like before," Lisa said. "It's like someone wants to point a finger at Ukraine. It's easy to imagine that might be Russia, given the tensions between the two countries."

"Unless *that's* what somebody wants us to think," Rawlings said.

"Right. So we're pretty much where we were before this attack—only now that a CyberCom employee has been murdered, we're going to have a lot more interference from the other agencies."

"They're probably going to call it assistance."

Lisa rolled her eyes. "I'm sure they will."

3

Lisa drove home and caught up on some sleep while Rawlings and his team completed their analysis of Rosenthal's computer and the deadly GIF. She couldn't get the image out of her mind of the CyberCom analyst's body lit by the flashing strobe, toggling between searing white light and darkness.

Despite Jon's concerns about her occasional binge drinking, Lisa had found a formula for combating depression that got her through most days—Zoloft, an active cybercrime investigation, and a daily spin session. Setting up her bike in the corner of his small apartment had been on her short list of move-in terms when they'd first gotten together in San Francisco. The bike was pricey on her federal salary, but it was better than a gym membership that she didn't have time to use.

After tossing down a cup of coffee, she climbed on the bike. The last rays of dusk were slanting through the blinds.

The bike had a large monitor mounted in front of the handlebars, where she could select from classes and instructors. For this session she chose a thirty-minute high-intensity interval training class with Robin Gutierrez, an instructor that she loved to hate.

The video began in soft focus and then resolved into high-def to reveal the instructor leading a prerecorded class in a New York City studio with a throng of riders in the shadows behind her.

The instructor stretched out her toned arms. "Are you ready to get your swagger on, hustlers?" She wore a stem microphone, branded workout gear, and a wicked smile. She looked like she had about .05 percent body fat.

I hate you, Robin. You know that, don't you?

Lisa warmed up, the bike set at low resistance. She was still tired from working the crime scene the night before—and frustrated at her failure to apprehend NatalyaX sooner and prevent Rosenthal's death.

For the past year, Lisa had tracked NatalyaX's movements across the Dark Web, searching for the clue that would reveal the hacker's identity or pinpoint her location. But Natalya remained a ghost.

"Now let's take that resistance up to forty-five to fifty for a thirty-second sprint. Cadence is one hundred. Get there." Robin looked into the camera and raised a peremptory index finger. "Yes, you can."

You're damn right I can.

Lisa was not a natural athlete and had struggled to pass the rigorous physical component of FBI Academy training. Her talents were at the keyboard, but still she had to find a way to maintain her qualifications as a field agent, and the bike workouts had helped build endurance.

Six intervals and seven minutes later, even Robin was sweating now, but that didn't stop her ridiculous patter. "Last interval before we're on flat road. I saw you dial down that resistance."

Bitch, please. You may be in better shape than I will ever be, but I know Krav Maga.

Lisa dialed up the resistance, her legs pumping slower now, like cycling through mud. She mopped the sweat from her face with a towel.

A message box appeared in the corner of her screen. Someone who was taking the online class at the same time had sent her a high five of encouragement. Not wishing to be inhospitable, Lisa clicked a high five in response, and the pop-up disappeared.

"Okay, let's take it out of the saddle. In four we rise, in three we rise, in two we rise . . . let's go!"

The soundtrack changed, the guitar riff kicking off Lenny Kravitz's "Are You Gonna Go My Way?"

"Adjust your crowns, hustlers," Robin said. "You know what's about to happen now."

Between gasping breaths, Lisa smiled. She was eighteen minutes into the ride, and the endorphins had begun to kick in. The instructor's inspirational hectoring was no longer so annoying, and she might have even laughed if she'd had the breath to do it.

Lisa turned up the resistance again, and for a few moments she wasn't thinking about the Black Dog, the killer she was tracking, or relationship land mines. She was thinking only of how far she could push herself.

"Now finish this thing up strong," Robin urged. "Be great. That's not a request; it's a promise."

The timer for the class ticked down to one minute, and Lisa coasted into the warm down. When the session was over, the instructor led a couple of minutes of stretches and deep breathing.

"You did it, my kings and queens," said the instructor. "Adjust your crowns. Respect your hustle. Empires have been built on less."

Lisa was standing up on the bike, hips resting on the handlebars and arms to the sky for a stretch, when the picture on the monitor crackled and disappeared.

Then the lights went out.

It was unusual to have a power outage in the winter, Lisa thought as she kicked out, unlocking her bike shoes from the pedals. At least it hadn't cut short the class. Her Black Dog was sleeping peacefully for the time being.

Lisa picked up her phone, which had been resting in the bike's cup holder, and tested the cellular data connection. Nothing. And no phone signal either. She'd wanted to call Jon to see if Quantico was also experiencing the blackout.

Trying to maintain the serenity she'd drawn from her workout, she found a flashlight and proceeded to light a few candles, expecting that she would be blowing them out again in ten or fifteen minutes. Then she showered quickly and got dressed.

Next Lisa went to the window to survey the colonial brownstones and apartment buildings near Dupont Circle.

Usually the windows around her would be lit with people returning home from work, fixing dinner, watching TV. But the apartment building across from her was completely dark, viewed through the first flakes of a light snowfall.

Her eyes drifted upward to the patch of the DC skyline that was visible.

Darkness.

For as far as the eye could see.

Even the traffic lights below were out.

Her pulse picked up. It was odd for both electricity and cell service to go down at the same time.

And if the power was out for long, the apartment was going to get awfully cold.

There was a knock at the door.

Lisa padded over silently. She peered through the peephole but wasn't able to see anything in the darkened hallway.

"Who is it?" she finally said.

"Special Agent Tanchik, this is David Gingrass, and I have my colleague Matthew Hebert out here with me. We're from CyberCom, and we need to speak with you."

I knew they wouldn't be happy that I took Rosenthal's computer, but showing up on my doorstep is a bit much.

She opened the door to two impatient-looking men in military fatigues.

"So this is about the computer from last night?"

"We need to bring you to Fort Meade." The older of the two, who had a pudgy face and close-cropped gray hair, was the one who had been doing the talking—Gingrass.

"That's not how this works," Lisa said. "Your boss needs to talk to my boss at the bureau and—"

"This isn't about the computer. Not exactly."

"What's it about then?"

"We're not at liberty to say, but you need to come with us."

"I have a class to teach tonight at Quantico."

"Trust me, Special Agent Tanchik; that class is canceled."

She was struck by the seriousness of his tone. "You realize that the elevators won't be working due to the blackout, right? You really intend to walk down twenty flights of stairs?"

"We won't have to," Gingrass said. "Our ride's on the roof."

4

They took the stairs up to the roof, the thwup of helicopter blades growing louder with every step. When they emerged into the night air, a sleek helicopter was idling, waiting for them.

"What did I do to deserve this special treatment?" Lisa asked.

"Tonight, this is the only way to travel," Gingrass responded. "Traffic lights are out across the city. Traffic's already a mess."

She recalled her view of the darkened DC skyline. "So this isn't just happening around Dupont Circle?"

"It's much bigger than that," Gingrass said, motioning to her to duck her head as they neared the chopper.

Before they could board, a man and a woman in their midtwenties emerged from the stairwell onto the roof. The man seemed to be able to tell that Gingrass was the leader of their little group; he went directly to him.

"Excuse me. Do you have room for two more?"

"I'm afraid we don't. This is a government helicopter, not a taxi service."

"But if you've got unoccupied seats . . ." The man paused. "We'll pay. We have money." He glanced at his wife, and she nodded, as if to confirm for the agents the state of their bank account.

"Why do you want on this helicopter, anyway?"

"Because some people are saying that this is a terrorist attack."

"And who says that?"

"CNN said it was a possibility. Before the satellite reception went out."

"And have you heard what the federal government is telling DC residents to do?"

"Shelter in place."

"That's right. This is your shelter. Stay in your place."

"If this is a terrorist attack, then DC is probably a target. We're better off away from here."

"You don't even know where we're going."

"Wherever it is, I'll bet it's safer than here."

Gingrass glanced doubtfully at Lisa and Hebert, and then said it anyway: "I wouldn't be so sure about that."

He motioned for Lisa and his partner to proceed to the helicopter, while directing an index finger at the young couple.

"Don't make me do something we're both going to regret," he said.

Once on board, Lisa strapped in and pulled on her headset, with Gingrass sitting next to her and Hebert opposite. An instant after they were settled, the gauges on the cockpit dash leaped, and so did her stomach. The chopper lifted off precipitously into the darkest night she had ever seen.

Lisa glanced down and saw the young couple grow smaller as they watched somberly, looking as if they had just missed the last airlift out of Saigon.

Soon the helicopter was passing over block after block of darkened buildings frosted in new snow. The only lights below were the headlights of cars.

A few minutes later, when they reached the outskirts of the District, Lisa peered out from the glass bubble of the passenger cabin at the thickening traffic on the Baltimore-Washington Parkway. It was the sort of traffic that you saw when people were evacuating from the path of a hurricane.

"Does this meeting have something to do with the blackout?" she said to her companions. The helicopter didn't provide much insulation against the cold, and her breath fogged before her.

"You'll be briefed when you get there," Gingrass said.

"C'mon, you've got to give me something here." She paused. "Was this blackout caused by a cyberattack?"

Hebert shot her a quick involuntary glance.

"Your partner doesn't have much of a poker face. I'm going to take that as a yes."

Gingrass did not take the bait.

"It's interesting that the cell towers are also affected," Lisa said. "I could see a cascading failure bringing down the electrical grid, but that shouldn't knock out cell towers, right? Two independent systems."

But Gingrass continued to ignore her theorizing.

The helicopter sliced through the sky, and fifteen minutes later they were circling the nine-story black-mirrored building that was the National Security Agency/CyberCom headquarters at Fort Meade, Maryland. CyberCom drew its resources from the NSA and shared the same director, but it was also a full and independent unified combatant command of the Department of Defense.

The chopper touched down on the roof helipad. A CyberCom agent was waiting for them—young, with short blond hair, wearing military fatigues and the empowered look that comes from being the assistant to someone important.

As soon as the helicopter that had deposited Lisa's group sped away, a sirocco whipped the rooftop as another helicopter landed on the helipad.

The young agent escorted Lisa, Gingrass, and Hebert to a stairwell door, pressing his thumb to a scanner and punching in a lengthy code. Electricity wasn't a problem here; it was no surprise that NSA/CyberCom headquarters was powered by backup generators.

Lisa looked back at the helicopter that had just touched down and saw a passenger staring back at her. He had a neatly trimmed black beard and mustache, bushy Groucho eyebrows, and a receding hairline crowned by dark, disheveled tufts. His pale features seemed to disappear behind this superstructure of black hair. Whoever the man was, Lisa figured that they must have something in common, because they had both received invitations to the same party.

After descending a flight of steps, she and the agents emerged onto the upper floor of the building, then boarded an elevator that again required a thumbprint and a passcode before descending to subbasement level.

Lisa studied her escort. There was something different about his fatigues—and her other two companions'—but it took her a moment to identify it. Instead of the rounded green and brown shapes of standard-issue camo, the patterns were broken up into tiny hard-edged squares. Digital camo.

"I'm Special Agent Lisa Tanchik, but I guess you already know that. And you are?"

"Brad Forrester."

"What's your position here?"

"Assistant to the director."

"And you're taking me to meet your boss?"

"Eventually. But I can't say when that's going to happen."

"And why not?"

"The director is extremely busy at the moment, as I'm sure you can imagine."

"You say that like you think I know what's going on. I haven't been briefed." She glanced at Gingrass and Hebert. "I'm in the dark here."

"Well, one thing that I can tell you is"—Forrester paused like he wasn't sure how the next words would sound coming out of his mouth—"we're at war."

5

Forrester deposited Lisa on a bench in a hallway with Hebert, while Gingrass took off for parts unknown. She watched as men and women—some in digital camo, some in suits, some looking like they had just been dragged out of bed—came and went from what appeared to be a war room. She played a mental game, trying to peg each visitor to the relevant agency. Judging by attire and demeanor, she thought she spotted CyberCom, NSA, army, CIA, and executive branch representatives entering and leaving the room.

She drew a few curious glances, but no one bothered to ask who was or what she was doing there. The visitors to the war room all had a similar stretched-tight look about them. They looked like people who were taking the most important test of their lives and failing miserably.

She turned to the young agent next to her. "Hebert. That's Cajun, right?"

"Yes, ma'am. Lafayette, Louisiana."

"Please don't call me *ma'am*. It's Lisa. Help me understand the difference between CyberCom and NSA, Hebert. You work out of the same headquarters, and you have the same boss, but you seem to be on different teams."

"Same team, but it's kinda the difference between playing offense or defense. The NSA is mainly interested in using cyber for espionage purposes. CyberCom, on the other hand, is about deploying those cyber assets to take specific actions against an adversary, like disrupting the development of nuclear weapons. The NSA tends to prefer just leaving malware and implants in place so that they can continue collecting intelligence indefinitely. With cyber assets, once you use it, you lose it, so the NSA sometimes pushes back on CyberCom's offensive maneuvers."

"And you wear fatigues, and they don't."

"Right. CyberCom is staffed by army personnel. Enlisted men and women and officers rotate through Cyber Mission Forces on two-year assignments. The NSA personnel tend to be lifers. That gives some of them a bit of an attitude when it comes to us."

"So what do you do around here when you're not shanghaiing FBI agents?"

"Developing my network security skills." He nodded at the closed door. "But mostly I'm trying to get inside that room."

"And what's in there?"

"That's CyberCom's command center."

"The war room."

"Basically, yeah. I wish I'd made it in there before this happened."

"And what is *this*?"

"You heard Forrester. Apparently it's the cyberwar that we've all been preparing for."

"And the people in that room are going to have the opportunity to distinguish themselves, earn promotions."

Hebert turned to her, making sure that he caught her eye. "That's not what it's about." He gave a slight shrug. "Well, not entirely. I'm here because I want to help keep this country safe. Does that sound corny?"

"Not at all."

Lisa might have been in that room if she had remained on her initial career trajectory. She had earned a scholarship through the federal CyberCorps program, which provided full scholarships to George Washington University for talented programmers and security professionals. In exchange for the scholarship, she was expected to use her cyber skills in the service of the federal government.

She'd recognized soon enough that she wasn't cut out for work in the clandestine services, whether it was CyberCom, NSA, or CIA. Too few moral guardrails. Espionage and national defense were vital, worthy services, but the work required a willingness to operate in gray zones, committing some evil for an arguably greater good. Lisa was self-aware enough to recognize the toll that sort of life would have taken on her. She'd convinced the CyberCorps scholarship panel to allow her to repay her debt to the federal government by working for the FBI, first as a civilian computer forensics contractor and eventually as a special agent. No law enforcement job was without its moral hazards, but putting cybercriminals behind bars was a mission that she could devote her life to without looking back.

"What do you know about the attack?" she asked Hebert.

"Not much more than you do, really."

"C'mon, how bad is it?"

He shook his head. "It's bad. I hear that the whole East Coast is dark, and that it's spreading west as far as parts of Ohio. I'm not talking out of school when I say that, because it's on CNN. My wife says the ATM machines are down. Most cell phones aren't working. Traffic signals and public transit systems are out. And this just seems to be the start."

"Did anyone see this coming?"

"You're asking the wrong person, ma'am. Sorry, I mean Agent Tanchik."

Their conversation was interrupted when a civilian emerged from the war room escorted by a general—judging by the decorations on his chest. Lisa immediately recognized the civilian as Tom Costa, the founder and CEO of SoftBlue, the world's largest software company. According to *Forbes*, Costa was one of the three richest men in the world, and he was red-faced, vein-bulging angry.

"You knew!" he shouted in a tinny, Kermit the Frog voice that was familiar to Lisa from his company's highly publicized product launches. "You knew all along, and you never bothered to tell us!"

"Mr. Costa, I advise you to watch your tone," the general said. "We don't work for you."

"But you work for the American people, right? And you knew!"

"You heard what General Holsapple said in there. You should take care when you issue your press release about the security patch. If you speak directly to the press, I strongly advise that you wait until you've cooled down."

"Two years! I can't believe you've known for at least two years!"

"I'm going to escort you back to your colleagues now, Mr. Costa." The CyberCom general touched Costa's arm, guiding him back to the reception area. Glancing around to see who might have overheard the exchange, the general glared at Lisa and Hebert for a moment before ushering the irate billionaire down the hall.

"I guess you don't need a security clearance to figure out what that was about," Lisa said.

"When you recall this conversation, please remember that I didn't say anything," Hebert said.

"Noted."

It was an open secret that the NSA and CyberCom collected software vulnerabilities. When the agency learned of a previously undiscovered security flaw in a widely used program like SoftBlue's word processing software, they had a choice to make. Alert the software maker to the error so that it could patch the flaw in the interest of national cyber defense? Or remain silent about the vulnerability so that the government could use it to penetrate the systems of adversaries?

The danger in the latter approach was that if you waited too long to patch the security flaw, you ran the risk that your enemies would use that same vulnerability against you. Judging by the conversation she'd just heard, the NSA and CyberCom had uncovered some chink in the digital armor of one of SoftBlue's products two years ago, and they had decided not to tell Costa and his company what they had found. Now that vulnerability was being used against the nation in a series of cyber-attacks. Someone was going to end up looking very bad when the story of this incident was told, and it would either be SoftBlue for producing a flawed product or the NSA and CyberCom for allowing that flaw to go uncorrected. Or perhaps both.

Once the general and Costa disappeared around a corner, Lisa said, "I can't stand just sitting here. Can you get me a laptop with internet access?"

Hebert nodded. "Maybe. If I can, it'll be satellite internet, which is slower because the signal has farther to travel."

"That's okay. Please do that. Now."

Hebert rose reluctantly and went off down the hall. Ten minutes later he returned with a laptop. "This is mine, but you can use it. It's been authorized."

"Does it have Tor?"

"Yeah," he said, sheepish. "I find it's a good way to understand what's going on in the world of cybercrime."

"I couldn't agree more. Good for you, Hebert."

First Lisa used the laptop to access the initial press accounts, which painted a disturbing picture of a massive and multipronged attack on everything from the electrical grid to public transportation and the banking system.

Next she opened the laptop's Tor browser, which was the gateway to the Dark Web, the universe of unindexed websites that was a playground for cybercriminals. Lisa employed a host of masterfully detailed fake identities whenever she traversed the Dark Web, and today she chose ShivaTGOD (short for Shiva, the God of Death), who purported to be a goth anarchist based in Berlin. She had been using the Shiva persona for several years on Dark Web sites, so she was a known presence.

She logged in to the BlackHoleSun chat board, which was frequented by criminally inclined hackers. If anyone there knew something about the ongoing cyberattack, they would almost certainly be bragging about it to enhance their cred. She found a thread that seemed to be discussing the attack and waded in.

> SHIVATGOD: So who knew that the cyber apocalypse would be this entertaining?

> DBASER: That's easy for you to say, Shiva. You haven't been without cell and Internet access.

DBASER was a whiny college girl attending an undisclosed East Coast university. She had pretensions of hacker grandeur but had never evidenced any real skills in her conversations on the board. At least that was who she appeared to be. As Lisa knew so well, you could never really tell who you were dealing with online, especially on the Dark Web.

> SHIVATGOD: And yet you're here, aren't you?

> DBASER: Starbucks Wi-Fi is like the cockroach that will survive even if we're entering a new digital dark age.

> SHIVATGOD: Thanks for your service, D. The struggle is real.

> HELENWHEELS: Shiva! Good to see you back on the board. I thought you must be dead or in jail.

HelenWheels, who was based in Detroit, had been a semireliable source of intelligence on the world of cybercrime for about a year and a half. She seemed to have some serious hacking chops and in the past had offered tips that suggested she had connections to Anonymous and WikiLeaks.

Helen's handle referred to the fact that a car accident when she was a teenager had severed her spine and confined her to a wheelchair for life. As far as Lisa could tell, she seemed to live her life on the Dark Web, where she found a freedom that eluded her IRL. There had been times when Shiva and Helen had been close online, sharing late-night intimacies, such as the time Helen mordantly joked about how her weight gain had forced her to trade in for the "Chevy Tahoe SUV" of wheelchairs. Lisa had in turn felt free to confide in Helen about her struggles with depression, albeit under the guise of Shiva. Sometimes Lisa suspected that her most frank conversations were conducted online with people that she didn't really know.

> SHIVATGOD: Still at large, my friend. Just busy sowing anarchy.

> HELENWHEELS: As one does.

> SHIVATGOD: I'm glad you're here. Was wondering what people are saying about the attacks. Got to be the Russians, right?

> HELENWHEELS: Ya think? They all but put their signature on it. I suppose China also has the capability, but these attacks look just like what the Russkies have been doing to Ukraine for years. But that's why some don't buy it. 4CHAN, as usual, is full of crackpot theories.

SHIVATGOD: But does anyone sound credible?

HELENWHEELS: What's with all the questions, Nancy Drew? You're starting to sound like LE.

Helen meant law enforcement. Lisa cursed herself for being so obvious. She needed to proceed carefully. Getting overeager could blow more than a year's worth of work building connections on this chat board.

SHIVATGOD: You really know how to hurt a girl. Seriously, how can you not be obsessed with this? Whoever is behind this is a freaking god.

HELENWHEELS: It is pretty sophisticated, no?

SHIVATGOD: What gets me is the variety of techniques being used. From what I can tell, it's like, symphonic. There are broad-brush viruses, targeted attacks, social engineering, all of it coordinated for maximum impact. At least that's what I was able to gather from the reporting posted on the New York Times site—before it was knocked down by a denial-of-service attack.

HELENWHEELS: It's next-gen, for sure.

SHIVATGOD: What does Anonymous have to say about all this?

HELENWHEELS: They're full of admiration, but don't really seem to know what's going on.

SHIVATGOD: How about WikiLeaks? They have known connections to Russia.

HELENWHEELS: Radio silence over there.

DBASER: Why don't you two just get a room?

HELENWHEELS: STFU, D.

SHIVATGOD: Second that.

DBASER: Why doesn't anyone ask me my thoughts on the attack?

HELENWHEELS: Because you know nothing, Jon Snow.

DBASER: I'm going to surprise you one of these days.

SHIVATGOD: And yet, you never seem to.

DBASER: I know when I'm not wanted.

HELENWHEELS: Good. Don't let the keyboard hit you on your way out.

SHIVATGOD: It feels like a new world out there now. Good thing I've got skills.

HELENWHEELS: Unlike lame-ass D.

SHIVATGOD: Right.

HELENWHEELS: Are you looking for opportunities?

SHIVATGOD: You mean participating in this attack?

HELENWHEELS: Maybe. I don't know. I'm hearing a lot of interesting chatter. If I come across something intriguing, would you like to know about it?

SHIVATGOD: Yeah, I think so.

HELENWHEELS: Give you a chance to show how good you really are.

SHIVATGOD: Try me.

HELENWHEELS: Okay. Look for me here and I'll reach out if I have something.

SHIVATGOD: Do that. Later.

At last, the door to the CyberCom command center opened, and Forrester reappeared. "The director will see you now." Lisa snapped the laptop shut, returned it to Hebert, and entered the war room.

6

CyberCom's command center pulsed with agitated conversations punctuated by shouting. One side of the large high-ceilinged room was covered wall to wall with enormous, brilliantly lit LED screens displaying maps of the US, with breakout images showing closer views of the grids of various cities. The maps were dotted with green, amber, and red lights. There was plenty of red across the board, which was probably not a good sign.

CyberCom officers in fatigues occupied rows of computer consoles, often accompanied by men and women in suits, apparent executive branch types.

Forrester led Lisa down to the front row of terminals, where a balding general was engaging in a heated exchange with two men in suits.

Forrester leaned in close. "Stick to the bullet points. He's not going to have a lot of patience for more than that."

The balding general finally looked over. Forrester said, "This is FBI special agent Lisa Tanchik."

"Tom Holsapple," he said, extending a hand and assuming that she already knew his titles as a five-star army general and director of the NSA and CyberCom. "So you were on the scene at Rosenthal's apartment?"

"Yes."

"And you've been pursuing the terrorist who uses those damn strobes?"

"That's right. I've been hunting her for about a year."

"Any progress?"

"Some. Not enough."

"Well, your investigation has just been given national defense priority. We're going to read you in."

"Does my director know about this?"

"Yes, and the bureau is on board. This is no time for interagency turf battles. We're at war."

"You're not the first person to say that to me, but what does that mean exactly?"

"I don't have time to give you a briefing, Agent Tanchik. One of my deputies will do that, to the extent that you need to know. But, to put it simply, we're experiencing a coordinated cyberattack on our critical infrastructure. We're still assessing the damage, but they've hit the electrical grid up and down the Eastern Seaboard, cell towers, the New York Stock Exchange, public transit systems, the ports, air traffic control centers, and many of our largest banks and hospitals. We're even getting suspicious reports from a nuclear power plant."

"Who's behind this?"

"It has to be a nation-state. No independent actor could accomplish something this huge and coordinated. We suspect Russia but don't have any hard evidence yet. That's where you come in."

"What can I do?"

"You can find the person who killed John Rosenthal. It's my understanding that you believe the attacker is based in Ukraine."

"The signs point to Ukraine, but that's probably intentional and consistent with Russian involvement."

General Holsapple nodded. "At first we thought that incident was a random event, but we now believe that the intent was to take out a key member of CyberCom's team and compromise our ability to respond to the attacks. Rosenthal was our best expert on Russian malware, which is another indication that Russia is behind this."

"So who do I report to?"

"Me and my team here. Deputy Director Emma Glass will be your primary contact."

Lisa started to say something, and Holsapple noticed.

"Do you know Glass?"

"Yes, but it's been a while."

"Is that a problem?"

"Not at all."

"You're free to report back to the bureau, but only to the director personally, no one else. And we'll be your first stop with any new intelligence."

"Yes, sir."

General Holsapple began to look around the room, moving on to the next crisis. "Where's Orlov?"

Forrester stepped forward. "He's here now, sir."

"Well, bring him to me."

Lisa guessed that Orlov must be the bearded fellow that she had seen staring out of the helicopter window.

General Holsapple glanced around impatiently at the scrum of men and women hovering nearby, each apparently waiting for an opportunity to give a report. His eyes settled on a middle-aged man in CyberCom fatigues with thinning gray hair and small round glasses. The man's face looked even grayer than his hair, and there was a sheen of perspiration on his forehead.

"Are you okay, Ruffalo?"

"Sorry, sir," he said, shifting unsteadily on his feet. "Not feeling well."

"Get this man some water and a chair," Holsapple barked at Forrester.

The assistant sprang to retrieve a chair, but before he could find one, Ruffalo lowered himself onto the polished concrete floor like a pilot executing a controlled crash.

"We need a doctor here!" Holsapple yelled as people dropped to their knees around Ruffalo to check his pulse and breathing.

Ruffalo grabbed a handful of his shirt over his heart.

A woman on the floor next to Ruffalo looked up at the closing circle around them and said, "He has a pacemaker. *He has a pacemaker!*"

Holsapple looked at Lisa. "Has your adversary ever hacked a medical device?"

"Not that I know of. Does anyone know the make and model of the pacemaker?"

Holsapple turned to another of his assistants, a younger, even more clean-cut version of Forrester. "That information would be in his personnel file, right?"

"I think so," said the assistant.

"Then go get it. *Now!*"

Ruffalo's eyes were closed, but he appeared to be breathing. Forrester administered chest compressions until a woman who said she had paramedic training relieved him.

Holsapple turned to one of the agents in his on-deck circle. "As soon as we know the type of pacemaker, I want you to work with the NSA to see if it has any known and unpatched vulnerabilities."

"Yes, sir."

With the exchange between the SoftBlue CEO and the CyberCom general in the hallway fresh in her memory, Lisa wondered if NSA had prior knowledge of the pacemaker's security flaw. That sort of edge might be useful if the NSA needed to remotely take out a terrorist with a weak heart hiding in the mountains of Pakistan, but it was very bad for someone like Ruffalo.

The woman stopped performing CPR on Ruffalo, looking up and through them with a bleak stare.

Holsapple knelt beside Ruffalo for a moment, and a shadow seemed to pass over his face. Then he stood and strode to the front of the room, taking a place in front of a podium with a microphone.

A dull, amplified thud as Holsapple tapped the mic, and everyone looked up from their monitors.

Holsapple cleared his throat. "Tony Ruffalo was one of our finest cybersecurity experts, and we will grieve for him. But we will have to do that later. We don't know Tony's cause of death, but we have to suspect that it was his pacemaker, and that it may have been hacked."

Lisa saw the anxious looks being exchanged around the room.

"Combined with John Rosenthal's murder, we have to assume that this attack is not limited to our critical infrastructure. It's also directed at us personally. Ruffalo was one of our best on protecting legacy infrastructure like power plants and public transit from cyberattacks. It's no coincidence that he was targeted. I'd like you to raise your hand if you have an implanted medical device, whether it's a pacemaker, an insulin pump, a defibrillator, anything with a wireless connection."

A few hands went up around the room.

"I'd like everyone who raised their hands to report to the infirmary now. We need to assess whether your devices are vulnerable. Go. Now."

A half a dozen people left the room hastily.

Holsapple continued, "You all know why the adversary is coming after us personally. It's to sow confusion, throw us off our game. Break our spirit.

"It's true that we're getting our asses kicked right now. There's no sense in pretending that we're not. This is the cyber Pearl Harbor that we've talked about for so long. But you know what came after Pearl Harbor—Midway, Guadalcanal, D-Day, the fall of Berlin. This isn't over, not by a long shot.

"We're professionals. We work the problem. This is what we've trained for. This is what the nation is expecting us to do.

"And I want everyone in the room today, including our guests from the executive branch and other agencies, to know that we're going to find out who's behind these attacks and bring them down—hard."

When Holsapple turned away from the podium, he had a look in his eye that reminded Lisa of Sonny Liston after Muhammad Ali had just demonstrated that superior size and strength weren't always enough.

"Let's get Special Agent Tanchik read in," Holsapple said to his immediate circle. He found Lisa's gaze. "You said 'her' earlier. Our adversary is a woman?"

"Yes, I'm fairly certain of that based on some comments I've seen from her in IRC chat rooms."

"Hmm." After a pause, Holsapple added. "It's good to find someone who knows *something* about what we're dealing with."

"I wish I knew more."

"Your director made a strong case that I needed to put you on this team."

"You mean my SAC, Pam Gilbertson?"

"I mean FBI director Louis Stevenson. I hope you live up to that introduction, Special Agent Tanchik. We really need you to."

7

Lisa was brought to an office on the periphery of the CyberCom war room. The sign outside the door bore a name from her past—Emma Glass.

Hebert gave a polite knock and deposited her at the door. A brusque "Come in" issued from inside.

"Good luck, Special Agent Tanchik," Hebert said as he withdrew. "From here you're on your own."

"Good luck to you, too, Hebert. I hope you get inside that room."

Glass rose and came around her desk to give Lisa a handshake. Lisa recalled that she was neither a hugger nor an air-kisser, but she was as beautiful as ever—shoulder-length red-blonde hair, blue-gray eyes, and a squared-off cleft chin that gave her a look both strong and feminine. Glass had lost every trace of her early-twenties gawkiness.

"Lisa! It's good to see you. Wish it could be under better circumstances. I guess I should address you as *Special Agent.*"

"And I guess I should address you as *Deputy Director*," Lisa said.

"Emma's fine." Her smile was colder than her words.

Lisa appreciated the civility, but it was hard not to recall their former relationship as rivals and competitors. They had been classmates at George Washington University, both scholarship students in the CyberCorps program and the most talented cybersecurity wonks in their class—a fact that irked many of their classmates, who would have been more comfortable if their male-dominated profession stayed that way.

You would think that would be enough to create a certain "us against them" esprit de corps between her and Emma. And it did, but only up to a point.

One of the highlights of their first year at GWU had been a capture the flag contest in which the class divided up into teams of two to attempt to crack a military-grade firewall. The task was complex and required them to work around the clock. Emma's and Lisa's teams were pegged by their classmates as early favorites.

Nearly thirty-six hours into the contest, Lisa's team was nearing a breakthrough. She tried to act nonchalant, but when she glanced at the other teams ringed around the computer lab, she locked eyes with Emma. Lisa hadn't yet perfected the poker face that would serve her well in the FBI, and she knew in an instant that she had somehow given away how close they were to victory.

A couple of minutes later, Lisa took a bathroom break while her teammate, Dez Moseley, ran some final scans. When she returned, Dez was in anguish, pacing around in front of his laptop and cursing.

"What happened?"

Dez wrapped his hands around his head like it was about to explode. "The scans were running. Everything was fine. I just closed my eyes for a minute, and I guess I must have nodded off."

"I'll repeat. What happened, Dez?"

"I startled awake and knocked over my bottle of Mountain Dew. It went right into the laptop and shorted it out."

There were damp paper towels stained with the radioactive-green soda all around the laptop. The keyboard was dry now, but the screen was black, and the damage was done.

Lisa looked to see if anyone had noticed their distress, but everyone was immersed in their work.

Except Emma. It was hard to tell from across the room, but Lisa thought she detected a slight smile on her face.

"Dez, do you actually remember knocking over your Mountain Dew? Did you see it happen?"

He shook his head. "I must have done it in my sleep. I woke up, and the keyboard was soaked."

"Could anyone else have seen it happen?"

"Nah, I don't think so." Then Dez reconsidered. "Emma was on her way to ask Professor Nance a question. Maybe she saw, but what's the point? We're toast."

"Yeah, you're right," Lisa said. "No point."

Lisa felt certain that Emma had sabotaged their project, even if she would never be able to prove it. She tried valiantly to redo their work on another laptop, but before she could get back to where they had been, Emma was raising her hand to call for their professor and claim victory.

Lisa and Emma never quite became friends, partly due to Lisa's suspicions about the capture the flag contest, but also because they were so very different. In many ways, Emma Glass was the anti-Lisa.

Dave Wu, another classmate, had made Lisa laugh by referring to Emma as "a super-together lady," and the description had stuck. She'd always thought of Emma as the epitome of one of those women who always looked perfectly put together, always said the right thing, never showed vulnerability. She understood why Emma constructed that facade in order to get ahead in a masculine, essentially military environment.

But, for better or worse, that wasn't Lisa's style.

"You're not catching us on one of our best days," Glass said.

"So I gathered. Did you hear what happened to that analyst, Ruffalo?"

"Yes. Absolutely shocking. He was a good man."

"I was there when it happened. I've never seen anything like this."

"Neither have we. Even in our tabletop exercises, we never really imagined that we would be the target of full-on cyberwarfare. We didn't think anyone who had the capability to mount this kind of attack would dare take us on in this sort of all-out way."

"Why not?" Lisa asked.

"Cyber is different from conventional, or even nuclear, war. There's a whole range of weaponry, much of it smaller scale in nature, capable of taking out discrete targets like a city government payroll system, stealing data about government contractors, or knocking out a polling station during an election. Our enemies use cyber because it's a way of undermining us without triggering an all-out shooting war. The tacit understanding among nations has been that cyberweapons can and will be used, so long as no one goes overboard."

Lisa nodded. "But now someone has thrown out those rules. So who's behind it?"

"We don't know yet. Russia is the obvious suspect, but they're denying involvement. Of course, that would be their tactic to delay a retaliatory strike."

"That's the thing about cyberwarfare, isn't it? The enemy isn't wearing a uniform or carrying a flag. It's often hard to know who you're fighting."

Glass nodded.

"But it almost has to be Russia," Lisa said. "Recent events would indicate that, right?"

The US president had recently sent troops into Syria that had pushed back Soviet-trained and armed Syrian brigades. When the US ambassador to the UN had followed that up by denouncing Russian aggression in Ukraine, Russian president Eitan Vasiliev had engaged in the sort of saber-rattling statements that usually preceded a declaration of war.

"But why would Russia risk the retaliation from the US that's sure to follow?" Lisa continued. "Even with what's been happening in Syria and Ukraine, wouldn't they keep things more small scale, like the 2016 election hack? Something that we wouldn't necessarily view as an act of war?"

Glass stole a glance at the monitor of her desktop computer, which was insistently pinging with incoming emails. "Yes, there is something else. I suppose I can tell you, since you've been read in."

"What is it?"

"There has been a nuclear event at a Russian reactor in Kostroma."

"How bad?"

"It wasn't anywhere near as bad as Chernobyl, but fuel rods were exposed, and there was a release of radioactive gas that's caused them to evacuate Kostroma and two nearby towns."

"That's terrible, but what has it got to do with the US?"

"The reactor malfunction was caused by malware that infected the nuclear plant's systems. That malware was based on the Stuxnet virus that we developed with the Israelis to destroy centrifuges used in Iran's nuclear program."

"Were we behind the reactor hack?" Lisa asked.

"No, of course not," Glass said. "But to the Russians, it looks that way. The Stuxnet virus didn't self-destruct as it was designed to do, so it's out there in the world. Just because we designed it doesn't mean we're using it against them now."

"Can't you reach out to them diplomatically and tell them that?"

"Believe me, the secretary of state is trying, but so far the Russians aren't even willing to acknowledge that there was a reactor event in Kostroma, much less that they're taking actions in response to it."

"And how do you know that it's the Russians that are attacking us?"

"About that," Glass said, returning to the seat behind her desk. "We think that your angle on the hacker who killed Rosenthal is one of the better leads we have."

"So you believe that murdering Rosenthal was the first wave in this broader attack?"

"Given the timing and Rosenthal's role at CyberCom, that's our working theory. Is that consistent with the other strobe attacks you've been investigating?"

"The previous attacks were all aimed at sowing political division. They were aimed at outspoken political commentators, particularly on the Left. We know why that would be in Russia's interest too."

Glass nodded. "We need you to find this attacker, and, maybe even more important, we need you to find the evidence that will draw a line between the attacker and Russia. It will need to be rock solid, because it may have to be the basis for a declaration of war."

"Is that all? You know I've been after her for a year now, and I'm not that much closer to identifying her."

"That's why we're assigning you a partner."

Lisa was grateful her poker face had improved. "I work better on my own."

"I remember that about you. But this order comes from General Holsapple. You really want to give him static at a time like this?"

"I'm just not sure that I need a partner." But she already knew this was a losing battle. "Who do you have in mind, anyway, and what do they bring to the table?"

"Your new partner is Arkady Orlov, the founder and CEO of Novo Security, based in Ukraine. Luckily, he was in the US for a conference."

"And he'll be useful to me how?"

"Orlov has some special knowledge of Russian cyber tactics. It'll be better if he explains. He's meeting with the director right now, and then he'll be joining us." Since this portion of the briefing was concluded, Glass swiveled halfway back to her monitor. "In the meantime, you mind if I . . . ?"

"No, sure."

Lisa would have considered this a power move on Glass's part, making her sit and stare at the walls while she worked, but not today. Lisa desperately wanted to check her emails and see if there were any new developments from the Quantico forensic lab, but she had been required to turn in her phone when she'd entered the CyberCom head-quarters. That was doubly frustrating because CyberCom was probably one of the few places where she could get online during the attacks.

Fifteen minutes later, there was a knock at the door.

The man with bushy eyebrows entered the room, planting himself in the chair next to her with a preoccupied air, as if it were his office and he already knew everyone. Lisa immediately recognized his type. Security consultants tended to be brusque know-it-alls who had to be the smartest guy in the room, especially when everyone else in the room thought *they* were the smartest.

Glass turned from her computer to face them. "Arkady Orlov, this is FBI special agent Lisa Tanchik. She's been pursuing the attacker who uses the strobe."

Orlov nodded, his eyebrows rising and falling. He was wearing a black shirt open at the neck, a gold chain whose medallion appeared to be lost in his chest hair, and black jeans. His entire outfit, if it could be called that, was black, except for a pair of traffic-cone-orange sneakers.

"How did your meeting with the director go?" Glass asked, shame-lessly fishing for information.

"It is shit show," said Orlov. "Absolute shit show."

"You're not wrong about that," Glass conceded.

"But it is shit show that I have seen before." He pulled a phone from his pants pocket and cued up a video. "Watch this."

Lisa resisted the urge to ask why he had been allowed to bring in his phone and she hadn't.

The video showed what appeared to be a control console with an array of meters, switches, and red and green lights. The console had a clunky, old-tech look, lacking the streamlined brushed-chrome design of the Jobs era. There was no technician behind the console, no figures in the frame.

"What are we supposed to be looking at?" Lisa asked.

"This is a transmission station just north of Kiev, operated by the electrical company Ukrenergo. Just wait a minute. You'll see."

Lisa sensed the movement before she could pinpoint it.

"Look at those switches on the right," Orlov said.

She watched the light on a switch flip from red to green, as if moved by an invisible hand.

And then another switch turned.

And another.

And then the entire console came alive, knobs turning and switches flipping like the keys of a player piano.

"With old technology like that they would have had to develop customized malware," Lisa said. "There's nothing off the shelf about that."

"Yes, they'd been planning it for a while. Just like they planned what's happening here now."

Glass clicked a few times with her computer mouse, then turned her monitor to face them. "Now watch this," she said.

In Glass's video, another control room came into view. It was a little more modern than the one they had just viewed, but not by a wide margin.

"What are we looking at?" Lisa asked.

"This is security footage from a control room at PSEG, the New Jersey power service. This happened in Newark three hours ago." She pointed at the screen. "Here it comes."

The central console came to life, precisely as in Orlov's video, dials turning and switches flipping without the aid of human hands. It would take time to study the malware at work, but it was clear the same enemy had orchestrated both attacks.

"After the power grid went down in New Jersey, the malware proceeded to disconnect circuits, delete backup systems, and shut down substations," Glass said. "As the final touch, the attackers shut down backup generators and left the PSEG team helpless in the dark. This was repeated at power plants up and down the East Coast."

"What happens in Kiev no longer stays in Kiev," Orlov said.

Lisa turned to him. "You sound like you know who's behind this. Who are they?"

"The Russians, of course," he said.

"Can you be more specific?"

"I believe this is the work of the hacker collective known as Sandworm. They've been practicing on my country for the past two years, developing their exploits, their tactics. And now you're seeing just how good they are."

Lisa knew some of the history. Moscow had long considered Ukraine its rightful territory, a strategic buffer between Russia and the NATO powers of eastern Europe, home to one of the region's few warmwater ports, and a lucrative pipeline route to Europe. A decade of tension between the two nations had finally erupted in the Ukrainian revolution of 2014, in which Viktor Yanukovych, the country's Kremlin-backed president, was overthrown. Immediately following the election, Russia had annexed the Crimean Peninsula in the south and invaded the Russian-speaking eastern region known as Donbass.

Since 2014, Russia had been waging an undeclared war on Ukraine, and much of that warfare had been conducted in the cyber realm. Lisa had heard about some of the better-publicized exploits, such as when the Russians rigged the website of Ukraine's Central Election Commission during the 2016 presidential election to declare ultraright candidate Dmytro Yarosh as the winner. The tampering had been detected only an hour before the election results were to be announced.

"Are they an independent group or state sponsored?" Lisa asked.

"They might as well be a branch of GRU. Yes, definitely state sponsored."

"Can you prove that?" Glass asked. "What makes you say they're state sponsored?"

Orlov shrugged. "You mean do I have an email from President Vasiliev giving order to hack Ukraine's electrical grid? No. But I have been watching them work for years. By their tactics, by their targets, by their sophistication, I know who I've been dealing with."

"So you can't prove it," Glass said.

"Not to your satisfaction, obviously," Orlov replied, his impatience showing.

Lisa decided it was time to intervene before the conversation became counterproductive. "You call them Sandworm. So you've seen those references buried in the code too?"

"What references?" Glass asked. "What's Sandworm?"

"It's from *Dune*."

Glass stared back at her blankly.

"Frank Herbert? Science fiction classic?" In tracking the strobe attacker, Lisa had noticed references to *Dune* buried in the coding, terms like *Harkonnen* and *Arrakis*, a desert planet where enormous sandworms roamed. If Natalya was connected to Sandworm, this was the biggest break she'd gotten in nearly a year.

"Okay."

"You are not the nerd I thought you were, Emma."

Glass smirked. "I can live with that."

"So your strobe attacker is a member of Sandworm?" Orlov directed the question to Lisa.

"It appears so," Lisa said, nodding, excited to finally be making progress in the case. "I believe the hacker I've been pursuing is a woman. I call her NatalyaX. She occasionally uses that name on hacker chat boards."

"I know that bitch," Orlov said, almost under his breath. "She tried to kill Ukraine's foreign minister by sabotaging the controls of his private jet."

"Do you know how to find her?"

"If I knew how to find her, she would be rotting in prison in Ukraine." After a pause, he added, "But I have some ideas."

Glass turned her monitor back around and started typing. "Clearly, you two are going to have a lot to talk about. Start by comparing notes, pool your knowledge, and prepare a report for CyberCom with everything that you've been able to piece together about Sandworm, these attacks, and NatalyaX. We need to know what you both know. And we need it now."

"How bad is this?" Lisa asked. "Because it looked pretty bad in that war room."

Glass stopped typing. "This makes the 2008 hack look like a minor setback."

"What happened in 2008?" Lisa asked.

"The Russians breached SIPRNet—the Secret Internet Protocol Router Network."

"That's one of your internal networks?" Orlov asked.

"It's *the* internal network. It connects the military, senior officials in the White House, and the intelligence agencies. The Russians had access to all of our most sensitive cyber defense communications."

"How did they gain access?" Lisa asked.

"That's the most embarrassing part," Glass said. "The Russians left USB drives containing malware in the parking lots and public areas of a military base in the Middle East. Some idiot picked up the drive and plugged it into a laptop connected to SIPRNet, and before long the bug spread, and the Russians had access to all of US Central Command."

"I never heard about that," Lisa said.

"It wasn't exactly our proudest moment. But this is far worse." Glass drew a long breath. "Without electricity and heating, people are going to start freezing to death in the northern states. With freeways jammed and trains out of commission, cities will start running out of food and essential supplies in a few days. And heaven help us if people start looting."

Lisa didn't know what to say to that.

But her new partner was not speechless. "It's the Gerasimov doctrine in action," Orlov muttered.

"And what is that?" Lisa asked.

"In 2014, Valery Gerasimov, Russia's top general, published an article in which he described a model for what he called hybrid warfare. Gerasimov saw war as a continuum that includes everything from conventional warfare to terror to economic pressure to social media propaganda and disinformation—and, of course, cyber."

"And Ukraine has been the proving ground," Glass said.

Orlov nodded. "Ukraine has been Russia's sparring partner for years, but we could see that they were pulling their punches. They show us that they can shut down our national power grid, but they only do it for two hours; then they turn it back on. They shut down our rail system, but only for a day."

"Why were they pulling their punches?" Glass asked.

"Because they didn't want to show you what they were capable of," Orlov said. "They were only practicing on us. They are not pulling punches now."

8

Sitting in a corner of the CyberCom command center, Lisa listened to an emergency television address by President Margaret Bilton, which was being displayed on the huge screen. The bustling war room paused as everyone stopped to listen. She wondered how many people on the blacked-out East Coast would actually be able to hear the president's words.

Lisa knew that there were some who would question a woman president's ability to lead the nation through the first real war fought on its own soil since the Civil War. As President Bilton began speaking, Lisa recognized with some relief that only the most partisan or sexist factions of the electorate could fail to get behind this leader.

President Bilton, sitting behind the Resolute desk in the Oval Office, spoke directly into the camera in a tone that was measured but steely.

When our nation was attacked on December 7, 1941, at Pearl Harbor, President Franklin Roosevelt called it a day that would live in infamy. Today is the dawn of a new day of infamy, perpetrated by cowardly and ruthless enemies. Citizens on our East Coast are experiencing a massive coordinated cyberattack that has damaged many aspects of our critical infrastructure: our electrical power grid, our water system, public transportation, health care, financial markets, communications. Our nation has experienced the loss of lives and enormous economic costs that will not be fully known for some time.

This is a new kind of warfare, but make no mistake—it is an act of war. And it will be treated as such by my administration. Unlike Pearl Harbor, we don't yet know with certainty the identity of our enemy. But I can assure you that it will not remain concealed for long. Our military and cyber defense agencies are bringing all of their resources to bear, and we will respond swiftly, decisively, and in kind. Our enemies will understand that attacking the United States of America is a mistake that they will pay dearly for.

The cyberattack is ongoing, and we cannot say at this time that it has concluded. Therefore, I am asking all US citizens, particularly on our East Coast, to stay inside their homes to the greatest extent possible. Monitor your local emergency broadcast system messages, and please obey them. Avoid driving because it may jam our roads and freeways, impeding the ability of our emergency aid workers to deliver much-needed goods and services.

We will provide further information in the coming days, but right now I want every American to know that this craven, brutal attack directed at our citizens will not stand.

Thank you, and God bless America.

9

Natalya moved through a pixelated urban landscape of burning cars and broken windows. She had adopted so many different identities that none of her given names seemed to fit anymore. So when she thought of herself, she used a name that she had chosen—NatalyaX, or just Natalya.

The brick and stone buildings on the screen were pocked with shell craters. It was dusk, and the air should have been hazy and filled with smoke, but instead everything seemed crystalline, every demolished wall and scorched sign lovingly rendered in 4K high-def. She could be in Belfast or Beirut or Nairobi, or some amalgam of all three. She had managed to access the internet by hacking a FEMA emergency relief headquarters.

At her side was some sort of military rifle of improbable firepower. She saw her legs moving, but they seemed to glide forward effortlessly, her POV Steadicam smooth. Natalya walked over broken glass, but it did not crunch beneath her feet.

Her avatar in this online game of *Call to Service* was "Sarge," a hulking brute of a man with a two-day stubble, a buzz cut, bulging biceps, and a scar underneath his right eye. She would have preferred a badass woman soldier, but that option had not been available.

Natalya strode boldly down the middle of the street. She did not attempt to hunker down behind cars or duck into entryways to avoid incoming weapons fire. Even though the streets were blazing around her as if the area had just been shelled, no other figures were in sight.

Then she detected a movement behind a burned-out chassis a half block ahead. A figure emerged from behind the car, possibly a Taliban fighter, wearing a camouflage fatigue jacket over white robes with a black-and-white checked kaffiyeh covering his head and face, revealing only the eyes. The Taliban had a rocket launcher hoisted on one shoulder.

He didn't open fire on Sarge but stepped out into the middle of the street and walked matter-of-factly forward. They met in front of an exploded café, whose scorched tables were overturned on the sidewalk.

"Hello, Natalya," said the Taliban. "You've gained weight."

"Hello, Kazimir. It's been a while. And it appears to be mostly muscle."

Kazimir, Natalya's handler at the GRU, Russia's foreign military intelligence agency, communicated with her through two-player online video games because it was one mode of messaging that was not monitored by the NSA. An FBI agent named Lisa Tanchik had been trailing her on the Dark Web, investigating her use of the strobes, but this was one place where even Tanchik could not find her. When he wanted to play, Kazimir would leave her a coded message on a Dark Web message board.

"The chief wants you to know that he was very pleased with the work you did in Newark," Kazimir said.

"I'm very glad to hear that."

"You're playing an important role, and your contribution will be remembered."

"I thought people like me didn't end up in the history books."

"Maybe not the official history. But in the secret history, the one kept by GRU and SVR, you will be recognized as a hero."

"I'll remember that you said that. When this is done."

"That's a conversation for another day."

"Understood. What do you have for me?"

"It's time to terminate your operation with Claremont Systems. We have other priorities now."

"Okay. I figured."

Kazimir proceeded to provide the details of her next assignment and some guidance on how to conclude her current project.

When they were done with the operations talk, Kazimir asked, "Did you take my recommendation when you were in New York?"

"Yes, I ate at Barney Greengrass."

"Ah, the Sturgeon King. And you ordered the nova lox platter?"

"Yes."

"Was it as good as I remember?"

"I don't know how you remember it, Kazimir, but it was very good."

"Just very good?"

"It was delicious."

"And you had it with the onion bagels?"

"As per your request."

"Good. You know I am living vicariously through you."

"I'm beginning to appreciate that." Natalya paused. "You know that your precious Barney Greengrass is shut down right now, in the dark."

"Nothing that good is ever gone for long."

"Doesn't that concern you?"

"We're not talking about Barney Greengrass anymore, are we?"

"No. We've kicked the hornet's nest. You, from a distance. But me, I'm right underneath it with a stick, poking."

"That's why you will be remembered forever, and I will be forgotten."

"Probably so, Kazimir. But I will never forget you. After all, you introduced me to Barney Greengrass."

"Run fast, and stay safe, my beautiful girl."

Kazimir turned and walked away through the devastated cityscape. He paused, aimed his rocket launcher at a three-story office building, and fired a shell, bursting the facade into flames and showering their avatars in pulverized plaster and gravel.

He turned back over his shoulder to look at her, the mask of the kaffiyeh accentuating his eyes.

"Sometimes," Kazimir said, "doesn't it just feel so good to blow things up?"

10

Natalya gazed at her date across the table of the Georgetown restaurant, watching him pick at his salad. The restaurant was fashionably gloomy on a normal night, but in the midst of the blackout it was operating by dim candlelight, and the patrons were wearing their winter coats at the tables. Until the food supplies ran out, restaurants like this one performed a kind of public service by staying open and feeding people who might not have any provisions at home.

Despite the candlelight, this was the opposite of a romantic dinner. Natalya was ending their relationship, but he didn't know that yet.

She had met Phil Memmott at the bar of the Mandarin Oriental Hotel in DC at a tech industry mixer. The Mandarin events were a miniversion of the famous pickup scene at the Four Seasons in Silicon Valley, where attractive young women showed up in clingy dresses to meet geeky tech entrepreneurs with new stock option wealth and impaired social skills. The Silicon Valley event was larger and boasted more IPO and near-IPO companies, but the DC event featured a higher percentage of companies with links to the Pentagon and the Department of Defense, so it had suited her objectives.

Natalya knew that she was attractive, but she had also recognized that she wasn't the most beautiful woman in that room. However, she had one critical advantage—she was probably a better coder than many of her targets. She could talk the talk, and that was how she had initially connected with the twenty-seven-year-old man-boy across the table from her. Natalya was able to supply the one component often missing from "the girlfriend experience" that young entrepreneurs were all seeking, even if they didn't realize it at first—the ability to fully appreciate their genius.

Natalya wanted Phil to know that she "got" him.

Oh, did she ever.

Phil was the CEO of Claremont Systems, a data analytics company that was on the verge of becoming a major contractor to the Department of Defense. Claremont was among a handful of companies that the DOD and, more importantly, CyberCom were using to develop the next generation of offensive cyberweapons.

That had always been the greatest vulnerability of the DOD, and now the NSA and CyberCom—the reliance on private firms as contractors. Just as companies like Lockheed Martin built fighter planes and General Atomics built drones, firms like Claremont Systems were designing and building the malware and other weapons that the Americans would use in "active defense," NSA-speak for offensive cyberwarfare.

While the private firms ran security clearances and took precautions against foreign espionage, they weren't nearly as rigorous as the agencies themselves. They should have learned that lesson from the Edward Snowden breach. As a contractor with Booz Allen, Snowden had been given shockingly wide-ranging access to NSA systems for someone who was not an agency employee.

Natalya had hoped to gain leverage over Phil in order to either use him to extract sensitive DOD data or infect his software to destroy US government systems. In an ideal scenario, her bosses might be able to plant a defect in a US cyberweapon developed by Claremont that would render it useless precisely when the Americans needed it the most. But playing the long game with Phil had ceased to be a priority now that the full-on attack was underway.

Unfortunately for Phil.

"And if the blackout weren't enough, three of my top developers delivered a letter to me today objecting to the use of our technologies for military purposes," Phil was saying, brandishing a fork. "I mean, they knew what they were signing up for. Making cyberweapons is *what we do*."

"They should be grateful to have a good job at a growing company like yours," said Natalya, nodding sympathetically.

"Exactly."

"You're defending America."

"Well, we're actually more on the offensive side of things. But yeah. In some ways it's the same thing. A good offense is the best defense."

"What are you going to do?"

"I'm going to try to explain the big picture to them. I shouldn't have to, but I will. I mean, it's not like we're making napalm. You heard the president's speech, right?" He didn't wait for her response. "If we can't attack whoever did this, then how will we deter anyone from doing it again?"

"It's a new arms race, isn't it?"

"You're damn straight it is. And you can't see another country's cyberwarfare capabilities the way you used to be able to spot missile silos with satellites . . ."

Natalya stayed silent, hoping that he would just keep talking. Even on this, their final night together, there was still the possibility that she might gather one last piece of valuable intelligence.

"You seem quiet tonight," Phil said. "Something wrong?"

"Yes, I'm afraid so, darling. This is going to have to end."

His fork froze halfway to his mouth, dangling spinach limp with salad dressing. "Carly," he said, using the name she had given him, "you're breaking up with me?"

"I've received a new work assignment. I'm going to be traveling all over the country for the next few months." Natalya always preferred to tell the truth when possible in order to keep her stories straight, and this was true. As the coordinated cyberattacks on the US increased in number and severity, she and the other members of Russia's network of sleeper agents were going to be very busy.

Phil seemed relieved. "I thought you were going to tell me that you'd found someone else."

"No, darling. It's not like that."

"Then can't we pick this up in a few months when things settle down for you at work? Are you coming back to the DC area when this is done?"

She had told Phil that she was a low-level programmer for a stealth start-up that was being spun off from a major tech company. It made her evasiveness plausible and gave him no means of verifying her story.

"I doubt it. The company is going to be based in Silicon Valley. I'm moving to Palo Alto."

"You're serious, aren't you?"

"Do you know me to be a kidder?"

"No, you never mess around." Phil smiled ruefully. "Except when you're messing around."

Natalya smiled back at him, not unkindly. He had been an enthusiastic lover, if a bit unskilled. She was going to miss him, at least for a week or two.

She had to think back to her teenage years to recall a relationship that was entirely genuine. Sometimes as she stared across the table at one of her targets, she felt a pang of profound loneliness. No matter how much she happened to like one of her assignments (and Phil was not an unlikable guy), she had to hold herself back, couldn't allow herself to feel anything. Otherwise, it would make what she had to do so much more difficult.

"I guess I'm asking if there can be a last time," Phil said. "Can we go back to my place?"

"I can't. I have to get up early to pack."

"It doesn't have to be sex. We could just watch a movie, hang out. I've been wanting to screen a true masterpiece for you—*Con Air*."

Phil had introduced her to the glories of the big dumb American action film, and they had spent many evenings on the couch at his apartment studying the works of Michael Bay, buffeted by the roar of explosions from the surround sound home theater speakers. She had been skeptical at first but was now a convert. As she well knew, there was a pleasure to be had in watching things destruct.

"I don't know this film. Who's in it?"

"*Everyone*. Malkovich. Buscemi. John Cusack. Ving Rhames. And, of course, the great Nic Cage."

"Ooh, I love him. I love the way he gets all intense at the end of a sentence." She flared her eyes and gave the last phrase a rat-a-tat cadence à la Cage.

"So that's a yes?"

She considered it, so much so that Phil nearly lived to see another day with that ploy. But she did not have time to waste. She had places to be.

"That is very tempting, but no. I can't." She was still finishing up a particularly virulent piece of malware designed to wreak havoc with an industrial facility.

"So this is it? I'm never going to see you again?"

"It really is, Phil. I'm sorry. It's been fun."

Phil pulled out his phone. "Then will you finally let me get a picture of us? I'd like something to remember you by."

"You know I'm self-conscious that way. I don't do social media."

"It's just for me."

"Right." She didn't believe him; the photo would be on Facebook and Instagram within the hour. Particularly now that the cyberattack had begun, she could not afford to leave such an obvious trail connecting her to a DOD contractor.

Besides, given what was about to happen to Phil, law enforcement was almost certain to examine his last posts, looking for clues to his death.

"You just want to show off for your friends," she added.

He was pulling out his phone, prepared to snap a solo shot of her across the table if necessary. "Even if that's true, is that so wrong? You're so hot, and if you're going to dump me like this, you've gotta give me something to remember you by. Let me make my friends jealous."

"I said no to the photo, Phil."

"The way you act, you would think you have something to hide," he said.

There was a large bottle of S.Pellegrino on the table, and she topped off their glasses. Phil took a sip. He had been alternating between beer and sparkling water throughout the meal. Natalya knew from experience that Phil had a small bladder, and it wouldn't be long.

Phil rose. "I have to hit the bathroom." He raised an index finger. "To be continued. I'm not giving up."

Natalya smiled seductively and nodded. She watched him wind his way across the darkened dining room, waiting until the bathroom door closed behind him.

Then she reached across the table to take a sip of Phil's beer. Anyone in the dining room who noticed would see it as a token of intimacy between a couple, albeit a sneaky one.

And then, in a sleight of hand that even a close observer would miss, she emptied a small packet of white powder into his glass. She swished the beer in the half-empty pint glass to dissolve the sediment that had gathered on the bottom.

The compound would induce a heart attack within two hours or so of being ingested. Kazimir had given her instructions on how to prepare it during their virtual rendezvous. The bitter taste of the powder would be masked by the beer. She didn't want something fast acting that would cause him to do a face-plant into his salad. She didn't need that sort of attention.

Phil returned to his seat a few minutes later. Now she had to keep him talking until he finished his beer.

"You know," Phil said with a keen look. "I actually thought things were getting serious. So serious that I had our director of security run a background check on you earlier today."

Natalya tensed. "Oh, really? What did you find?"

"Not much. But that in itself was kind of troubling."

"How so?"

"Well, there just isn't that much about you on the internet, at least not much that dates back more than a year. Sure, you have accounts on social media, but they were all opened about the same time, and there's not a lot there."

"I'm a private person, Phil. I thought I'd give the whole social media thing a try, but it just didn't take. Is that so wrong?"

"No, I get that. But my security director said that your profile had some of the earmarks of a professionally constructed fake identity. A good one."

"So what are you saying? Does your security director require that I take a polygraph to be your girlfriend? Or maybe there's just a form you'd like me to complete."

"It's just procedure. You know there are people who would like to get close to me. Because of my job."

"That may be true, but if I was one of them, would I be breaking up with you?"

Phil stared at his plate and nodded. "You've got me there. Look, I'm sorry I said that. You've just got me rattled. I don't want this to be over."

Natalya raised a hand to call their waiter to order another glass of wine. She hoped that would prompt Phil to drink up.

Sure enough, Phil downed the rest of his beer in a couple of quick gulps and began to order another while the waiter was at the table.

Natalya reached across to take Phil's hand. "You know, I've changed my mind about that glass of wine. We really shouldn't prolong this, and I do have to get up early tomorrow."

Phil gazed back at her with what appeared to be genuine sadness; then he turned to the waiter. "I guess that'll be it. We'll take the check."

She was tempted to follow Phil and observe her handiwork, see if he collapsed on the sidewalk or made it all the way back to his apartment. But that would not be prudent. If the police managed to figure out that his death was not an accident, then she didn't want to give them the opportunity to find CCTV camera footage of her trailing the victim. Some of those cameras would still be operating on battery power, at least for a while.

As they exited the restaurant, Phil said, "I'm going to miss you, Carly. And I really mean that. If you change your mind, you know where to find me."

She touched his arm. "I do. And I'll miss you too. It was just bad timing."

She watched Phil walk away, headed to the parking garage to retrieve his car. She hoped that the drugs didn't take effect while he was driving. Collateral damage was messy and unprofessional.

She hadn't been lying when she said she would miss him. She hoped that after her role in the ongoing cyberattacks was completed, she might return to sleeper status, maybe start a new relationship, one that was not an assignment. However, she also knew that if she ever made that daydream a reality, it would probably have to be in another country. Because the list of tasks that she had been assigned to perform in the coming days would ensure that US law enforcement agencies would never stop hunting for her, especially Special Agent Lisa Tanchik.

Her work with the GRU had been rewarding, but it had also left her in a kind of limbo. She was an American by citizenship and culture, but not an American. She was Russian by heritage, but not a Russian. She was a spy, but she felt like a civilian most of the time.

Maybe for people who were truly singular, the only true allegiance was to yourself. Because who else would understand?

There was, however, one person she'd encountered who seemed to be just as singular as she was.

Natalya resolved to do something about her. That would be a start.

11

Day Three

This is Don Hansberry at the CNN News Center in Atlanta reporting on America Under Attack. The electrical and cell service shutdown that began yesterday evening continues all along the Eastern Seaboard, from Maine to South Carolina, with blackouts extending as far to the west as eastern Ohio. Utility crews are working around the clock to restore power and communications before more lives are lost to the brutal January cold.

FEMA has confirmed forty-one deaths attributed to the blackout and cyberwarfare campaign, but that is obviously incomplete information. We will continue to share the latest reports with our listeners as they become available, for those who are able to hear them.

President Bilton and the State Department have yet to identify the enemy behind the concerted cyberattacks on the East Coast, although it is widely speculated to be Russia. There is a growing outcry from the public and in Congress for a declaration of war. Senator Willard Nevins from Kentucky strongly criticized President Bilton from the floor of the Senate last night, charging that the president "is too weak and indecisive to be the commander in chief" and should "stop preventing her generals from doing what needs to be done."

In a new and deeply disturbing development, three prominent Americans are included in the death toll: Supreme Court justice Arnold

Denton, New York senator Louise Salinger, and US Army general David Esposito. Each of those three deaths resulted from a malfunction in a pacemaker that had been infected with malware. In our next segment, we will provide details on the brands of pacemaker that may be subject to this form of hacking, and what you can do if you may be vulnerable.

We urge everyone who can hear this to stay inside and stay safe. Also, for those who are considering driving west out of the attack zone, please be aware that we are hearing unconfirmed reports of car navigation systems being hacked, causing accidents. That's why it's so important to follow the advice of President Bilton and FEMA—shelter in place.

12

Lisa and Orlov were working in a conference room at CyberCom in the early morning hours, comparing notes and preparing their report on the hacker known as NatalyaX. Glass's assistant checked in to see if they needed anything.

Lisa rubbed her tired eyes. "We need to review the security camera footage from the Newark power plant for the forty-eight hours preceding the event."

"I don't think you're authorized for that," said the assistant, a young woman who seemed to be trying on a less persuasive version of her boss's no-nonsense demeanor.

"You have two choices here," Lisa said. "You can interrupt the very important work that Emma is doing right now. Or you can give us what we need to perform the critical task we've been assigned. Which do you think is going to show Emma that you know how to perform in a crisis?"

Lisa stared at the young assistant, wondering whether underlining that she and Glass were on a first-name basis was too obvious.

"I'll get you that footage," the assistant said, backing out of the room.

When the conference room door closed again, Orlov said, "You would do well in Ukraine. Much bureaucracy. To get anything done you must be unstoppable, like snowplow."

"Did you ever get the impression that NatalyaX was in the US?" Lisa asked.

"No, but I was never able to get very far tracking her online. Always with the proxy servers."

When the assistant returned with the Newark footage, they divided the files between them and began scanning.

"What are we looking for, anyway?" Orlov asked.

"I don't know, but I think we'll know it when we see it."

Lisa fast-forwarded as technicians came and left the control room, ticking along at a rapid clip like mechanical toys that had been too tightly wound. Then the lights dimmed, and the cleaning crew came and went.

Nothing out of the ordinary as far as she could tell.

At the desk across from her, Orlov was concentrating just as intently on his work.

Lisa thought she noticed something and froze the video.

Orlov heard that her keys had stopped clicking and turned to face her. Without the patter of the keyboard, the room was so quiet that she could hear the ticking of carbonated bubbles inside the aluminum can of soda beside her.

"Something?"

"I'm not sure," she said, studying the image.

Minutes before, the night crew working the control room had abruptly left, leaving it empty. Then a tall woman wandered in, head on a swivel, like someone who didn't belong there. The dark-gray sweatshirt and hoodie that she wore marked her as an outsider. The woman seemed to know where the security cameras were and avoided looking into them, with the hoodie pulled up and her head down. But Lisa could tell that the person was a woman from the way she moved and her long slender hands. Lisa scrolled backward and forward through the footage but was unable to make out her features.

This woman looked nothing like the engineers, technicians, and nerds that made up the control room staff, who generally wore either hard hats or pocket protectors.

"Could that be her?" Orlov asked.

Lisa brought her face closer to the monitor. "Maybe. She certainly stands out. Let's see what she does next."

Lisa let the video resume at regular speed. The woman sat down in a chair in front of the control console, still keeping her face out of the camera's view.

She removed a flash drive from her pocket and plugged it into a port on the console. Then she waited a couple of minutes for the malware to download, unplugged the drive, and walked out of the control room.

"The plant administrator reported that someone set a fire in a trash can around the same time," Orlov said. "Maybe she set it as a diversion to get the technicians to evacuate."

"Simple but effective," Lisa said, consulting one of the files.

Lisa scrolled the video forward and backward, watching the woman's movements and gestures, trying in vain to get some sense of who she was.

Was she nervous? She didn't appear to be.

Was she armed? It was difficult to tell if she might have a weapon tucked away in her jeans or the front pocket of her hooded sweatshirt.

If someone had interrupted her, would she have killed to complete her mission? It was impossible to say, but Lisa was going to guess the answer to that question was yes.

Lisa paused the video. "I think you have the security footage from the room where the fire started."

Orlov examined the flash drive containing the raw materials they had been given. "I'm looking for that feed."

Fifteen minutes later, Orlov uttered some sort of guttural exclamation in Ukrainian.

He motioned for Lisa to join him at his monitor. Orlov played the video, which showed the woman in the sweatshirt pulling a handful of loose papers from a desk, placing them in a wastebasket, and lighting an entire book of matches and tossing it in. Black smoke immediately began billowing.

A minute later, the smoke detectors went off, but the woman was already gone, headed for the control room.

"She probably posed as someone with access rights to get in the door," Lisa said. "Given the way she's dressed, and her obvious skills, she might have presented herself as a software vendor on-site for an installation or maintenance."

"We must have a copy of the facility's visitor logs," Orlov said. "But how far do you think that's going to get us?"

Lisa ran a hand through her black hair. "Not far, I'm sure."

"Do you think we can even get the visitor logs given the current state of things?"

"I'll bet we can."

"And why is that?"

"Because CyberCom is affiliated with the NSA. And the NSA knows all."

"I don't like Big Brother," Orlov said. "But sometimes it is helpful to be his friend."

After a beat, he asked, "So do you think that's her? NatalyaX?"

Lisa stared at the frozen image on the screen. Despite her evasive maneuvers, one camera had captured a partial side view of the woman's face. Lisa thought she detected a slight smile playing on the woman's lips as she strode out of the smoke-filled room.

"She thinks she's winning. That they're winning."

Orlov turned to look at her. "Aren't they?"

Lisa stood. "We need to speak with Glass."

13

Emma Glass had moved to a temporary cube-like office that opened directly on the CyberCom war room. As an aide escorted Lisa and Orlov through the command center, it was clear that the pandemonium had not lessened. If anything, the room seemed more chaotic. Lisa hated to apply the word *panic* to people in charge of national defense, but that was what it looked like.

The giant LED screen spanning the rear wall displayed a map of the US power grid. The screen then shifted to a diagram of the nation's banking networks. Each screen was filled with red warning indicators.

As they entered Glass's office, she was pacing around her desk, listening to a conference call in which several male voices were carrying on an argument. She looked visibly distressed as she waved them in.

"Chief Perotta," she said, interrupting the argument, "we were told there was a train collision with mass casualties, at least twenty-five, and a three-alarm fire."

"We're on the scene at Penn Station now," said a voice from the speaker. "There's nothing here. It's dark, and no trains are moving. I don't know who's responsible for this, but you need to fire their ass."

"I'm going to put you on hold for a minute."

"You know we have other crises to deal with here, right? Fires to put out—literally. Real ones."

"I know, and I'm as upset about this as you are."

"Are you, Deputy Director Glass? That's good to know."

"I'm going to let you go now."

"Okay, you do that. And I hope you have your shit together if I ever speak to you again."

Glass hung up the phone, looking stunned. "We've lost confidence in our command and control," she said.

"What does that mean?" Lisa asked. She and Orlov remained standing. It didn't seem right to sit down while Glass was pacing about.

"Our agents can't trust command and control."

"Yes, you said that. But what does it mean?" Lisa asked.

"It means that the attackers have compromised our communications systems. We can no longer trust the reports we're getting from our agents and army officers out in the field."

"Meaning one of your agents' email was spoofed," Lisa said. "You got a report from an agent about a collision at Penn Station."

Glass nodded. "As if this crisis wasn't bad enough, we now have to question the legitimacy of every message, every bit of information, that we receive. Without effective command and control, we're virtually helpless."

"This happened in Ukraine," Orlov said.

This got Glass's attention. "What did you do about it?"

"We tried introducing an encrypted verification code that our people could use to confirm that they were legit."

"Did it work?"

"No. The Russians just hacked the verification codes."

"So how did it end, your situation?"

"They stopped," Orlov said with a shrug. "They tested their techniques, achieved proof of concept, and then stopped."

Glass nodded. "Because if they had persisted, the US might have eventually taken notice. Spent more time developing countermeasures."

"*Da,*" Orlov said. "The Russians were correct that the world community didn't care so much about Ukraine. We were their laboratory, their—how do you say it?—guinea pig."

"They're reporting attacks that haven't occurred, diverting our resources, so that we aren't dealing with the attacks that are actually underway, such as the situation at the Beaver Valley nuclear facility in Pennsylvania."

"What's going on there?"

Glass shook her head. "A near meltdown. It's going to be okay—I think. But that's not our subject right now. I don't have time to give you two a full briefing."

"We have some footage we'd like to show you from the Newark power plant."

Orlov cued up the footage on a laptop and set it on Glass's desk. They sat down and watched as the woman in the gray hoodie set the fire in the trash can and then installed the flash drive in the plant's control room.

"Do you think that's NatalyaX?" Glass asked when the clip was done.

"Possibly, but we don't know."

"In our investigation we've been focusing on known and suspected Russian sleeper agents. It's more likely that the Russians would use an operative who's been here for a while that they believe is not under surveillance rather than trying to get someone into the country undetected."

"Sleeper agents?" Lisa said. "Really? I thought the Cold War was over."

"It's nothing new. In 2010, we expelled ten Russian sleeper agents who were arrested in New York, New Jersey, and Virginia for trying to steal classified information. Cold War or not, espionage goes on."

"If you know of people who are Russian sleeper agents, why haven't you done something about them?"

"That's not my call to make. Sometimes State and DOD decide it's better to just observe them and see what we can learn about their network. In some cases we're not entirely sure that they are operatives."

"Can we see the profiles?" Lisa asked.

Glass handed them each a thick folder. As Lisa took the file, she noticed Glass's perfectly manicured glossy-red nails. They made Lisa feel uncharacteristically self-conscious about the fact that her nails were worn down to uneven blobs of gray polish.

"These are printouts of the most recent intelligence," Glass said. "But we've also set up a data room with pretty much everything we've collected on these agents over the past three years."

"You mind if we . . . ?" Lisa said, nodding at the file.

"Go ahead. Dig in," Glass said. "I have to get security to start scanning all accounts and devices."

Glass swiveled around to face her monitor, while Lisa and Orlov raced through their copies of the file in an unspoken competition to be the first one to find something significant.

After ten minutes of perusing the file, Lisa said, "Here."

Glass and Orlov looked at her.

"I think this agent, Hannah Price, is NatalyaX," she said.

"And what's your basis for that?" Glass asked.

"Credit card bill. She purchased a pair of shoes from the shop of a Tokyo designer, Toshio Shinkai."

"And that is significant because . . . ?"

"NatalyaX once mentioned that designer in a post on a Dark Web site where she was listing people that she considered creative geniuses, along with William Gibson, Neal Stephenson, and Jonathan Ive. Including Shinkai on that list stood out. I looked him up, and it turns out he's a relatively obscure designer who's known mainly among hardcore fashionistas."

"Never heard of him," Glass said. "But then again, I wouldn't. How much were the shoes?"

"Fourteen hundred dollars."

"Then I guess I won't be buying a pair."

Lisa motioned to a laptop on a side table. "Can I use this? I'd like to look up the model online right now."

Glass nodded.

After Lisa spent a minute on Shinkai's minimalist website, she found the shoes that Hannah Price had bought.

"How do they look?" Glass asked.

"Uncomfortably conceptual," Lisa said.

"It's a bit tenuous, but worth pursuing," Glass said.

"So you think Hannah Price is NatalyaX?"

"It seems likely," Lisa said. Orlov nodded.

Lisa removed a black-and-white surveillance photo of Hannah Price from the file. It had been taken a couple of years earlier when she was in her early twenties. Hannah was a US citizen, born Svetlana Gromyko to Russian parents who had since returned to Moscow. She had fine, pale features, blonde hair, and light-colored eyes that stared opaquely back into the camera, giving nothing away.

"How long has Hannah Price been under surveillance?" Lisa asked.

"Five years or so."

"How certain are you that she's a Russian operative?"

"Fairly certain, based on a few contacts that she's made with known GRU associates. But she's been largely inactive until now. State Department thought it was best to just keep an eye on her and see if she led them to other members of the network."

"So you could have grabbed her up long before she participated in this attack."

Glass scowled. "Wasn't my call. And I'd advise you to watch that sort of comment around here."

Lisa laid the thick file on Glass's desk. "With this much intelligence you should be able to bring her in."

Glass shook her head. "We lost track of her two days before the attack. She's in the wind. But I have a mission for you." She reached into a drawer of her desk and removed two satellite phones, then slid them across. "We want you to find NatalyaX and stop her."

"Stop her how?" Orlov's fingers began to flutter on the arms of the chair, like they wanted to make some big emphatic gestures. "I'm a security consultant. I'm no field agent."

"No, but your partner is," Glass said.

"You carry a weapon?" Orlov asked Lisa.

Lisa nodded.

"You ever fire it? Outside of a firing range?"

"Once or twice."

"This does not reassure me."

"We need to stop NatalyaX from doing more damage. But, even more important, we need to establish a clear link between the Russian government, Hannah Price, and NatalyaX. So far we don't have the smoking gun to prove that Russia is behind the cyberwarfare attacks. Without that, it's difficult for the US to launch a full-scale counterattack. You can start by going back to the place where Price is living in Falls Church. See what you can find."

"There won't be anything there," Lisa said. "She would have had every opportunity to clean house before launching the attack. She would know that we'd go there."

"If the Russians had her walk into that Newark power plant, there's a good chance they assume we haven't identified her as a sleeper agent. Every other law enforcement agent on the East Coast is dealing with the blackout. I can't pull anyone away from that, and most of them wouldn't have a clue what to look for. If there's anything there that points to her involvement in the strobe attacks, the sabotage at the power plant, or anything else, the two of you will find it."

Orlov scratched his beard. "We've got CyberCom and NSA surveillance files, but if it's as bad as you say, how do we know that they haven't been compromised?"

"You mean the false crisis reports?" Glass said. "The data room files are clean. I can't assure you of much, but I do know that."

"Is shit show," Orlov said.

"Yes," Glass nodded. "It is a shit show. But have you got a better idea?"

14

Lisa and Orlov stood on the roof of the CyberCom headquarters as the chopper's blades began to beat the air, starting slowly and then accelerating into a blur. Lisa hefted her backpack, which was equipped as if they were on an expedition into the Alaskan wilderness rather than suburban Virginia. Their gear included military rations, flashlights, sleeping bags, knives, guns, flares, lighters, and satphones. They were starting out in midafternoon but had to prepare for the possibility that their expedition might extend overnight.

"I don't like it," Orlov said as they waited for the helicopter pilot to wave them in. "This feels like a camping trip. I hate camping."

"Do I look like a girl who belongs in the great outdoors?"

Orlov acknowledged the point with his customary shrug.

"How far do you think things have deteriorated out there?" Lisa asked. "I mean, it's only been a day since the attacks began."

"I saw it happen in Kiev in 2016. A large city is entirely dependent on logistics, the flow of goods by train, plane, truck. Once you shut that down, it doesn't take long for things to start falling apart. There's a run on the grocery stores, and there's nothing to restock the shelves with. Then the restaurants begin running out of food in a couple of days. Then the gas stations run out of gasoline, and the cars stop working. Highways get jammed up, and everything grinds to a halt."

"And then things must really start to deteriorate."

"In a worst-case scenario."

"I was in New York City during Hurricane Sandy," Lisa said. "I've witnessed something similar."

"It is not pretty," Orlov said.

"No it's not."

"But I still wish they hadn't given me a gun."

"It's just a precaution. Ever used one?"

"No. In Ukraine, ordinary citizens don't carry guns. In Ukraine, we don't all think that we are cowboys."

As the helicopter lifted off, Lisa looked down at Maryland's suburban sprawl, now strangely lifeless in the wintry afternoon sun. There were very few cars on the freeway below.

She felt as if she were about to be air-dropped into some decimated third world country. And, in some ways, her home turf had become a foreign country. Everything that she thought she knew now seemed suspect.

She looked over at Orlov, insect-like in his noise-canceling earphones, watching him watch the landscape roll past beneath them. She assumed this must all look even stranger to him. But, in Orlov's typically laconic fashion, he wasn't letting on.

After a thirty-minute trip, the helicopter slowed to a hover and descended onto the asphalt expanse of a shopping mall parking lot. There were some parked cars but no human figures in sight.

The pilot's voice came through her headset. "This is Falls Church. I can't get you any closer than this."

"Couldn't you land it in the street right outside the house?" Lisa asked.

"We have orders not to do that," the pilot said. "We have to stay out of close quarters. People might rush the chopper, trying to get a ride out. That's been happening. Panic's starting to set in out there."

Lisa and Orlov climbed out of the chopper and did 360-degree turns, looking to see if the sound of the helicopter had attracted any threats. Everything seemed perfectly quiet and still. She zipped up her parka against a bitter wind that hit her like a slap.

If anyone was observing them, they were doing it from a distance.

The chopper lifted off, enveloping them in a gritty wind. They took a moment to watch the helicopter grow smaller and then disappear into the overcast sky, headed back to Fort Meade.

Once it was gone, they were both quiet as the recognition sank in that the relative safety they had enjoyed at the CyberCom headquarters was gone, and they were now on their own.

Lisa removed a map of Falls Church from her jeans and traced a route from where they stood to the address, which she had marked with a red ballpoint *X*.

"We're probably only ten or fifteen minutes away," Lisa said, hoisting her pack. "Best to keep moving."

They set out across the mall parking lot toward the residential neighborhood that lay beyond. As they passed by a mall entrance, Lisa saw that the glass doors were shattered, and a trail of merchandise was scattered on the pavement, low-value items that had been discarded as looters loaded their take.

"We should keep moving," Orlov said, his hand reflexively touching the jacket pocket that held the handgun.

A metallic rattling came from the other side of the lot, where a couple of teenagers pushed a loaded shopping cart with a wobbling wheel. The two parties eyed one another for a moment, then kept moving in their respective directions.

"Where are the police?" Lisa wondered.

"Occupied," Orlov said. "Saving property is a luxury when lives are in danger."

"I suppose."

"But I understand that the shopping mall is a sacred place for you Americans. This must feel like a violation, like the sacking of a temple."

"Please save the cultural critiques for when we get back," Lisa said. "Right now we need to concentrate."

She consulted her map. "Over there." She pointed at the street ahead.

They walked past an empty gas station and fast-food restaurants that ringed the mall, toward a series of apartment buildings. Several of the buildings had small bands congregated in front of them, huddled around burning dumpsters and trash cans for warmth.

Lisa was relieved that none of the locals tried to engage them.

They turned a corner onto a residential street of one- and two-story houses, lined with oak trees. Midway down the block they arrived at their destination—a large redbrick house with a white wooden porch. According to the surveillance files, Hannah Price rented a room here.

"This is it," Lisa said.

"Looks deserted," Orlov said.

"Every place looks deserted when the electricity's out. That doesn't mean it is."

Lisa led the way up the wooden front steps, which emitted a creak announcing their arrival.

In response to the sound, there was a rustle of footsteps from inside the house, and a querulous old man's voice shouted from behind the door. "Who's there?"

"We're friends of Hannah. Is she there?"

"No, I haven't seen her since the blackout. You need to move along."

The wooden steps groaned as Lisa advanced another step.

"You stop right there, you. I have a loaded shotgun, and believe me, I know how to use it."

Lisa couldn't see the man behind the thin curtains over the windows on either side of the front door. "We don't want any trouble. We just need to have a look in Hannah's room."

"I don't think she'd want that."

"It's okay. I'm with the FBI. If you come out, I can show you my badge."

"What's your name?"

"Lisa. My friend's name is Arkady."

"You a Russian?"

"I am Ukrainian," Orlov said. "Fuck the Russians."

A pause from behind the door. "Say your name again?"

"Lisa."

"Lisa Tanchik?"

"Yeah." Lisa was growing uneasy, not sure where this was headed.

"Hang on. Hannah left a package for you. Has your name on it."

Lisa and Orlov exchanged looks, and then they heard the man's retreating steps in the hallway. It took Lisa a couple of seconds to react, and then she was bounding up onto the porch and shouting to the man.

"Don't touch the package! Don't touch it!"

She tried to knock down the door, but it wouldn't yield to her shoulder.

They heard a loud thud beyond the door, and when they finally managed to get it open, it was partially blocked by a body.

A thin man in his late fifties with a full head of gray-white hair was sitting on the floor, looking ashen. A package the size of a hatbox was on the hallway's oak floorboards, where it had been dropped. The label, which was faceup, read, *For FBI Special Agent Lisa Tanchik.*

"Don't touch it," Lisa said to Orlov. "And don't touch that man."

"You think it's—"

"Yes. Novichok." A nerve agent manufactured in Russia and one of the deadliest substances on earth, it had been used by the GRU against defectors and spies. Even a microgram dose could be lethal, and it was extremely fast acting.

The old man's eyes were glassy, and spittle flecked the corners of his mouth. Lisa and Orlov watched in stunned horror as his hands and then arms began to twitch. His eyes closed, his breathing stopped, and, in a matter of minutes, he was dead.

And they had no choice but to watch. They couldn't raise a hand to help him, because if they made contact with the Novichok, they would meet the exact same fate.

15

Natalya watched anxiously as Agent Tanchik approached the front steps of the house. She was surprised to see that the FBI agent was accompanied by Arkady Orlov, who was well known to Natalya and her handlers for his role in Ukraine's cyber defense. It was quite possible that she might take out two of the GRU's most skilled adversaries with a single neatly wrapped brown-paper package.

The sun had descended below the low clouds, bathing the scene in cold, late-afternoon sunlight. She was positioned in a third-floor window of an abandoned apartment building a half block away from her former residence.

This was the rare occasion when Natalya felt like a real spy, the kind that clashed with opposing operatives in the physical world. Usually her exploits were carried out from behind a keyboard from hundreds or thousands or hundreds of thousands of miles away. Even when her work involved a specific human victim, as opposed to a system that was breached or destroyed, she rarely had the opportunity to view the mayhem in real time.

It was thrilling. She found it hard to suppress a smile. It was the same feeling she had in a darkened theater, not knowing what was coming next.

But then she saw the pair pause on the steps and exchange words with someone inside.

She smacked the windowsill with the palm of her hand when she realized that it was George, her landlord. He had told her that he was leaving to stay with his niece in Silver Spring for the duration of the blackout.

He was going to ruin everything.

Tanchik was supposed to enter the house, where she would proceed to Natalya's room and find the package addressed to her. When she picked it up to take it back to the FBI's forensic lab, she would be infected by the nerve agent and dead in moments. Natalya had not told her landlord about the package; she'd assumed that he wouldn't even be at the house when the FBI arrived.

Instead, she watched through the open doorway as her landlord writhed on the hallway floor. George must have entered her room and seen the package. He had always been nosy, but in a harmless, kindly way. It was his way of showing that he took an interest in her.

Tanchik and Orlov didn't even attempt to perform CPR, which signaled that they knew they were dealing with Novichok or some similar substance.

It felt odd to see Agent Tanchik IRL. The FBI agent had trailed her online for so long that she had almost ceased to think of her as a physical being. It was easier to imagine her as an avatar, operated remotely by a faceless intelligence service.

Natalya removed a small pair of binoculars from her purse and trained them on Tanchik.

The Dark Web was a two-way mirror. While Tanchik had been tracking her, trying to get a glimpse of her in the chat rooms and online forums that Natalya visited, thinking she could see through the masks that Natalya wore online, she probably didn't appreciate just how closely Natalya had, in turn, been observing her. They were like two guests at a costume party, moving through the crowd, each trying to recognize the other by a snippet of conversation, a turn of phrase, a look in the eyes.

They had similar talents and interests, Natalya had learned. They even shared a sense of humor. But Tanchik was leading the relatively uncomplicated American life that Natalya had been denied. If Natalya had been given the same opportunities as Tanchik, she wouldn't have squandered them by allowing depression and alcohol to constantly send her life spinning off its axis.

Natalya watched as Tanchik looked up and down the street. Her eyes scanned suddenly upward, and Natalya crouched lower beneath the window frame so that the lenses of her binoculars wouldn't catch the sunlight, revealing her position.

Could Tanchik actually sense that she was there on the scene, observing her handiwork? The thought gave her a thrill.

Tanchik didn't look depressed tonight. If anything, she seemed energized. *She could definitely do a better job with her makeup—if she even wears any—and her hair,* Natalya thought. She had the look of someone who didn't feel the need to dress for the eyes of men. She probably assumed she was so good at her job that she was above all that. But anyone who thought they didn't live in that world was operating under a misunderstanding.

If Tanchik and Orlov decided to search the building that she was in, she would have no means of escape. But their attention was focused on the deadly package.

Natalya watched as they tied napkins around their noses and mouths and donned latex gloves. Tanchik cut armholes in a black plastic garbage bag and used it as a makeshift hazmat gown to keep dust from the nerve agent off her clothes.

Then the FBI agent reached into the hallway and ever so carefully opened the box, snipping the string with a knife that she removed from her bag. She lifted the lid in painstaking slow motion, fearful of disbursing the toxin. Inside, they found the note that read:

Greetings, Special Agent Tanchik! Very pleased to inform you that you are about to die a horrible death. Take comfort in knowing that it will be very quick.

She had been tempted to sign the note NatalyaX but didn't want to help Tanchik make her case. The FBI agent would know who had left her the present.

Natalya had taken extensive precautions when she'd prepared and deposited the package, wearing a face mask, gloves, and coveralls that left no exposed skin. An open vial of the Ebola virus wasn't as toxic as her tiny packet of Novichok. She had asked Kazimir whether they really wanted to use the nerve agent, which was produced only in Russia and was associated with the SVR, Russia's foreign intelligence service. She had been told that the decision was "above her pay grade," as the Americans would say. Like so many elements of the ongoing cyber-warfare attacks, Russia wanted both attribution and deniability. They wanted everyone to know that Russia was behind the attacks, without leaving any definitive proof.

Once again, Tanchik stepped out onto the front porch, gingerly carrying a white plastic garbage bag that must contain the poisoned package. Tanchik set the bag on the porch and looked up and down the street, then studied the surrounding buildings again. Her instincts were correct, of course. A trap like this was too good not to witness in person.

Natalya's pulse thrummed, caught up in the game of cat and mouse. She realized that Agent Tanchik must consider her the most evil creature imaginable, but she didn't think of herself that way. And, if Tanchik gave it enough thought, she would probably reach the same conclusion.

In this world, sides had to be chosen. Sometimes you had the liberty to choose your side, but more often the decision was made for you.

NatalyaX had been born the daughter of Russian scientists—her mother, Petra, was an agronomist, and her father, Yakov, was a chemical engineer—who had been studying at Johns Hopkins. They had christened her Svetlana Gromyko, a name that she considered hideous. She'd first attracted the attention of the SVR when she'd aced math and science apti-tude tests in sixth grade. A man in a dark suit, named Kostya, had arrived one day at her parents' apartment in Baltimore to ask her a battery of very intrusive questions. He had a deeply lined face and penetrating eyes.

Natalya didn't know who Kostya was, or what the test was designed to evaluate, but she sensed that something important was at stake.

Whatever this prize was, she instinctively and desperately wanted to win it.

"Do you like it here in America?" Kostya asked.

"Yes," she said. "It's fun, and I love my mom and dad."

"Aside from your mom and dad, what do you love about this country?"

"Oh, lots of things, I guess. My friends, and my tumbling class, and FAO Schwarz, and the Saturday-morning cartoons."

"What do you think about Russia? Do you think Russia has those things?"

She thought about this. "I don't know. Maybe not the same things. Maybe different, better things. Maybe in Russia they have a toy store that's bigger than FAO Schwarz."

"Well, it is different, and in some ways it is better. I guess it depends a bit what you're used to."

He had the most penetrating eyes. They could be cold and apprais-ing one moment and warm and friendly the next, and she had abso-lutely no idea which of those looks was genuine.

She put on the best performance that she knew how to give. By her preteen standards, Natalya thought that she was, by turns, charming and funny, thoughtful and sincere. She tried so hard to gauge which responses elicited the man's approval.

Apparently, he had liked her answers, or at least had liked her enthusiasm and determination to persuade him.

At the end of the visit, Kostya left her sitting on the threadbare couch in the living room and visited with her parents. When her parents returned, her father told her that she had done very well, and that things were going to be different for her because of it. Natalya's mother was crying.

"Different and better?" Natalya asked.

"Yes." He nodded. "So much better."

"Then why is Mom crying?"

"Your mother is crying because she's happy for you."

Her parents hadn't exactly been spies, but they'd cooperated with the SVR, leaving her behind in the US at age fourteen with an "aunt" when they returned to Russia after working for several years at the same chemical company.

Losing her parents and essentially being recruited as a future spy when she was only a child had taken its toll. She had been a wild, and sometimes violent, teenager, but that had also served her well later.

Looking back on that early interview with Kostya, Natalya could see that life was like computer code—you could either be a one, or you could be a zero. Even at twelve years old, she'd known that she wanted to be a one, whatever the cost.

And now the cost of being chosen was destroying the country she loved.

Natalya's thoughts snapped back into present tense when she noticed that Tanchik continued to study the surrounding buildings.

What was she looking at?

Maybe she'd caught a glimpse of the binoculars, or maybe Natalya had been right earlier, and Tanchik had somehow sensed her. Either way, the FBI agent, Orlov in tow, began walking purposefully toward the building that Natalya was hiding in. Natalya's fingers reached for the long thin knife in the inside pocket of her jacket, confirming that it was in easy reach, and then she removed the Sig Sauer P225 from her backpack.

She wasn't looking for a direct confrontation with her pursuers, but if they found her, she was going to make them sorry that they had.

16

"What are you staring at?" Orlov asked.

Lisa studied the darkened facades of the buildings facing the house where NatalyaX had lived. Now that she was standing still and the fear and adrenaline had subsided, she felt the cold sinking into her bones. Lisa suspected that someone who would set a trap like the package dusted with Novichok would want to observe the outcome, if possible.

And if she were NatalyaX, which building would she choose? There was a small ranch house directly across the street, but that was probably too close, too exposed. It would be easy to spot a figure in one of those windows, or even a rustling of the curtains.

No, she would prefer to observe from a bit of a distance, and at some elevation, perhaps with a pair of binoculars.

She studied each of the nearby apartment buildings, calculating the sight lines. As dusk descended, NatalyaX would have to be fairly close to be able to make out what was happening at the house. She would know that Novichok was extremely fast acting, and they wouldn't get far if they were exposed. They would have died in the foyer of the house like her landlord, or perhaps made it to the front porch. Which building would afford the best view of the mayhem?

There was really only one viable candidate—a four-story redbrick apartment building across the street and a bit to the left. The building appeared to be unoccupied.

Lisa removed her gloves and the garbage-bag smock and set off across the street.

"Where are you going?" Orlov asked.

"I think she might be here."

"Who?"

"NatalyaX."

"You think she'd want to watch what happened?"

"I think she'd find it irresistible."

Orlov hurried to catch up. "And what if we find her? She's probably armed, right?"

"Probably," Lisa said. "But so am I."

"Shouldn't we call for backup?"

"Under current conditions, that could take forever." Lisa was standing at the front door of the building. She tried the door to the vestibule and confirmed it was open; then she studied the security camera mounted overhead.

"Why don't you see if the recordings from that camera are stored on-site," Lisa said, anxious to give Orlov a task that would get him out of harm's way. "If it's still working on battery power, maybe it captured an image of her."

They stepped inside the darkened lobby. There was a wall with mailboxes, an elevator that was not working, and a doorway that led to stairs.

"Okay, I'll see if I can find a security station. And what are you going to do?"

"I'm going to take a look upstairs. If you hear someone coming back down who doesn't sound like me—hide."

"How will I know what you sound like?"

"I'll announce myself."

Lisa pushed through the door to the stairwell, gun raised. Night was falling, and it was nearly pitch black on the stairs, except for a bit of pale twilight from a skylight on the roof. With the elevator out, the stairwell was probably the only route out of the building from the upper floors.

She stepped quietly up to the first landing, then got off on the second floor. She walked the hallway, testing each doorknob.

When she found an open door, she stepped inside and cleared the apartment. She opened the closets, gun still drawn. Then bathroom door. Then bedroom door. Underneath the bed.

Clear.

Lisa proceeded to search each open apartment, working her way up to the third floor. She figured that if NatalyaX was there, she would be in one of the units that offered a view of the house where she had lived.

After clearing another apartment on the third floor, she found two locked units, and then went on to the next.

Her fingers rested on the doorknob. She quietly tested it, and it turned, but she did not open the door.

17

Inside the room, Natalya watched the doorknob twitch and tightened her grip on the pistol.

It required a conscious effort not to hold her breath. Natalya forced herself to breathe easily. Being too tightly wound when the time came was how errors occurred.

She considered whether she should fire through the door but decided that was too risky. Tanchik was an experienced agent and was probably standing away from the door as she tested it, anticipating gunfire from within.

No, if Natalya was going to take a shot, she knew it had to find its target. Head or center mass. When dealing with professionals, you could not give them a chance to return fire.

She cursed herself for allowing Tanchik to corner her like this. It had been a foolish indulgence to observe them picking up the package. But there was no time for recriminations now. There was only the moment at hand and the faint ticking sound of the FBI agent in the hallway, shifting her weight from one foot to the other on the hallway's wooden floorboards, deciding what came next.

18

A shuffling sound, and then a thud. Lisa removed her hand from the doorknob. She thought the sound had come from one of the units down the hall. She walked cautiously toward it, gun still drawn, careful not to stumble in the gloom.

As she approached the source of the sound, a scrawny tabby cat emerged from the apartment into the hallway. Lisa peered inside but saw no other signs of life. The cat skittered off into the darkness.

She was about to turn to resume her search of the previous apartment when she heard a door creak and quick footsteps.

Lisa instinctively ducked as a gunshot boomed in the confined space, and the wood of the doorframe splintered next to her head.

She turned in time to see the figure of a woman at the other end of the floor near the stairwell.

NatalyaX.

Lisa managed to squeeze off a shot, but it was too late. NatalyaX was bounding heavily down the stairs, from the sound of it taking them two and three at a time.

Orlov. He was in danger. She ran to the stairwell so that her voice would carry to the ground floor.

"Orlov! She's here!"

Lisa heard another gunshot crack and raced down the stairs.

When she reached the lobby, it was empty. "Arkady?"

She heard a rustle from the rental office near the front door, and Orlov lifted his head above the surface of a desk.

"Are you okay?"

"No, I am not okay. That bitch tried to kill me."

"You're not wounded?"

"No."

Lisa nodded to the lobby doors. "She went this way?"

"I think so. I heard the door slam, but I didn't see. I was busy trying to avoid getting my head blown off."

Lisa peered out through the glass at the street and the surrounding buildings. No sign of NatalyaX, but she could be lying in wait for them.

She pushed the door open slowly, gun still drawn, then hurried for cover beside an SUV parked in front of the building. She stayed there for a moment, listening to her ragged breathing.

Lisa looked up the street and then, after circling around to the front of the SUV, checked out the reverse angle. There was no movement anywhere. The group of locals who had been warming themselves over a garbage can fire down the street had vanished at the sound of the gunshot.

Orlov appeared in the building's doorway.

"Stay back," Lisa said. "She might still be around."

But her instincts told her NatalyaX was gone. Who knew when they would again come so close to apprehending her?

She removed the satphone from her backpack and contacted CyberCom. "We're ready for pickup. And the helicopter pilot who comes for us should be wearing hazmat gear. We'll be bringing back a package that's been dusted with a nerve agent."

"Sorry, Special Agent Tanchik, but that's not going to be possible," said the dispatcher. "All of the choppers are out for the next few hours. You have no idea what we're dealing with tonight."

"What do you suggest?"

"Shelter in place, Agent. I'll reach out on the satphone when we can lift you out. Did I hear you correctly that you may be bringing back a sample of a nerve agent?"

"You heard right."

"Do you know what kind?"

"I'm not certain, but we think it may be Novichok."

"Jesus. You two stay safe, and we'll lift you out as soon as possible."

"What do they say?" Orlov asked when she turned off the phone.

"They say we're spending the night here."

Orlov shook his head. "I don't like it. NatalyaX could still be watching us, waiting for another chance to sprinkle her fairy dust on us."

Lisa looked up and down the block. Though she saw nothing suspicious, she knew that didn't mean they were safe.

NatalyaX had surprised her. Lisa had assumed her skills as an operative were exclusively in the cyber realm, but she had looked awfully comfortable with a gun in her hand. Perhaps she had received training as a field agent and knew how to conduct surveillance, how to kill.

"I think you're right," Lisa said. "If she's following us, it will be easier to spot her if we're on the move."

"So which way?" Orlov asked.

"Back toward the mall, I guess. At least we know that there are plenty of landing spots for the chopper over there."

They shouldered their packs and started back the way they had come, using cars and buildings for cover as much as possible. The suburban streets were eerily quiet. Most people must have moved into the local disaster shelter, where there was electricity from a backup generator and food.

The adrenaline spike that followed the gunshots was dissipating, and in its wake Lisa could feel the depression creeping in. It took the form of a gnawing hopelessness, a feeling that all her choices were the wrong ones. She quickened her pace.

"Hey, wait up," Orlov said as he fell behind.

When they reached the shopping mall, there was renewed activity. Even though the place had been extensively looted, a new wave of scavengers seemed to be passing through.

A group of about twenty suburbanites were wheeling shopping carts in and out of the mall entrance. This group didn't look like looters, more like people who were doing what they needed to do to survive during a crisis with no end in sight.

"It would be good to find a place with a view of the mall parking lot so that we can see the helicopter arriving," Lisa said. They walked across the street to an International House of Pancakes with a front door that was shattered.

There was no one inside. Lisa checked the freezer and cabinets but found no food, apart from some jars of maraschino cherries and some spoiled containers of pancake batter.

Orlov stretched out in a large booth that occupied one corner of the restaurant. "At least this is a comfortable place to wait out the night." He pointed to an impossibly vivid poster of a stack of pancakes with strawberries and whipped cream. "I just wish I didn't have to stare at that. I'm starving."

Lisa reached into her pack and tossed Orlov a protein bar.

"Thank you," he said without enthusiasm. "Another metaphor for America." He waggled the bar. "This is a perfectly acceptable form of nutrition, but after looking at that poster, all I want to do is gorge myself on a huge plate of pancakes buried in whipped cream and powdered sugar."

"Please, Arkady. Really? America didn't invent advertising, or restaurants, or being hungry."

Orlov shrugged. "Okay, but there's a certain type of excess that is uniquely American, and I think that poster is representative."

Lisa turned the cardboard poster to face the wall. "You know what I don't understand about what happened tonight?"

"What's that?"

"How did NatalyaX know that I would be the one who visited her apartment?"

"She knows that you've been pursuing her for a year."

"True, but there are a lot of agents involved in this effort now. I think it's odd that she was so certain that it would be me who'd be there to pick up that package."

"What are you saying?"

"I'm saying it was like she had inside information."

"Yes, that's what hackers do. They breach systems and extract information."

"I suppose."

Lisa glanced at her watch and realized that Jon would be worrying about her. "Excuse me for a minute. I need to call someone." Lisa went to the opposite side of the restaurant, near the front doors.

Out of earshot of Orlov, she tried to reach Jon using the satphone. Surprisingly, the call went through.

"Jon?"

"Lisa!"

"I can't believe I got you. I'm using a satphone, but on your end . . ."

"Cell service is starting to come back in DC—at least in some areas. I guess we're getting priority treatment so that government operations can be restored. But how are you? Are you okay?"

"I'm fine. I'm out in the field tonight. In Falls Church."

"Overnight?"

"Yeah, I'm afraid so."

"Are you in a secure location?"

"Yes, I'm fine. A chopper's going to pick us up in the morning."

"Us? You with another field agent?"

"No, I'm here with Arkady Orlov. He's a Ukrainian security consultant. And definitely not trained for the field."

"Hmm. He doesn't sound like someone who's going to be very useful if things go south."

"No, but he is kind of amusing."

"So at least there's that. Tell me that what you're doing is safe. I know you probably can't tell me what your mission is."

"I'm safe. The hazardous part of the assignment is already done."

"So it *was* hazardous."

"Yes, but clearly I'm still here."

"And that's supposed to make me feel better?"

"I really am fine. And I'll see you tomorrow and tell you everything that I can."

"Can I send a dog photo to the satphone you're using?"

"You're still researching dogs in the middle of a national emergency?"

"Mostly I've been defending against attacks on the New York City subway system. But I do have some downtime."

"So you still want to adopt one?"

"Yeah," Jon said, "because if we don't, you know . . ."

They said it together. "The terrorists win."

"Love you," Lisa said.

"Love you too."

Lisa signed off and returned to Orlov, taking the other side of the cushioned booth. Ignoring him for the moment, she checked out the sight lines to the mall parking lot.

Her thoughts turned, not for the first time, to the sight of Tony Ruffalo clutching his chest in the war room after his pacemaker had been hacked. There was something particularly horrifying to her about a threat that came from within your own body. She was glad that she had no implanted medical devices, no insulin pump or pacemaker, because it might have driven her mad knowing that NatalyaX or the Russians could turn those devices against her. This new form of biological terror was a little like the horror movie trope when the terrorized heroine realizes that the call is coming from inside the house.

"This actually may be too comfortable," Lisa said. "It's going to be hard to stay awake here."

"So we talk," Orlov said. He reached into his backpack and removed a bottle of Stolichnaya vodka. "And we drink."

"My poison," Lisa said. "You were only supposed to pack essentials."

"*Da*. That's why I only brought one bottle."

Lisa found a couple of glasses. Orlov poured them triple shots and then placed the bottle on some unmelted ice in the restaurant's walk-in freezer.

They clinked glasses, and both took big swallows.

"*Na zdorovye!*" Orlov said.

The vodka burned going down, and it made Lisa recall her last argument with Jon before she had been drawn into the current crisis. Would he tell her that she was putting herself and Orlov in danger now?

"Okay," Lisa said, the shot already calming her jangled nerves. "Here's something to get you started. You love to criticize America, but there must be a few things that you love about this place. Name one."

"You misunderstand me. I love America. I love your movies, your music, your television. *Godfather*s *I* and *II*. Scorsese, Ford, Welles, Mr. P. T. Anderson, Ms. Kathryn Bigelow."

"That's refreshing to hear something positive from you about the US."

"I could go all night on the subject."

"Music?"

"Coltrane, Sinatra, Otis Redding. Hendrix."

"And from this century?"

"Taylor Swift. She is American princess."

"And television?"

"*The Wire*, of course. And *The Sopranos*. *Mad Men*. *Miami Vice*."

"You had me until that last one."

"What do you mean? Michael Mann is goddamn genius. Have you seen *Last of the Mohicans*? *Heat*? *Manhunter*?"

"Okay," Lisa said. "So you have some sense of what we're about here in the US."

"Who doesn't? You like to think that you're the good guy, but you also want to be the freethinking, wisecracking outlaw. You're Han Solo, Jack Nicholson, Deadpool. You want to run the world *and* be the scrappy underdog too. You can't have it both ways, but somehow you manage to."

"I don't want to hear you trash-talking Han Solo—or Nicholson."

"What about Deadpool?"

"Say what you want about Deadpool."

Orlov nodded, absorbing and acknowledging that statement. "My son, Alyosha—big Deadpool fan."

"Oh, I didn't realize—"

"That I had a family? What, you think I am just comic sidekick to American FBI agent? Believe it or not, I have a whole life—and family—that you know nothing about."

"My apologies. Sounds like you've got more of a family than I have."

"I'm sorry to hear that. What about your mother and father?"

"My folks had me late in life. Mom had a heart attack when I was fourteen. My dad died six months later. They said that was a heart attack, too, but I think he just didn't want to live without her."

"No brothers or sisters?"

"There was a sister, Jess. But she died when I was still in high school."

"What happened, if you don't mind me asking?"

"OxyContin and alcohol. That's what happened." She poured another shot of vodka. "That's why I stick to alcohol."

Orlov stared at her for a moment with a look that she couldn't read.

Ready to move on from the recounting of family histories, Lisa said, "So despite all your anti-American snark, you seem to have some feeling for what's happening to my country."

"I do, and I don't."

"Please explain, because that sounds pretty callous."

Orlov raised a hand in concession. "Of course, sure, I hate seeing all this panic and suffering. No one deserves that. But there's a part of me that is kind of glad to see the US get a taste of what it's like to be Ukraine."

"And what does that mean exactly?"

"It means that no country is immune anymore. The mighty US, the not-so-mighty Ukraine, doesn't matter."

"You act all cynical, but I get the impression that you're really a patriot at heart. You're probably a national hero back in Ukraine," Lisa said.

Orlov sat up in the booth and rubbed his beard. "I suppose some people know what I did. But I failed. I was unable to stop them. And now it's happening again. And again, I can't stop it."

"No matter what happens, you should be proud that you stood up and fought back."

"That's a nice thing to say, but you have no idea what you're talking about."

"So tell me," Lisa said. "We've got all night."

Orlov poured two more shots. "For that, I'll need more vodka."

After emptying his glass, he said, "I could have done better."

"Who doesn't think that? You were going up against one of the world's most sophisticated cyber actors, with all of the manpower and resources of the GRU behind the attack. You had an impossible task."

"That's not what I mean," said Orlov.

"Then what do you mean?"

He seemed to be considering a response, but the more he contemplated it, the darker his expression grew. Finally, he waved a hand in dismissal. "I don't want to talk about it. This is depressing enough."

Lisa wondered what secret Orlov might be harboring, but she knew that she couldn't pry it out of him. It was unsettling him so much that it would eventually have to come out like a loose tooth.

She yawned. It wasn't going to be easy to stay awake all night to guard against looters or a return visit from NatalyaX.

"Why don't you get some sleep?" Orlov said. "I'll stand guard."

"Are you sure?"

"No problem. I don't think I'll be sleeping anyway. Every time I close my eyes, I see that crazy bitch running down the stairs and taking aim at me."

"Was that the first time someone has tried to kill you?"

"Yes. You know, I talk about cyberwarfare like I'm some kind of veteran. But it's different when someone aims a gun at you and actually tries to blow your head off."

He was staring out through the large plate glass windows at the road and the shopping mall parking lot beyond. Lisa saw their reflections superimposed over that image, mirrored back at them darkly.

19

This is Don Hansberry of CNN reporting on America Under Attack. The cyberattacks on America by an unknown adversary continue. Progress is being made in restoring electrical power and cellular service in pockets of East Coast cities, including certain portions of Washington, DC, New York City, and Boston, but much of the Eastern Seaboard remains without power in the middle of one of the coldest winters on record. Given the nature of the crisis, the government has been unable to provide definitive estimates of deaths or property damage, but White House press secretary Sandra Turner conceded today in a briefing that there is no question that the death toll is mounting.

While electricity and cellular service are beginning to return, that progress is overshadowed by news of continued attacks. Multiple sources have confirmed that a nuclear power plant in Beaver Valley, Pennsylvania, has been placed on high alert, with personnel being called in on an emergency basis to respond to a crisis. It is important to note that there have been no reports of a release of radiation from the facility.

20

Lisa awoke at first light because there was no place to escape the bright sun. With its large plate glass windows, the IHOP was like a glass box open on three sides.

She glanced over at Orlov, who was wearing the same brooding expression that he'd had when she'd fallen asleep, only now the circles under his eyes were darker.

Lisa glanced around the diner and rubbed the sleep from her eyes. "Where's my waitress? I need a refill on my coffee."

"She is bringing it with my pancakes and bacon," Orlov responded grimly.

Lisa reached into her pack and tossed him a protein bar.

"That is your answer for everything, isn't it?"

She shrugged. "When's pickup?"

"The chopper's on the way," Orlov said. He walked over to the window and studied the horizon.

"Is the package secure?"

Orlov nodded to the white plastic garbage bag on the floor near the cash register.

"I bagged it two more times and sealed them all tight. I was worried that when we get in the helicopter, all that wind might kick up some loose particles."

"Good idea," Lisa said. She nodded toward the road and the shopping center. "You see any activity out there last night?"

"A few cars. Some looters over at the mall. No one tried to come over here."

"You think things are starting to settle down out there?"

"Hard to say."

Fifteen minutes later, Lisa heard the sound of a helicopter approaching. They shouldered their packs and went across the street into the mall parking lot to wave down their ride.

"When we get back, I'm going to sleep for the rest of the day," Orlov said.

"If they let us."

What Lisa thought was, *When we get back, I'm going to take my antidepressants.* She had missed two days of Zoloft and was starting to feel it. While missing two days wasn't necessarily debilitating—antidepressants had a cumulative effect—there was no denying that the Black Dog was her constant companion now. He lay at one end of the booth, gnawing on a tear in the Naugahyde upholstery with single-minded focus.

She needed a stiff drink. That would send Black Dog slinking back to his crate, at least momentarily.

"What's the first thing you're going to do when you get back?" Orlov asked.

"A long hot shower."

"This is where you ask: 'What are you going to do, Arkady?'"

"What are you going to do when you get back, Arkady?"

"A burger and a beer. So American, but so good."

Orlov seemed exhausted but in good spirits. He did not know Lisa well enough to spot the change in her. When she got back home, Jon would recognize the indicators in an instant. He probably wished that he didn't know her that well.

On the ride back to CyberCom headquarters, she observed the snarled and unmoving traffic on the highway below.

"Why are the freeways blocked?" Lisa asked the pilot, using her headset.

After a crackle of static, he responded: "Gas stations are running out of gas now. Once cars start running out of gas in the middle of the road, it doesn't take long before the whole freeway is impassable."

Lisa was relieved to see the CyberCom/NSA headquarters come into view. The black-mirrored windows of the building glinted with a coppery sheen that was intended to block the signals of rival intelligence agencies. They landed on the roof, and she and Orlov were once again escorted downstairs.

They were brought to Emma Glass's office first. A man with sandy hair in a charcoal pinstripe suit was standing in the corner near the door, intently tapping away on his phone. Glass didn't introduce him, and they didn't ask.

After Lisa and Orlov had briefed her on their encounter with NatalyaX, Glass said, "So you had her right in front of you, and you let her go."

"Well, she had a gun, and she tried to kill me," Orlov shot back.

"I'm not talking to you," Glass said. "I'm speaking to Special Agent Tanchik. Who has a gun. And supposedly knows how to use it."

"You're right," Lisa said. "I should have had her."

"If you had captured NatalyaX, we might have the intelligence we need to link this attack to the Russians. We're at a critical juncture now."

"How so?"

"POTUS has to decide whether or not to treat this as an act of war by Russia. It would be nice to know that the country that we're about to declare war on is actually responsible."

"That hasn't stopped you in the past," Orlov said.

Glass ignored the remark. "I think I'm going to have to bring you two into a classified meeting."

At this point, the man in the corner stopped typing and lowered his phone. "They do not belong in the meeting. Especially a non-US citizen," he said, glaring at Orlov.

"You all invited *me* to participate in this investigation," Orlov said.

"Who are you, anyway?" Lisa asked the man.

Glass fielded the question, as if her guest was above explaining himself. "This is Geoffrey Tobin, deputy national security adviser. This meeting is with senior executive branch staff, including the secretary of defense and secretary of state."

"They do not belong in the meeting. I don't think they even belong here at CyberCom," said Tobin. "One is FBI and lacking the appropriate security clearance; the other is a foreign national."

"We're in the room," Orlov said.

"The decision makers are going to want to question them directly," Glass said. "Tanchik has been pursuing NatalyaX for a year now, and Orlov knows more about Russian cyber tactics than anyone on our team. No written briefing is going to cover everything. This is a decision on a declaration of war, and I won't be accused of holding back any information that may prove relevant. Do you want that responsibility?"

Tobin's jaw clenched, and finally he said, "They can come to the briefing, but they don't speak unless spoken to."

Glass nodded. "Okay, let's go."

Glass and Tobin rose and left the room, and Lisa and Orlov followed. They took an elevator to the top floor and a conference room that looked out on rolling hills dotted with patches of snow and a freeway in the distance. A group of twelve was sitting or standing around a long mahogany table, waiting to get started. Lisa could tell that the composition of this group was different than in the CyberCom war room, because the suits outnumbered the khakis.

General Holsapple was at one end of the table. At the opposite end sat Margaret "Maggie" Bilton, the president of the United States. Lisa felt as if the nightly newscast had just come to life.

Holsapple called the meeting to order. First came a briefing on the state of the nation in the wake of the attack, which was dire. As the presentation wore on, Lisa and Orlov sat in silence, trading occasional stunned looks.

Holsapple flipped through PowerPoint slides filled with charts and graphs detailing the impact of the attack on electrical power, clean water, phone service, trucking and rail deliveries—and it all seemed disturbingly antiseptic. But after having been out in the field that morning, Lisa knew what those primary-colored pie charts and bar graphs meant.

After the facts and figures, Holsapple finally addressed the human toll, saying, "You may think that because our enemy has not launched a missile and wiped out one of our cities that this war does not have casualties. That is a mistake. If anything, this attack is more deadly than a missile strike, because the damage is not isolated to a blast zone.

"The elderly are freezing to death in their apartments. The sick are dying because they were unable to reach a hospital to treat medical emergencies. Those that reach a hospital are often dying because healthcare workers lack medications, supplies, or electricity. Some people are being shot as looters. Stores are running out of food, and people are going hungry. Controllers that regulate oil and gas pipelines have been disabled, cutting off heating in several East Coast cities. A fire in New York City started by a blown electrical substation is spreading unabated because the fire department can't reach it through streets filled with abandoned cars. People are dying in those fires. I could go on, but you've all seen the reports.

"The bottom line is that this is a deadly attack on American citizens, and it calls for a commensurate response."

Finally, they had reached the question that was at the heart of the meeting: Should the US go to war with Russia? And, if so, what sort of war should be waged?

"No one disputes that, Tom." Lisa recognized Secretary of Defense Richard Stansfield, wearing his dark suit with the rigid posture of the former five-star general that he was. "The question is, Who do we strike? I still haven't heard confirmed attribution that Russia is behind this."

"And even though it might feel good to launch some form of attack on Russia, we all know where that will lead," said Secretary of State Mona Washington. "President Vasiliev has based his entire political career on not being seen as weak with the US. He will feel compelled to respond in kind—or up the ante."

"But there is such a thing as a proportionate, measured response," said National Security Adviser Alberto Molina. "How certain are we that Russia is behind this? Eighty percent certain? Ninety percent? God, I hope we're not at forty percent."

Stansfield stood up with his fingertips on the table. "I think Al's right. There's a proportionate response to be made here, and I think it probably involves a response in kind, a cyberwarfare counterstrike. Or maybe it's sending missiles to take out strategic military targets. But we have to know that we're attacking the right actor. And if we're not certain, we need to factor that into our response."

President Bilton had remained silent through the discussion, occasionally whispering comments to an aide who sat beside her. She finally interjected, "So what is it? Forty percent certainty? Ninety percent? I'm not hearing the facts that would help us resolve that. Who can tell me that?"

Holsapple took this as his cue. "Madam President, the malware that was used in the attack on the power grid and the public transportation systems in New York and Philadelphia is nearly identical to malware that has been linked to the GRU in the past. We believe it was originally developed by the Central Scientific Research Institute of Chemistry and Mechanics in Moscow, which is owned by the Russian government."

"But that doesn't necessarily mean that Russia is behind this," Molina interjected. "That malware is available to terrorist organizations on the Dark Web."

"That's true," Holsapple said, frowning at the interruption. "But the sheer sophistication and coordination of this attack could only have been accomplished by a state-sponsored actor."

"We can't forget that Russia has ample motive, in their mind at least, to attack us," Stansfield said.

"What's the current status of Kostroma?" President Bilton asked.

"The Russians aren't providing details—just accusations. They're clearly downplaying the damage to the facility and the casualties, but we can see from satellite images that there's been a release of toxic radiation."

"The Russian ambassador is adamant that the US is behind the malware that sabotaged the nuclear plant," Secretary of State Washington said. "They know we created the Stuxnet virus with the Israelis, but they're completely ignoring the fact that it doesn't just belong to us anymore. It's out there in the world."

"The same defense they're going to use if we accuse them of distributing GRU-made malware now," Bilton said. "Do we know who was behind the Kostroma attack? Maybe if we had some evidence, we could convince them."

"We're working on that," Holsapple said, "but we don't have anything yet. And we're stretched pretty thin as it is."

"I want resources deployed from other agencies if necessary," Bilton said. "If we can get the Russians to stand down and cease these attacks, then that has to be our highest priority."

"Yes, Madam President."

With that, the discussion paused as the cabinet officers around the table looked at one another. Finally, Secretary of State Washington spoke. "While the human toll is our paramount concern, we also can't ignore the financial cost of these attacks. The malware has wiped out the hard drives of thousands of businesses, destroying data. Many companies are working to replace their equipment, but the world's available supply of hard drives has been exhausted."

"What's the solution to that?" President Bilton asked.

"The Chinese have already identified the opportunity and have cranked their hard drive manufacturing into overdrive."

"Have to give them credit," the president said. "Look, I'm hearing some new information, but most of this is already in my briefing. Is this really the best you've got? None of this gives me any sort of comfort level launching an attack on a nation that has an unpredictable leader and significant nuclear capabilities."

Holsapple cleared his throat and swallowed. "I'm afraid this is the nature of cyberwarfare, Madam President. There is inevitably less certainty when war is being waged in the fourth domain."

"Fourth domain? I don't know that term."

"War has traditionally been fought in three domains—land, sea, and sky. Cyberwarfare is the new, fourth domain."

"I don't care what you call it, General; we still need to know who we're fighting, and we need to know that we're striking back at them, and not some unrelated party."

"As we proceed with considering offensive options," Holsapple said, "it's important to remember one thing."

"What's that?" Bilton asked.

"That when we launch a cyberattack, it's a little like throwing stones from a glass house."

"How do you mean?"

"I mean that the US is one of the most modern, internet-enabled nations on earth. In most cases, that's a good thing. It makes our factories and our networks more efficient and modern. But it also makes them more exposed. If we get involved in a full-scale cyberwar with Russia, the fact that much of their infrastructure is dependent upon systems and equipment that are decades old actually becomes an advantage for them. They have fewer attack surfaces than we do."

"I take your point," said the president. "But if we confirm that the Russians are behind this, what choice do we have?"

The aide at the president's side said, "From a political standpoint, we—"

The president raised a peremptory hand. "I'm going to stop you right there. This is not a political decision. I don't want anyone in this room to mention politics or polling data. We don't go to war on that basis."

The room fell silent for a moment. No one was willing to be the next to draw incoming fire.

"So what else have you got?" the president asked.

"Well," Holsapple said, "we haven't fully debriefed them yet, but FBI special agent Lisa Tanchik and security consultant Arkady Orlov were in the field pursuing an operative known as NatalyaX. We believe that NatalyaX is Hannah Price, a known Russian sleeper agent. We also believe that she is the hacker who was spreading the strobe attachment that killed John Rosenthal."

"Why don't we hear from them?" The president turned her gaze to Lisa and Orlov.

Lisa looked at Orlov, who nodded for her to go ahead. She gave a précis of her yearlong pursuit of NatalyaX and the links they'd found between her and the Sandworm hacker collective, a known tool of the GRU.

Lisa had the rapt attention of the room. When she finished describing the death of Hannah Price's landlord, she turned to Holsapple. "Has the substance been confirmed as Novichok?"

Holsapple turned to one of his deputies and, after a whispered conversation, nodded. "Yes, it was Novichok."

"That's the substance that the GRU used to assassinate that former party official who was living in England, right?" the president said.

"Yes, that's correct," Holsapple said.

"Have we ever seen a case where an agency other than the GRU used Novichok?" the president asked.

"I don't know the answer to that question, Madam President, but I suspect that someone in this room does."

One of the men at the opposite end of the table spoke up. "Ross Ehrenreich, CIA. We're not aware of any case where Novichok was linked to an actor other than the GRU."

"Thank you." The president turned to Lisa. "If you've been tracking her for over a year, you must have gotten some sense of her. Were there ever any giveaways that she is a Russian?"

"Madam President, I don't think she is a Russian. If, as we suspect, Natalya is Hannah Price, she has Russian parents, but in attitude, temperament, and tastes, she's an American. She has never lived in Russia. She likes American things."

"But not enough to stop her from destroying them. If you encounter her again—"

"That's not an *if*, Madam President; that's a *when*—"

"Okay. Good," President Bilton said. "That's helpful. Now I'd like to hear more about how close the match is between the malware used against us and malware that we've associated with the GRU. We need to reach a decision here."

Tobin, who had been silent thus far, spoke up. "As we finish this discussion, shouldn't this be limited to the highest security clearance?" He was looking at Lisa and Orlov.

"Yes, you're right," Holsapple said. He whispered a few words to one of his aides, and then Lisa, Orlov, and three others were ushered from the room as the conversation continued.

Tobin personally escorted Lisa out. "That was impertinent," he said when they were in the corridor. "You don't talk to the president like that."

"I didn't get the impression that she had a problem with it," she said. "And since you're not my supervisor or the FBI director, I don't take orders from you."

"You watch yourself, Special Agent. I don't think you have any idea what I can and can't do."

As she and Orlov returned to their temporary offices, Lisa clenched her teeth, thinking about how close she'd come to apprehending Natalya. The president and her advisers had a difficult, if not impossible, decision to make—whether or not to declare war—and she might have made it much easier.

Maybe she still could.

21

After her expedition into the now-lawless wilds of Northern Virginia, Lisa was given an opportunity to return home to her apartment for a night of sleep in her own bed. She needed to recover her antidepressants and other medications, so CyberCom gave her a lift in one of their helicopters, depositing her on the roof of her building. The pilot would return in the morning, part of an impromptu shuttle service that they were running for CyberCom and NSA personnel.

On the ride over, as the grid of DC streets glided past below in the umber light of dusk, the pilot's voice popped in Lisa's headset.

"You heard the news?" he asked.

"What happened?"

"We're at war. With Russia. Officially now."

"Is it just cyber?"

"Far as I know. That's what the president said in the official declaration. But I guess you never know when troops or missile strikes might be involved."

"God, I hope not," Lisa said, gazing down and imagining the impact of an ICBM on her Dupont Circle neighborhood.

"Didn't think I'd see something like this in my lifetime," the pilot said as he spiraled down to the roof of her building. "A war on our soil."

As the helicopter hovered and descended, Lisa saw curtains open in some of the windows of the surrounding apartment towers, faces peering out. Maybe they were hoping for rescue; maybe they were just glad that the chopper didn't signal some sort of attack.

No one knew what to expect in this new world, including Lisa.

When the helicopter touched down on the roof, Jon was already waiting for her, drawn by the noise.

They kissed briefly, and he held her by the shoulders, at arm's length. "I wasn't sure you were still okay."

"I'm fine, but it's like the Dark Ages out there. How are you?"

"I'm fine. The academy is shut down. We were all told to just stay home until they called us in. My biggest challenge has been finding something decent to eat with the grocery stores all empty. But you, I knew you'd be in the middle of things."

She smiled. "I kinda was, but I'm okay."

They descended the stairs to their apartment. He watched her go straight to the medicine cabinet in the bathroom and swallow a pill. "How are you feeling?"

"A little wonky, but nothing that can't be put right."

She sensed his worry, and she knew it was a sign of how much he cared. So why did it feel so much like mistrust? "Have you got enough of everything? I'm not sure how you'd refill a prescription right now."

"I think I'm good on everything for now. Besides, there are doctors on staff at CyberCom who should be able to provide meds if I need them."

It felt good to be back in their apartment after sleeping in a booth at IHOP, knowing that her rest could be interrupted at any time by looters or a Russian operative spreading deadly toxins. The apartment was lit by candlelight and smelled of wax. Blankets were piled on the bed, and Jon kept his down vest on.

"Still no electricity?" Lisa asked.

"It came back for about fifteen minutes yesterday, then went out again. At least cell service is mostly back."

Lisa headed for the kitchen. The main compartment of the refrigerator was at room temperature, and anything that could spoil had. But the freezer still had a block of ice—and a bottle of Ketel One vodka.

"Hello, friend," she said, pouring a stiff shot into a tumbler. She settled into the couch and stared about the room.

"And . . . there's no TV. How have you survived?"

"It's been hell."

"We may actually have to talk to each other," Lisa said.

Jon leaned over and kissed her. "Let's not go there just yet," he said.

22

Day Five

This is Don Hansberry reporting from CNN headquarters in Atlanta. Yesterday President Bilton officially declared war on Russia, naming that country as the perpetrator of the ongoing cyberattacks. Ordinarily, when war is declared, CNN would have a correspondent on the scene where the bombs are falling and the troops are marching. But Secretary of State Mona Washington has stated that the US is responding in kind with cyberattacks on Russia's critical infrastructure. We await word from the Bilton adminis- tration on the progress and success of those attacks.

In the meantime, the destruction continues to mount in the series of cyberattacks that has crippled the entire East Coast and extended west as far as portions of eastern Ohio, Kentucky, and West Virginia. Electrical power, cellular connectivity, public transportation, and other essential services are beginning to be restored to pockets of certain cities such as Washington and New York, but the progress is painfully slow as the human and financial toll mounts. FEMA reports one hundred and eight confirmed fatalities, most from hypothermia as temperatures dropped as low as ten degrees last night in Boston. At least thirteen deaths are attributed to looting and riots that have broken out in several cities. When asked yesterday when the electrical grid will be fully restored, Homeland Security director Shane Willett responded, "It's impossible to say at this time. Some of our power grid infrastructure dates back to the fifties. Once it has been knocked down, it is not so easy to stand it back up." Nevertheless, White House officials that we spoke with stated that they are cautiously optimistic that the worst of the attacks are over, and that the East Coast has turned a corner and is on the path to recovery and restoration of services.

One of the most alarming new developments is a video that has become a worldwide internet sensation. It purports to show a White House address by President Bilton in which she admits that the US has engaged in cyber-warfare tactics against Russia, China, North Korea, and Iran, and that the US "deserves the attacks it has experienced as retribution in the past several days, and sincerely apologizes to our friends and enemies for our pattern of unprovoked cyber aggression."

Experts quickly debunked the video as a so-called deepfake, a near-seamless digital alteration of previous addresses by President Bilton. The technique, also known as human image synthesis, uses artificial intelligence to combine and superimpose existing images onto source images. The White House immediately issued a strong repudiation of the video as false pro-paganda designed to weaken our country during a time of crisis. That has not stopped several foreign governments, including Russia and Iran, from treating the video as a legitimate statement from the US president and expressing outrage.

Our guest is Professor Calvin Folger from the Stanford Center for Internet and Society, an expert in deepfake technology, here to deconstruct this video and explain how this footage varies from President Bilton's facial and verbal characteristics, which are a kind of digital signature. Thanks for joining us, Professor Folger . . .

23

When Lisa awoke in the morning, she was still on the couch, but Jon had supplied a pillow and blankets. The Black Dog was there, curled into her knees, softly snoring. She felt low, like a device with a depleted battery.

When she sat up and laid her bare feet on the cold floor, she realized just how hungover she was. Maybe she'd drunk more of the vodka than she remembered. When she saw the empty bottle on its side at the foot of the couch, that suspicion was confirmed.

"Hey," Jon said, poking his head out of the kitchen. "You up for some breakfast?"

"Not just yet," she said, squinting in the too-bright sunlight from the window. "Could you pull those curtains?"

"How are you feeling?"

"You're going to hate me for this, but do we have anything else to drink around here?"

"A skunky bottle of chardonnay that's been open for a while."

Lisa went to the refrigerator. "Any storm in a port."

"I know you don't want to hear this but—"

"Any sentence that starts like that should end right there."

"Drinking right now?" Jon said, undeterred. "On top of missing your antidepressants for two days? That's a recipe for disaster. You know this."

"I'm not saying you're wrong. And I'm happy that you're an even-tempered, well-adjusted guy who thinks that *CSI: Miami* is dark. But you don't know how I feel."

"I don't need to understand things the way you do. I'm an FBI agent too. I wouldn't want someone in your condition standing next to me if shots are being exchanged."

"You're not my supervisor," Lisa said, opening the fridge. "It's not for you to judge whether I'm impaired or not."

"I know things your SAC doesn't know, though, don't I? I know that you drink before you go into work some days. I know that you've gone out into the field still feeling the effects from the night before."

"Those have been rare occasions," Lisa said, frustrated. "I've never endangered anyone. And that's not your business."

"It actually is. I have a responsibility to the bureau, and to my colleagues. If the SAC learns about what you're doing, they'll assume that I knew and didn't say anything."

"If you're so worried that I might reflect badly on your career, then there's one way to fix that," Lisa said, taking the bottle of chardonnay off the door.

"That's not what I'm saying."

"Then what are you saying?" Every time they had this argument, it was like a chess game; each match produced some new variation, some twist.

"I guess I'm saying that if you don't take care of this, I might have to report you to the SAC."

And there it was. Jon had never crossed that line before.

Lisa set the bottle carefully on the counter. Then she turned and stared at him for a long moment. "You would do that to me? Then why don't you report Gillmartin? Judging by the way he looks in the morning, he has a far worse problem than I do."

"I don't live with Gillmartin. And I don't care about him."

She turned her back on him. "Oh, so this is caring? You're willing to get me kicked out of the bureau because you care so much about me. Thanks, friend. You have my permission to care a little less, okay?"

"You wouldn't be kicked out of the bureau. There's a diversion program. You could get clean and come back."

"Not if you out me to the SAC. I would probably need to come forward myself to get that sort of treatment."

Jon nodded. "Maybe that's what you should do then."

"And is that substance abuse diversion program going to cure my depression, too, which I've had since I was eight years old?"

She poured some chardonnay into a coffee mug, then poured the rest of the bottle out in the sink and tossed the bottle in the recycling bin. "Later this morning a helicopter is going to pick me up and take me back to CyberCom. I can help stop what's happening to this country. If you really care about me, you won't stand in my way. Because if you do, I don't think I could ever forgive you."

She drank down the cup of wine and chased it with some water. And then she pulled on some workout pants, climbed on her exercise bike, and selected a class. Overnight, electrical power and internet had been restored, at least in her neighborhood. She was sure that DC had been a priority in the recovery efforts. She placed a bottle of water in the bike's cup holder.

Okay, Robin. Bring it. Let's sweat out some vodka.

As the bike pedals began to spin, Lisa forgot about Jon, forgot about the cyberattack, and let the endorphins take over.

She wasn't long into her ride when a high five popped up on her screen. She reached over to click a high five back, and that was when she noticed the other rider's screen name.

She hit the red brake button and brought the bike to an abrupt halt. The rider's ID was NatalyaX.

24

Lisa had an hour before the helicopter from CyberCom arrived to pick her up, so she took the opportunity to walk around her neighborhood. In some ways it looked the same, but in other ways the rhythms were all off. The traffic lights were still out, and only a few cars moved haltingly through the intersections, unsure of the new rules of automotive etiquette.

There were people walking on the sidewalk, but far fewer than usual. And those that she passed were often loaded down with items they had scavenged to help them weather the ongoing crisis—blankets, six-packs of bottled water, sleeping bags.

Lisa popped in her fully charged AirPods, hoping some music would distract her. When she got into the office, she'd request the bike company's accounts, but she already knew they would only lead her to a dead end of false IDs and proxy servers.

NatalyaX had brought the war into her home.

She felt a disproportionate surge of relief when she saw that her favorite local coffee shop was open for business. A tall dark roast was not enough to put her right, but it was definitely a step in the right direction.

As soon as she reached the counter, the barista she saw most of the mornings she came in said, "Tall dark roast with room?" It was more of a statement than a question.

"You know it," Lisa said. "And a shot of espresso on the side."

"A twist. I love it when you surprise me."

Lisa had to pay cash because payment card readers were not working. As she made change, the barista smiled and looked like she was about to say something, but then decided not to.

Lisa waited for the barista to drop off her drink at the other counter, and when she picked up the cup, she noticed the writing in marker on the side:

FOR LISA—FROM NATALYA

Lisa glanced quickly around the coffee shop and then out at the sidewalk, making sure that this message wasn't a prelude to some sort of ambush. Once she was confident that no one was bearing down on her, she said, "What is this?"

"It's a surprise. From Natalya." The barista saw the look on her face and added, "It's okay, right?"

"Is Natalya here?"

"No, she called here about two weeks ago. She said that she was a friend of yours and wanted to give you a little surprise, asked me to write her name on your coffee cup the next time I waited on you." The barista was frowning now, worried she'd done something wrong.

"Did she say how she knew I was a regular here?"

"No."

Two weeks ago. Well before the Rosenthal attack. Well before the blackout.

The only explanation that made sense was that she'd been hacked. Which would also explain how Natalya knew which spin class Lisa was taking.

"What else did she say?" Lisa asked. "Was there some message for me?"

"She just wanted me to say that she hopes you have the best day ever. She sounded like a good friend. Did I do something wrong here?"

"No, no, it's fine," Lisa said, smiling. "I was just surprised. If Natalya reaches out to you again, could you give me a call?" She slid her card across the counter. "I'd like to return the favor and surprise her."

"You two are so cute. I wish I had a friend like that."

"Yeah, Natalya is very special," Lisa said, then left the coffee shop.

Out on the sidewalk, her neighborhood, which had seemed off kilter before, now seemed to be positively swarming with hidden currents and undertows.

She scanned the shops, the apartment buildings, and the offices as she headed back to the apartment. She'd had an instinct in Falls Church about the vantage point that NatalyaX had been using to observe her. Could she summon those instincts again?

Lisa studied the people who passed on the street as they hauled groceries and survival gear back to their homes. She paused in the middle of the sidewalk to gaze up at the surrounding rooftops as pedestrians coursed around her.

There was no sign of NatalyaX, and Lisa had no sense that she was near. Like the high-five message, showing that she knew her favorite coffee shop was just a parlor trick, a taunt. As she walked on, Lisa wondered what else the Russian operative knew about her.

25

By the time Lisa arrived at the conference room at CyberCom where she and Orlov would be working that day, she had developed a theory about how NatalyaX was tracking her.

Before Lisa could begin, Orlov held aloft some sort of orange pastry. "Have you had one of these?"

"No. What is that?"

"Is a breakfast muffin. It has a whole poached egg inside it." He gazed at it admiringly, as if he was about to launch into a soliloquy.

"And I take it that you like it?"

"It is magnificent."

"I'm very happy for you, but there are some new developments that we need to discuss."

After bringing Orlov up to speed on NatalyaX's messages on the exercise bike and at the coffee shop, he said, "You two are developing such a close relationship I feel left out."

"I wouldn't be so sure she isn't tracking you too."

This gave Orlov pause, and he placed the half-consumed muffin on a napkin.

"How would she know that I visited that particular coffee shop?" Lisa continued. "My neighborhood has half a dozen of them in a three-block radius."

"Educated guess? Maybe she tried leaving messages at several coffee shops in the area, until someone recognized your name and confirmed that you were a customer."

"Possible, but that seems like a lot of trouble for very little return. No, NatalyaX was showing off by sending that message. And tracking me down in that way isn't particularly elegant. It doesn't reflect favorably upon her skills as a hacker."

"So how do you think she knew? Oh, wait, of course."

"Yes, she's accessing GPS data. Think about the spoofed email that she sent to John Rosenthal with the strobe attachment. She knew that he wasn't with his wife. She knew that he was working away from home and would be quick to open an email from her."

"So you don't think she has somehow placed a tracker on you or simply hacked your credit card?"

"I just did a search of my purse and all my belongings, with the help of the CyberCom staff. It came back clean. And it would have to be more than just a single credit card. I think the Russians are going to the source—one of the major data brokers."

"The ones that online advertisers use?"

"The same. She's also tracking my online accounts somehow. She found my spin class account and sent me a high five."

Orlov considered that. "Did you high-five her back?"

"Yeah, before I knew it was Natalya."

"Don't do that."

Lisa scowled at him.

Orlov grew animated; his hands started moving in vague, excited gestures. "If the Russians have hacked one of the major data brokers, then they would have access to—"

"Everything about everyone."

"With full GPS data, they can know where we live, who we visit, where we shop, our habits—"

Lisa raised her cardboard cup. "Where we buy our coffee."

"We need to find out which data broker the Russians have penetrated."

Lisa nodded. "Exactly. If we can identify the GPS data that they're working with, we'll have a better sense of the tools at their disposal and what their next moves might be. And maybe we'll have a way of tracking back to the perpetrators."

"How do we run this down?"

Lisa smiled ruefully. "We're working with the NSA, remember? You really think they don't already have that access?"

"Your country scares me sometimes, Agent Tanchik."

"Until we've sorted this out, I think we'd both better stop using our phones. We need to get a couple of burners."

"Shouldn't we tell CyberCom about the threat?"

"Of course, we'll report this to Glass, and she'll tell Holsapple, but I'm not sure we have enough evidence at this point to convince him to tell everyone in both agencies to abandon their phones."

She pinched off a piece of Orlov's breakfast muffin. "But what they *can* do is get us access to the data brokers."

After Lisa and Orlov shared their theory with Emma Glass, it didn't take long for the NSA to come back with an answer.

Lisa and Orlov were in Glass's office, hearing a report from a top NSA official, Cedrick Tompkins. He had the build of a linebacker but the demeanor and sartorial sense of a policy wonk, with wire-rimmed glasses and a sweater-vest beneath his suit jacket.

"When we reached out to the major data brokers, it quickly became clear that our questions made one of the companies, Ubi Mobile, very uncomfortable, and for good reason."

"They've found a security breach," Lisa said.

"Yes," Tompkins replied. "A massive one."

"Can they link it to the Russians?" Orlov asked.

"Not definitively, but that's what the security firm they've hired is suspecting."

"Who did they hire?" Orlov asked.

"Pendragon."

"They're okay." Orlov had clearly been primed to trash a competitor firm, so this mild praise spoke volumes.

"I'm glad you approve," Tompkins said.

"Can you get us in?" Lisa asked. "We need to see the evidence, and the database."

"That can be arranged," Tompkins said. "But no looking up your ex."

Lisa smiled tightly and held her fire. She needed Tompkins's cooperation.

"So can we go now?"

"Chopper's on the roof," Tompkins said.

Forty-five minutes later, the three of them touched down in a parking lot near the offices of Ubi Mobile, a data broker that collected geolocation data from millions of phone users around the country so that businesses could deliver targeted advertising and services. Ubi Mobile's headquarters were in a nondescript mirrored five-story office building in Fairfax, Virginia, one of dozens of similar structures that were scattered alongside the highway, distinguishable only by the Ubi logo on top.

In Ubi's lobby on the third floor they were greeted by Ken Steadman, the company's tanned, smiling, sport-coated chief operating officer, who made a point of shaking hands with everyone.

"You're going to have our full cooperation in this matter," said Steadman. "We take our responsibilities as a custodian of data very seriously."

"We appreciate the access," Lisa said.

"Not many third parties get inside our data center, but any friend of Cedrick Tompkins is a friend of ours."

The executive led them into a vast high-ceilinged room filled with office workers at desktops, each with multiple monitors. As they walked across the floor, Steadman said, "We track about two hundred million mobile devices in the US here, with information collected from more than five hundred apps."

"What sort of apps?"

"Oh, all sorts; a lot of them deliver local news, weather, or sports."

"What types of data do you collect?" Lisa asked.

"You have a phone, don't you, Agent Tanchik?"

"Yes."

"Well, that phone probably checks in with us more than fourteen thousand times in a given day. As you go about your daily routine, we can probably trace your location at any time to within a few yards."

"Do you have my name?"

"Probably not, but we don't really need it to target you. As long as we know your IP address, we know where to deliver the ads. And if we do want to target you more personally, your address is a matter of public record."

"And what if it isn't?"

"Then we just watch to see where your dot sleeps at night."

Lisa shot a shuddery, skeeved-out look at Orlov.

They entered a private room off the main floor, where Steadman sat down in front of a cluster of monitors, inviting them to do the same. The monitors all had the same image of a map covered with red dots.

"We can match your name to one of these dots and know quite a lot about you. Or we can just watch the behavior of your dot and use it to spot trends in overall consumer behavior. Hedge funds pay us good money for that sort of information. With it, they can tell whether shoppers are turning out at the mall during the holiday season, or whether they're visiting a particular store and how long they're staying there. They can also tell if a manufacturing plant is working overtime or slowing down, whether they're working night shifts or not."

"But consumers have no idea what you're up to here, do they?"

"Every one of the mobile apps that we work with has a privacy policy. You click your acceptance when you use them for the first time. It pays to read them."

"But even if you read the policy, would you really have any idea that all of *this* is happening?" Lisa gestured to indicate the room full of data analysts.

"Well, perhaps not," Steadman conceded. "But does anyone ever really want to know how the sausage gets made? They just want the convenience of their phone and their apps. But there's a trade-off, and it involves less privacy. We all know it's happening, and we all buy in, to one degree or another."

Sure, Lisa had clicked her acceptance to more than her share of app privacy policies, but she had never agreed to allow Steadman and his minions to watch her sleeping dot, to know how long she slept, when she got up and where she went, and when and where she was sleeping with another dot.

"So you believe you've been hacked by the Russians," Tompkins said, getting down to the business at hand.

"Yes, we think so, but we're still completing our forensic investigation. We were going to come to you as soon as we had completed our work." Steadman was watching them carefully as he said this. He clearly didn't want his company to be pilloried in the press for compromising the nation's cyber defense, or for standing in the way of CyberCom's investigation.

"Of course you were," Tompkins said in a neutral tone. "We're going to need full access to your investigation reports, along with the underlying audit trails, screenshots, everything."

"Of course."

"Tell your consultants at Pendragon to share those materials with the CyberCom team, which will be led by Special Agent Tanchik and Mr. Orlov."

"Will do."

"But for now, give us the highlights."

"Well, ever since the attack began, cellular service has been down pretty much all along the East Coast, and we saw a sharp decline in data collection. So you would figure that there would also be a corresponding drop in our internal usage and analysis of data."

"Yes," Orlov said, leaning in now.

"But the overall level of data usage didn't drop nearly as far as we were expecting. There was activity on our servers that we weren't initiating. That was when we realized we had an intruder."

"Have you isolated the malware?"

"Yes, they were using a program that is known as Zeus Matrix. Pendragon tells us that it's associated with a hacker collective called Sandworm."

Orlov and Lisa nodded.

"How long have they been on your system?" Lisa asked.

"We're still trying to establish that, but it's been at least eight months, and perhaps much longer."

"So you're treating it as a security breach, right? You're going to notify your customers?"

"We're still completing our investigation and talking to our privacy counsel about that."

Lisa knew what that meant, and it made her angry. "Just so you know, I believe I was targeted by a Russian operative based on the information they obtained from your database. I also believe that a CyberCom official may have been murdered using that data. You're going to need to inform people about this." Faced with the prospect of notifying the hundreds of thousands, or even millions, of customers as required by state security-breach notification laws, companies all too often strained to conclude that notification was not legally required.

Lisa's words appeared to have the desired effect. Steadman looked shaken. "We're going to do the right thing here."

"Can you tell what information they were targeting?" she asked.

"No, that's hard to say."

"Can you show us the information you have on a particular address?"

"Definitely. While our real-time data collection has obviously been impaired since the cell towers went down, we still have very robust historical data."

Lisa scribbled an address on a scrap of paper and slid it over to Steadman. "Show us this."

Steadman spent a few minutes entering the coordinates, and then a location in Maryland appeared on their monitors, centering on a complex of what appeared to be office buildings.

"What are we looking at?" Steadman asked.

"This is us," Lisa said. "The headquarters of CyberCom and the NSA. Those red dots are agents and agency employees." She asked Steadman, "Can you show us this in time lapse?"

"Okay."

Steadman typed in some additional search terms, and the red dots began to move over the course of a recent forty-eight-hour period prior to the attacks. The red dots flowed in like a tide at eight o'clock in the morning, and many flowed back out around five o'clock.

"Zoom out from five to seven p.m.," Lisa said. "Let's see a surrounding twenty-mile radius."

The view widened out to show the freeways and open spaces of suburban Maryland. The red dots that were leaving the CyberCom/NSA headquarters were dispersing and coming to rest at various locations throughout the suburbs of Odenton, Annapolis Junction, Jessup, and Columbia.

"They could identify everyone who works at CyberCom and NSA, and then follow all of their movements when they leave headquarters, including to their home address. This was how they knew that John Rosenthal was living apart from his wife in that apartment in Columbia. They knew he would open that spoofed email from his wife without looking too closely."

Tompkins's jaw clenched, and he looked stricken. "They know where our people live. All of them. I have to call the director."

Tompkins rose to leave the room, but Lisa got up quickly and blocked his path.

"What are you going to tell him?" she asked.

"That all personnel need to disable geolocation tracking on their phones immediately."

"I don't think that's a good idea."

"And why is that?" Tompkins asked impatiently.

"Because if you were watching this screen, and all of those red dots vanished at once, what would you think?"

Tompkins's posture changed, and he no longer looked like he was about to barrel through her to get to the door. "I'd think that we'd discovered their tracking."

"If we know, but they don't know that we know, that's an advantage, and we haven't had many of those since the attacks began."

"I see your point," Tompkins said. "But this decision is above both of our pay grades. I'll pass your comments along to the director."

Steadman added, "You know, if they're watching you all that closely, then they probably already know that you're here visiting us."

"No they won't," Lisa said. "We all left our cell phones behind at CyberCom headquarters. As far as they know, that's where we are right now."

"Do you think Sandworm knows that you've identified their presence on your systems?" Orlov asked.

"Pendragon says they might not. And even if they do, they don't know that we're cooperating with CyberCom and the NSA. We're about to begin a process that would purge any malware from our systems."

"You should maintain the status quo for now," Lisa said. "We may be able to use this."

"That's a dangerous game," Steadman said.

"What part of this is *not* dangerous?" Orlov asked.

26

Emma Glass drove her Mercedes down the Russett, Maryland, Main Street on her way to CyberCom/NSA headquarters in the midafternoon. She was listening to the *New York Times* podcast *The Daily*, playing through the car's speakers via her phone's Bluetooth connection. Her thoughts were on the latest series of cascading crises that she was dealing with as the cyberattack continued into its fifth day. The *Times* was reporting that day on how the climate of fear and uncertainty was impacting the financial markets, and how the media was reflecting, and perhaps ratcheting up, the nation's collective anxiety level.

The dulcet tones of the host were interrupted when the podcast abruptly stopped playing. Emma pressed play on her phone, but nothing happened. There must be a problem with the Bluetooth connection.

She switched over to talk radio and drove on past coffee shops and convenience stores.

The screen on the dash that displayed the radio station call letters briefly went blank, as if experiencing some sort of short circuit, and then came back online. This was the same screen used by the car's navigation system, which she didn't need because she could drive the route from her house to CyberCom headquarters in her sleep.

Once again the car's display screen went black after a white electrical flash of static.

When the screen came back this time, it bore a message:

You've been owned, Emma Glass. Please brace
for impact.

She tapped the brake with her foot, but there was no resistance. It was a sick, empty feeling, like testing your footing at the edge of a cliff and finding only air.

Her pulse raced as she eyed the speedometer. The car was doing thirty-five miles per hour, but was accelerating.

She began flashing her headlights at oncoming cars to warn them. Some drivers flashed their lights back in reply. Some stared at her in consternation as they passed. One driver flipped her off.

A thirty-five-miles-per-hour crash was probably survivable. At fifty or sixty miles per hour, it might not be.

She noticed a tiny amber light on the dash that read: "Driver Side Airbag Not Activated." She felt like slamming the steering wheel in frustration, but there was no time for wasted movement.

She needed to slow the car's momentum by any means necessary.

Emma tested the steering wheel, but it was barely responsive. There was a row of parked cars on the street, so she put all her strength into turning the wheel. The Mercedes swerved a bit, grazing one of the parked cars with a grinding shriek of metal on metal and the smack of a driver's-side mirror being knocked off.

The car slowed a bit, but not enough.

She tried the demolition derby maneuver again, and the brutal impact shivered through the steering wheel and into her forearms.

The car's momentum had slowed slightly.

She saw a light post fifty yards ahead and tried to turn the Mercedes toward it.

In her mind, two phrases kept repeating as the collision neared, and she put her arms up in front of her face to attempt to do the job that the airbag would not:

This is survivable.

Please brace for impact.

This is survivable.

Please brace for—

27

When Lisa and Orlov reported back to Glass about their trip to Ubi Mobile, the first thing she noticed was that the deputy director had a large gauze bandage on her forehead.

Then Lisa saw her eyes. She seemed shaken; it was a new look for her. The Super-Together Lady had the appearance of someone who had just been taken apart and reassembled, with a few pieces missing.

"What happened to you?" Lisa asked.

"Car accident. I ran into a light pole."

"Are you okay?"

"Yes, I'm fine. Just a few stitches. No concussion."

"If you don't mind me asking, what happened?"

"My car was hacked. I was driving, and I got a message on my navigation system telling me that I'd been owned. All of a sudden it was like the entire electrical system went out. I wasn't able to operate the brakes and could barely turn the wheel. I completely lost control of the vehicle."

"You were lucky you got out of it as well as you did."

"You're not kidding. If I hadn't managed to execute a controlled crash, I'd be in the hospital. Even the airbag was disabled, so this came from bouncing my head off the steering wheel," she said, pointing to the bandage. "I think they intended to do some real damage."

Glass was trying to be her usual impervious self, but there was a quaver in her voice that gave her away, along with the darting eyes. Lisa couldn't help but feel sympathy for her, and it was a strange sensation. She was certain that was the last thing that Glass wanted from her.

"I've heard that the GRU is able to hack into cars through the web-enabled navigation system, but I'd never seen them do it," Orlov said. "This is one technique that they didn't test out on Ukraine."

It wasn't hard to see the connection between Glass's car accident and what they had learned earlier that day at Ubi Mobile. If the Russians followed the red dots leaving CyberCom, they would have identified everyone's home address. By cross-checking to public property records, they could have figured out which red dot belonged to Glass. And with that information it would have been easy to locate the signals sent by her car.

"First Rosenthal, then Ruffalo, and now you," Lisa said. "Holsapple needs to be briefed on this so he can try to anticipate who might be next."

"I'll be speaking with him after we're done here," Glass said. "I'm going to recommend that our people not use their cell phones when they're away from headquarters. Burners will be issued."

"But everyone should leave their phones on for the time being, so long as they don't use them or take them off the grounds."

"So we don't tip the Russians that we know they're tracking us."

"Right," Lisa said. "They'll figure it out soon enough when the phones don't leave these grounds, but we shouldn't make it any easier for them. But you should know that it may already be too late to protect your staffers. If the Russians have had access to that geolocation data for months, they probably already know where your people live, what they drive, their habits. They may already have plans in place to do to them what they did to you."

"I'm quite aware of that," Glass said. "I'm also going to recommend that our people vary their routines, drive other cars, sleep at other places if possible. CyberCom and NSA are making arrangements for staff to sleep in their offices if they're more comfortable with that. In fact, it's going to be encouraged. Most of us are working around the clock anyway."

"I hope you're taking your own advice," Lisa said.

"Yeah, I'm using a burner phone, and I'll be driving a rental car and staying in a hotel—when I'm not sleeping here." She nodded to the leather couch in her office, which had a folded blanket and pillow at one end.

Lisa nodded, but she had no intention of deactivating her own phone. She wanted NatalyaX to know her location. It increased the likelihood that NatalyaX would come for her, and Lisa welcomed that.

"We have offensive cyberweapons too," Glass said. "They're going to find that out." Glass's expression hardened. "They may know who we are, but we know who they are too. Don't think we don't. If they're coming for us, then you can rest assured that we'll be coming for them."

Orlov nodded. "I used to think there were no real casualties in cyberwarfare," he said. "Or if there were, they were indirect."

Lisa nodded, thinking of the message in the coffee shop that morning, wondering when NatalyaX would attempt to weaponize the information that she had about her. She had to assume that NatalyaX knew nearly everything about her, from her medications to where she parked her car. "This sort of targeting feels more personal than some enemy launching missiles at you or aiming a high-powered rifle."

Glass nodded and then touched a finger to the bandage on her forehead and winced. "I have another assignment for the two of you. I'd like you to go to Brooklyn—Brighton Beach."

"What's there?"

"The Russian community in Brighton Beach and the surrounding area has the greatest concentration of potential GRU sleeper agents and sympathizers. I'd like you to visit some of these addresses." She slid a folder across her desk. "See if you can identify anyone who's actively participating in the attacks."

"Why us?" Orlov asked.

"Well, for one thing, you shouldn't stand out in Brighton Beach. You speak the language."

"I am not Russian. I'm Ukrainian!"

"You speak the language, though, right?" Glass asked.

"*Da.*"

"Then you're Russian enough for this assignment."

"You seem pretty Russian to me," Lisa offered.

Orlov glowered at them.

28

Earlier that morning, just after sunrise, Natalya had parked her rental car in a gas station across the street from the North Hudson Sewerage Authority in Hoboken, New Jersey. She had gone inside the gas station to find a snack, but the shelves had been empty; she hadn't even been able to find gum or mints. At least she had been able to fill up her gas tank. Most stations were out of fuel at this point.

Disappointed, she had returned to her car and watched the first wave of plant workers arrive for the morning shift on a gray day in which the sun was the color of a worn nickel. Maybe it was overstating it to call it a wave; the parking lot wasn't nearly full, probably because many employees weren't able to make it in during the cyberattack. Nevertheless, for critical infrastructure like the water purification plant, simply shuttering until the crisis was past was not an option.

There were high fences around the actual facility, but the parking lot was open to anyone. A security guard was stationed at the entrance gate on the far side of the lot.

The initial wave of cyberattacks had largely crippled the East Coast, shutting down the electrical grid, air traffic, public transportation, financial markets, and the health-care delivery system. But it was her understanding that was just the prelude. While the GRU would never brief her on the overall plan because of the possibility, perhaps even likelihood, that she would end up in the hands of the Americans, it wasn't hard to figure out that this next phase would be the masterstroke. In one encrypted message that she'd received, her next task had even been referred to by Kazimir as the "final blow."

A plant like the Hoboken facility stored thousands of tons of the chlorine gas used in the water purification process. The chemical was deadly when inhaled.

While the Americans had a defense system that could mitigate the impact of Russian missiles, there was no such defense for an airborne toxic event. An enormous toxic cloud of chlorine gas had the potential to cause fatalities on a scale that no onslaught of ICBMs could match. Only wind currents could dissipate such a cloud, and by the time it drifted out over the Atlantic and dispersed, the damage would be done.

The GRU's intelligence showed that while the water purification plants had been identified as a potential target by the Americans, there was a greater focus on defending chemical-manufacturing plants, and defense resources were being prioritized elsewhere.

Natalya knew that she wasn't the only operative with a similar mission. A coordinated attack of this scale could never be dependent on one person. There had to be multiple fail-safes, multiple targets. There was probably a targeted chemical plant in or near each major metropolitan area on the East Coast. Developing tailored malware that would knock out legacy systems across the entire country was simply too great a task even for the GRU, but by focusing on the heavily populated East Coast cities, her handlers hoped to maximize the damage. She could imagine a series of chemical clouds creeping up the coast and through Washington, Philadelphia, New York, Newark, Providence, and Boston, mingling to form a giant toxic cocktail.

Natalya reached inside her purse to touch the cold slimy rubber of her gas mask. Soon everyone would be clamoring for one of those, and they would be in very short supply.

Her long delicate fingers moved from the mask to the stippled grip of her gun. Both objects gave her a tactile sense of comfort, and both would be indispensable when the event occurred. It would be best to be off the street and out of sight when the gas was released, because even her gun might not be enough to protect her against people facing impending death and determined to take her mask.

Twenty-four hours or so after the event, once things had thinned out, she might be able to venture out into the street to greet the dawning of a new world. She imagined walking down Fifth Avenue in her mask and visiting all of the most fashionable shops, strolling past the counters where the clerks were slumped on the floor, and filling her shopping bag with the most beautiful clothes—vibrant silks, lush cashmeres, sleek and ingeniously engineered shoes.

No lines.

No price tags.

No hovering salesclerks asking if they could help her.

Whenever she watched a film or TV show about the end of the world, the most thrilling part was always the obligatory montage of the empty urban landscape, blissfully quiet, the architecture taking on a new, eerie beauty in the absence of people. Once the chemical-plant attacks began, the East Coast would look like the product of a zombie apocalypse, but without the hoi polloi of pesky and disgusting zombies.

Natalya drove her car across the street into the Hoboken facility's parking lot and pulled into a spot. Through the windshield, she took a closer look at the plant's perimeter, trying to spot security cameras. She eyed the guard, who was posted on the other side of the lot at the gate that led into the plant.

There were a couple of cameras trained on the parking lot, but they appeared to be trained on the area immediately in front of the facility's gates. They would not record activity in the rear of the lot, where she was.

Natalya removed from her purse a clear plastic bag that contained six flash drives. Each one had a piece of paper taped around it bearing the North Hudson Sewerage corporate logo. She got out of her car and strolled around the middle of the lot, still far away from the security cameras. In case she was being observed, she made a point of looking about conspicuously, as if she were trying to remember where she had parked.

As she walked around the lot, she let the flash drives slip one by one from her hand to the asphalt. The flash drives were bright red and black, so they stood out. They should attract the attention of anyone who saw them as they walked across the parking lot.

Like many critical infrastructure targets, the Hoboken plant's computers were air gapped, meaning that they were not connected in any way to the internet. Because if a computer had access to the internet, then every hacker in the world potentially had access to the equipment that it controlled.

The flash drives that Natalya had deposited in the parking lot were loaded with malware specifically designed by the GRU to target the facility's controllers. All she needed was for one worker to pick up a flash drive and plug it into a computer inside the facility to see what was on it.

In that moment, the air gap would be overcome, and the malware would infect the plant's system, causing the tiny mechanical controllers that regulated the chlorine tanks to malfunction. Then the clock would begin ticking down to the explosion that would release the toxic gas.

This sort of ploy was not new, and it no longer worked with sophisticated targets, such as CyberCom and NSA staffers. However, the workers at the water purification plant would not be that tech savvy—at least not all of them.

Seeing the corporate logo, an employee might want a reward for retrieving proprietary company data that was somehow misplaced in the parking lot. Or perhaps they might plug in the flash drive hoping that they would gain access to something intriguing, such as the salaries of their coworkers. Or maybe they would just be motivated by simple, dumb curiosity.

Natalya just needed one employee to plug in a flash drive.

Once the drive was activated, the employee's monitor would fill with a series of hard-core pornographic images. The employee would likely be shocked and would not report the discovery of the flash drive to a supervisor or anyone else. At that point, the employee's primary concern would be the fact that he or she had just used a company computer to view highly obscene material, which could be grounds for termination.

After Natalya had distributed the six flash drives around the parking lot, she returned to her car. She knew that she should leave immediately in case someone recognized her as a stranger to the facility.

But she couldn't help but linger for a few minutes, watching the workers march toward the plant's entrance on autopilot, many with earbuds on.

Natalya noticed a middle-aged man with a comb-over in a navy-blue windbreaker and tan pants pause for a moment on his walk across the lot.

The man leaned down to pick something up, and then he looked around to see if any of his coworkers had noticed.

He thinks he might have discovered something valuable, Natalya thought.

His hand rested at his side for a long moment, and then, in a slow and inconspicuous movement, he placed the object in his pants pocket and proceeded toward the entrance gate.

In her business, Natalya found that the most valuable skill was an appreciation of the things that consistently motivated people—greed, lust, love, curiosity. After watching the way the man pocketed the flash drive, she knew with absolute certainty that he was not going to simply turn it over to his supervisor. No one looked that sneaky when they were doing the right thing.

No, he was going to plug it in and see what it contained.

And, with that small act, the man in the blue windbreaker was going to be complicit in the deaths of hundreds of thousands of people within a twenty-mile radius.

29

It was early evening, and Lisa and Orlov were driving north on I-95 toward New York City and Brighton Beach to visit the addresses of some possible sleeper agents. Lisa was driving because Orlov had demonstrated in a mere fifteen minutes behind the wheel that he was a menace.

She listened to a radio station broadcasting the same panicked news report about the cyberattack on an endless loop. All the stations were like that now. It was white noise to her, but still an improvement over silence. After spending time in the CyberCom war room, she and Orlov knew much more about what was happening than any journalist.

As she drove slowly along the freeway, steering around the vehicles that had run out of gas or been abandoned, Lisa's thoughts kept returning to something that Orlov had said to her that night in the IHOP in Falls Church. It seemed to be a sensitive topic, but after an hour of turning it over in her mind, she finally felt compelled to pose the question.

She switched off the radio.

"Arkady, you said that you could have done better defending Ukraine against the Russian cyberattacks. I've been wondering what you meant by that."

Orlov didn't turn to face her. He kept staring out the window, seeming to find something fascinating about the nondescript trees and green reflective exit signs.

"I know you probably don't want to revisit the past, but if there's something there that would help us now . . ."

"It would not help," Orlov said. "What, you think the Russians have some secret weakness that only I know about, and that I have been keeping it to myself? No."

"Well, what is it then?"

More silence, filled only by the sound of the tires humming on the road.

"I helped them," Orlov finally said, quietly.

"What do you mean? You helped the Russians? Helped them how?"

"Before the attack, they knew that I was their primary adversary, key to Ukraine's cyber defense. Twenty-four hours before the attack began, I received an anonymous IM with photos of my son, Alyosha, who was eight years old then. Photos of him at school, playing with his friends, with my ex-wife, who has custody."

"What did they want you to do?"

"They didn't ask that I actively participate in the sabotage of our systems. They wanted me to stand down during the attack, not try too hard, call in sick, whatever. Their primary request was that I not go public with any evidence directly linking Moscow to the attack."

"And you complied?"

"They were threatening my son. What was I supposed to do?"

"I don't know."

"But you judge me. I can hear it in your voice. It's easy for you because you don't have anyone, no family of your own."

That remark stung Lisa, but she knew that was just the way Orlov reacted to the pain of remembering. "So you've been carrying the guilt, feeling like you let your people down."

"It is not a feeling. I *did* betray my country."

"You know you couldn't have stopped them anyway."

"That is the kind of thing that all collaborators say. I could have fought harder, could have prevented some of the damage. There were five elderly people who died of cold when the power went out."

"That's not on you," Lisa said.

"You weren't there. You don't know."

They drove on down the dark, desolate freeway for another ten minutes.

Finally, Lisa had to ask the inevitable question. "Have they threatened you since you came to the US?"

"No. They don't have any more leverage."

"Your son?"

"Leukemia. Eight months ago."

"I'm so sorry. Your wife?"

"Ex-wife. No, that she-wolf hates me, and the feeling is mutual. I'm alone in the world like you are. We have nothing to lose."

"We all have something to lose," she said.

They drove on for a while, both concentrating on the patch of road illuminated and disappearing in the cone of the headlights.

"Now that I've told you, what are you going to do with this?" Orlov asked.

"I should report it to CyberCom."

"Yes, that is what you should do."

"And Emma Glass would immediately have you pulled from this assignment."

"Yes, she would, and I couldn't blame her for it."

"And they'd probably lock you up for good measure, at least until the national crisis was past."

"When someone gets locked up as a potential threat to national security, whether it's in the US, Russia, or Ukraine, they usually don't see the light of day again for quite a while, regardless of the evidence."

Lisa hesitated. Was turning him in any different than Jon threatening to report her? Orlov couldn't change his past, just like she couldn't turn off her depression. All they could do was move forward, try to make some kind of peace with themselves. "I think we have a better chance of catching NatalyaX if we work together," she finally said.

"That is definitely true."

Lisa rolled her eyes at Orlov's estimation of his skills as a cyber investigator, but she couldn't disagree with his conclusion.

"You are wishing that you hadn't asked the question now, aren't you?"

"A little bit, yes."

"So what are you going to do?"

"I think for the moment we're going to pretend this conversation never happened. You can't change the past. None of us can."

"It's true you can't change the past," Orlov said. "But you never stop paying for it, do you?"

30

Natalya walked around the block three times before she approached the front door of the brownstone in the early evening. Kazimir had given her this address in Williamsburg, Brooklyn, as a place where she could find shelter while she waited to confirm that her mission at the water purification plant was completed. When the malware began transmitting signals back to the GRU's team of hackers in Moscow, then Natalya would know that she could move on to the next assignment.

Jamie and Michelle Pennebaker were known to be Russian sympathizers of some sort. Coming here had been a calculated risk—if their identities were known to US intelligence agencies, then they would be under close surveillance—but it was less risky than attempting to avoid detection by the NSA while out on the streets.

She looked up and down the block, which was lined with similar brownstone walk-ups. A gust of frigid wind blew down the dark corridor of buildings. The streetlights were out, and there were no signs of electric light on the block, no pedestrians, no people inside the parked cars. When she was convinced that no one was watching the house, Natalya walked quickly up the front steps and pressed the buzzer.

A woman in her late thirties with short blonde hair and cat's-eye glasses peered through the partially open door.

"Yes, can I help you?"

"I'm Natalya."

The woman studied her for a moment and then opened the door wider, motioning her inside. "We were expecting you earlier. Has anyone followed you here?"

"No."

"Are you sure?"

"I know my job."

She nodded. "Of course. Come in."

Once inside, the woman called out, "Jamie, she's here! Natalya's here!"

From the back of the house, a man entered, also in his late thirties, with a neatly groomed beard that had two gray stripes at the chin like fangs.

"You should have called for me first, Michelle."

"What was I supposed to do, leave her out on the front porch to attract attention?"

Jamie turned to Natalya. "You weren't followed here, were you?"

"We've already done that," Michelle said.

"I wasn't followed," Natalya repeated.

The living room was lit by candlelight and lined with overstuffed bookshelves, and there was a turntable and a long shelf of vintage vinyl. The furniture was French country and mildly distressed, like her hosts. She didn't need to ask if they had children, because it was not that sort of home. On the walls were framed black-and-white photographs of New York street scenes and original, but mediocre, abstract paintings. Natalya sized them up in an instant, sensing that they had only recently outgrown their PBR caps and Chuck Taylors. They almost certainly had tattoos, but now wore their clothes to conceal, rather than display, them.

They were unlikely Russian spies, but so was she. She wondered how the GRU had recruited the couple but didn't want to ask. The less she knew about them, the better.

"We were told to put you up for as long as you needed," Jamie said. He and Michelle sat down on a couch in the living room, and Natalya took the armchair across from them. "They said you have a mission in the area."

"Yes."

"Of course you can't talk about it," Michelle said. "And we don't want to know. Well, we actually do want to know, but we understand that we can't."

Natalya wondered if the couple had ever been tasked with any actual espionage assignments, and whether they could be trusted.

"Were you born here?" Natalya asked.

"Yeah," Jamie said. "I'm from Florida, and Michelle is from Vermont."

"I grew up here too. Have you ever visited Russia?"

"I spent six months in Moscow as part of a student exchange program when I was nineteen," Jamie said. "Michelle's never been."

"I haven't been either," Natalya said. "What was it like?"

Jamie considered and then said, "I don't know. Things seemed cleaner, simpler there somehow. Maybe it just seemed that way because I was nineteen."

"Have you two been at this long?" Natalya asked.

"We were both recruited six years ago, and we've been married for three," Jamie said. "But we probably shouldn't share too much about our backgrounds."

After an awkward pause, Michelle said, like she was commenting on the weather, "Exciting times."

Natalya smiled ruefully. "Very."

She couldn't be sure, but an expression flared on Jamie's face that could have been a scowl.

"You can have the guest bedroom, first room up the hall on the right," Jamie said.

"Thank you," Natalya said. "I really appreciate this. I need to stay off the streets as much as possible right now."

"We're happy to help," Michelle said. "It's an honor."

And there was that expression on Jamie's face again. There was no mistaking it. What was his problem?

"Can we get you something to eat?" Michelle asked. "Glass of wine? Beer? You must be tired."

"I wouldn't turn down something to eat," Natalya said. She was famished. It had been hard to find something to eat in Hoboken, despite power being restored. Restaurants and grocery stores had run out of food, and there weren't that many good dining options in New Jersey even when it wasn't under attack.

Michelle heated up a bowl of pasta and served it up with a glass of pinot grigio. Natalya thanked her hosts and took it back to her bedroom with a flashlight.

When she was done, she promptly fell asleep on the bed with her clothes still on. About two hours later, she awoke in the middle of the night, with the aftertaste of wine soured in her mouth.

It took her a moment to orient herself and recognize what had interrupted her deep, hard sleep. There were sounds coming from another room. Jamie and Michelle were arguing. They were clearly trying not to be heard, but voices carried in the old brownstone.

She had to listen closely, but when she did, she heard every word.

"Who knows what she's here to do," Jamie said. "People are dying in these attacks. Mrs. Pleskow down the street had a heart attack, and there was no way to get her to a hospital because of the traffic and the power outage. She died as a direct result of the attack."

"What did you think we were doing when we allowed ourselves to be recruited?" Michelle responded. "This is what we signed up for. This is it."

"This isn't what *I* signed up for," Jamie said. "I thought maybe I'd have an opportunity to provide some useful information, perform some small service. More than anything, I saw this as a way to express just how damn disappointed I am with the direction this country is headed in. But how are you going to feel if she's here to plant a bomb or start a fire that's going to kill our friends and neighbors?"

"I don't know how I'll feel. Part of something important? Something bigger than us?"

"I know you, babe. And I know how you'll feel. You won't be able to live with it."

"Even if that's what this is, I can live with it," Michelle said. "Haven't we talked about how our country has stopped being a force for good in the world? I'm not naive about Russia's flaws and problems. But this is a way of saying no to our country. Before a nation can change direction, it has to be stopped in its tracks."

"You want to look at this in big-picture geopolitical terms, but it's a lot simpler than that. People are going to be hurt, and they're going to die because of what we're doing right now. The question is, Do you want that blood on your hands?" Jamie's voice grew louder as he posed the question.

How could they not know that she could overhear them? These two wouldn't last a week in the field on a real assignment. If they were this indiscreet, could they even be trusted to provide her with a secure hiding place?

"You think the US doesn't do the same thing?" Michelle said. Michelle's voice dipped, but Natalya heard the word *Iran*.

"Yes, I agree that the US has been wrong about so many things," Jamie said. "In abstract terms I believe it, but I'm not willing to kill for it."

Natalya had to admit that Jamie was a pretty good debater, but she was rooting for Michelle.

"We're not going to kill anyone."

"But she is," Jamie said. "She may look all cute and harmless when you first meet her, but it's not hard to see that she's a killer. And if we harbor her and assist her, then we're accomplices to murder."

"You've waited kind of late to say this to me," Michelle said.

"This has been coming for a while, but having her here just crystallized everything in my mind. She has to go."

"Are you planning to report her to someone?"

There was a long pause, and Natalya leaned close to the bedroom door to hear every word.

"No," Jamie finally said. "I don't think so."

That was not the definitive answer that she had been hoping for.

Natalya knew she would not be spending another night with the Pennebakers.

31

Day Six

This is Don Hansberry reporting for CNN on America Under Attack. While the East Coast urban centers from Atlanta to New York slowly regain electricity, internet, and essential services, our sources at the State Department are telling us that the public should not assume that the attacks are over, and should remain vigilant. In fact, Department of Homeland Security units and city police departments have been placed on high alert based upon intelligence indicating that more attacks are planned. One highly placed State Department official said to us off the record that, and I quote, "The worst may still be ahead of us. The next forty-eight hours will be critical."

32

Natalya rose early, showered, and dressed. She entered the small kitchen at the rear of the house to find Michelle stirring a pan of eggs with a wooden spoon. The room was filled with the strong aroma of brewing coffee.

"You want some breakfast?" Michelle asked. "Cage-free eggs. Vegetarian fed. No hormones. And I make a mean scramble."

Natalya sat down at the table in the breakfast nook in the corner of the kitchen. The sun felt good on her still-damp hair. "Yes, thanks, that smells great."

Natalya brought over a plate of scrambled eggs with diced orange peppers and green onions. The aroma was wonderful.

"Where's Jamie?"

"Sleeping in."

"Were you two up late?" Natalya asked. She watched Michelle consider how to respond, telegraphing every emotion. Definitely not spy material, though her heart seemed to be more or less in the right place.

Before Michelle could respond, Natalya added, "It's okay. I could hear you two talking."

More complicated emotions flashed across Michelle's face as she tried to decide whether Natalya could have somehow overheard their heated exchange.

"How much did you—"

"More than enough."

"If you knew Jamie, you'd know that he talks like that sometimes, but it doesn't mean anything."

"He said he was thinking about reporting us to the government. Do we really want to take that chance?" Natalya floated that *we* out there like a lifeline and watched to see if Michelle would take it.

Was Michelle with Natalya, or was she with Jamie? Whether Michelle realized it yet or not, her life depended on it.

"What are you suggesting?" Michelle asked, tossing a quick glance at the door to the hallway to confirm that Jamie wasn't standing there.

"You know that we're all US citizens, so what we've been doing is treason, which is punishable by death. If we're captured, the GRU will disavow us. There won't be any exchange of prisoners, no bargaining for our release. We don't have any margin for error."

"I understand," Michelle said. The words were like a puff of smoke that barely carried across the kitchen table before dissolving. "But I'm still not sure what you're asking."

Natalya reached into her purse and removed a folded knife. With the click of a button she exposed the long, slender blade. She slid the knife across the table to Michelle.

"He's sleeping. It won't be difficult. Just put it in his throat." Natalya wasn't about to offer Michelle her gun, because there was a chance she might turn it on her. Michelle was no threat to Natalya with a knife.

Michelle didn't look Natalya in the eye, because her gaze was fixed on the blade. "I don't think I can do that."

"Why not?"

"Because he's my husband. I love him. And he would never really turn us in."

"But he said that he might."

"He's an idiot. He says a lot of things, but I know when he really means something."

"You may think you know that, but what am I supposed to think? Should I risk my life for him? Risk the mission? Or trust that you know him well enough to know that he wouldn't do it?"

"He's the one who recruited me," Michelle said. "He wouldn't betray us."

Natalya could tell she knew it wasn't a persuasive argument from the way she said it. She noted that it was the second time Michelle had used the word *us*. It had taken only five minutes together in the sunny breakfast nook, but already she and Natalya were speaking like fellow conspirators.

It was almost enough, but not quite.

"Forgive me for saying this, but you two don't look like a couple of Russian spies," Natalya said.

"Isn't that the idea?" Michelle said while Natalya spread orange marmalade and butter on a slice of wheat toast. "But Jamie has always been obsessed with Russia. He's been reading Marx and Lenin since he was in high school, and it sort of became his thing, you know? It was cute."

"Hmm. Cute." Natalya nodded, biting into her toast to suppress a smile.

"And sure, he doesn't approve of everything that Russia does, what with the autocratic leaders and the oligarchs. But he believes that Russia still offers a great hope for the world, a force that can counterbalance our out-of-control capitalism."

Natalya thought the couple's misplaced idealism was, to use Michelle's word, cute, and also a little sad. And no one was more unreliable than a disappointed idealist.

If Michelle had been willing to kill her husband, Natalya might have let her live.

———

Natalya finished her scrambled eggs, seasoning them with a few drops of Tabasco. She searched the pantry for some snacks for the road and found some apples (organic, no doubt) and breakfast bars, packing them into her purse.

She pulled the blinds to ensure that neighbors couldn't see Michelle's body lying on the tiled floor of the kitchen, the red splotch of a bullet wound staining her Brooklyn Bowl sweatshirt.

Natalya grabbed her by the feet and dragged the body into the pantry. She had put Jamie's body in the master bedroom's walk-in closet. She had taken the bloodstained bedsheets and tossed them in with the body. If someone conducted a cursory examination of the house, she hoped that they would conclude that the couple had fled to the west like so many others to escape the fallout from the cyberattack.

She rinsed the blood off her hands in the master bathroom, regretting that it had come to this, but regretting even more that she had not been better prepared for the situation.

She wished that Kazimir had let her know that her hosts were little more than sympathizers, not fully committed, field-tested operatives. If she had known that going in, she would have planned to kill them from the outset.

It was sloppy, in the way that a handler who was not risking his own life could afford to be sloppy.

As she locked up the house behind her, Natalya pulled one of Jamie's baseball caps lower over her eyes in case someone was observing. She resolved to never again trust her fate to amateurs.

There was no substitute for professionalism.

33

The drive from Fort Meade to Brooklyn had been slow due to stalled cars blocking I-95. Lisa and Orlov had caught about three hours of cold and uncomfortable sleep in the car before proceeding north at sunrise. They were passing by Trenton, New Jersey, only about two hours from their destination.

"I would kill for a cup of coffee," Orlov said.

"Me too," Lisa said. "But first we have to find a place that's open."

"Maybe in Brighton Beach I can get a proper Russian cup of coffee. Perhaps even some pierogies."

"I thought you hated the Russians."

"I don't hate their food. When the US has a trade war with China, do you stop eating egg rolls?"

"Point taken. Could you dial up our NSA contact on the satphone and put it on speaker?"

Orlov punched the numbers and then held up the satphone.

"We're going to be in Brighton Beach in probably less than two hours," Lisa said. "You've been monitoring the Russian community there. Anything of interest? If you don't have any better ideas, we're going to start at the address of Sacha . . ."

"Fedorov," Orlov said, glancing at the file.

"Well, I don't have the sort of data feeds that I'm accustomed to," said Marcus Stone, the young NSA analyst who was their point of contact for the assignment. "A lot of CCTV cameras are disabled now, and NYPD still isn't online in many precincts—"

"Why don't we start with what you *do* have?" Lisa said.

Silence on the line and the sound of shuffling papers. Then: "Well, I have a double murder in Williamsburg. A couple named James and Michelle Pennebaker. Reported less than an hour ago. The wife's sister had a key and found the bodies when she was checking in on them."

"Do they have any Russian ties?"

"Not that I'm seeing. But wait a second."

"Yes?"

"We have some very old records on James Pennebaker. Back in 2006, he visited Russia. Some sort of Columbia student exchange program."

"That's it?"

"Yeah."

"What about the murders? Was it a robbery? Something to do with looting?"

"The only notation that we have from Brooklyn PD is that it looks professional."

"I'd like that address," Lisa said.

———

When they rolled up in front of the brownstone in Williamsburg, the police were still on the scene.

As Lisa approached the yellow crime scene tape that barred the open front door, she was met by a lanky middle-aged officer whose lined, drawn face made her tired just looking at him.

"Hold up there, you two," he said. "Don't you know what the tape means? This is a crime scene."

Lisa flashed her FBI badge. "Special Agent Lisa Tanchik."

"Well, hello there, Special Agent. Detective Aaron Steinmetz, Brooklyn PD. What does the FBI want with this? It just looks like a robbery slash looting incident that turned deadly. Unfortunately, there have been plenty of those lately."

"We're running down a lead, and we'd like to take a look."

The detective lifted the crime scene tape with an index finger. "Okay. Suit yourselves."

As Orlov ducked under the tape, Steinmetz asked him, "You FBI too?"

"I'm a consultant," Orlov said.

"And trusty manservant," Lisa added.

She didn't need to look to see Orlov's scowl.

Steinmetz smiled to himself, like someone in a dysfunctional relationship who took some small solace every time he saw another mismatched couple.

"You said this was a shooting, right?" Lisa asked.

"That's correct."

"We're pursuing someone who has used an extremely deadly nerve agent to kill. You haven't seen any signs of that sort of thing, have you? Any white powder?"

Steinmetz frowned. "No, I haven't seen any white powder. I guess if it was here, I'd probably already be dead, right?"

"Most likely. Walk us through it?" Lisa asked.

"I suppose so," the detective said.

Steinmetz led them down the hallway, past the living room, and into a small kitchen at the rear of the house. The room smelled of stale eggs, and something else.

He pointed to the open pantry door. "The wife was found in there with two bullets in the chest. No muss, no fuss. Very precise. No forensics yet, of course, but looks like a small-caliber bullet."

Lisa and Orlov peered into the narrow pantry at Michelle Pennebaker's body on the floor next to the recycle bins and beneath rows of canned goods, her sweatshirt drenched in red. That was the smell that was mingled with the aroma of stale eggs—blood.

"Any shell casings?"

"No. And no fingerprints. Which is saying something because there's an unmade bed in the guest bedroom. It's possible that the killer slept in it."

"That doesn't sound like a looter," Orlov said.

The detective nodded. "True, but we don't know when the bed was slept in. Maybe a looter killed the couple and then got a little rest here before moving on."

"That would be pretty cold," Lisa said.

"Or pretty exhausted," Steinmetz said. "We've seen all sorts of strange behavior since the attack. People are tired; they're desperate; in many cases they're hungry. Even regular citizens can lose it under those conditions. Maybe a neighbor sought shelter or assistance here, and when they got turned away, they killed the couple."

Orlov walked over to the skillet and stared at the eggs.

"Don't eat that," Steinmetz said, maintaining a straight face. "It's evidence."

"That's a lot of eggs for one person," Orlov said.

Lisa emerged from the pantry. "Maybe the killer was a guest who slept upstairs in the extra bedroom, came down this morning, and had breakfast prepared by the wife, and then murdered them both."

"If so," Steinmetz said, "that's some cold shit."

"Where's the husband?" Lisa asked.

"Upstairs," said the detective, leading the way out of the kitchen and up the stairs.

In the master bedroom on the second floor, the bed was unmade. There was a bloodstain on the right side of the bed and on the pillow.

"So the husband was sleeping there when he was shot?"

"Yeah, it appears so." He led them over to the walk-in closet, where a man in his midthirties was sprawled on the floor faceup, two entry wounds in the center of his forehead.

"Once again, very precise," Steinmetz said. "No messing around, no hesitation. Which makes me think it wasn't just a neighbor who flipped out."

"Right," Lisa said. "Someone who hadn't killed before would be more likely to hesitate, wake up the victim, have to chase him around a bit. Or at least they wouldn't display such good aim."

"That's my thinking too," Steinmetz said. "Is that the kind of person you two are pursuing?"

"Yeah," Lisa said.

"Does it have something to do with the attacks?"

"I don't think you need to know that."

"I figured that it must if the FBI was devoting resources to this in the middle of a national emergency."

"Have you noticed anything unusual around here? Anything that didn't seem to fit?"

Steinmetz glanced around the bedroom and shook his head. "Nah. Everything I've seen so far suggests that this is just your average childless, aging hipster couple. Typical Williamsburg."

"Nice stereotyping, Detective," Lisa said.

Steinmetz nodded in mock appreciation of her mock compliment. "But you're free to have a look around—as long as you don't muck up our crime scene." Steinmetz went back downstairs to rejoin his team in the kitchen.

Lisa and Orlov donned latex gloves that they had grabbed from a box downstairs and split up to cover the house.

"Why don't you start with the guest bedroom, and I'll do this room," Lisa said. If it was Natalya who had slept there, she knew that Orlov wouldn't find anything—unless Natalya wanted them to.

"Da," Orlov said as he left.

Lisa started with the nightstands, opening each drawer. Nothing out of the ordinary. A vibrator, some condoms, lubricant, a couple of paperback bestsellers, some loose change, some collar stays.

She always felt a little uncomfortable rifling through the possessions of a victim. She knew some agents and police who never missed an opportunity to make a joke about the embarrassing or awkward facts that inevitably turned up in this sort of close scrutiny of a life. Lisa felt that those sorts of insensitive remarks just victimized the victim all over again. She tried to remember that her own life barely withstood the minimal scrutiny of her coworkers—and probably wouldn't fare so well under this sort of lens.

Lisa made a slow circle of the room, not sure what she was looking for. Then she returned to the walk-in closet. For the moment, she forced herself not to stare at the victim, avoiding his black hole gaze.

She looked at the shoes arrayed in racks along the floor, the handbags and sweaters lining the top shelf. There was a plastic file cabinet uncomfortably near the body. She managed to open a drawer without disturbing the position of the body and found only old tax returns.

Lisa ran a hand through the shirts and blouses hung in the closet. As the cottons and silks rippled beneath her fingers, she noticed that there was a shelf in the closet that was hidden behind the clothes. On the shelf were stacked more sweaters, scarves, and winter wear, but when she followed it to its end in the corner, she discovered something else.

A small stack of books.

She lifted them out with both hands.

Karl Marx's *Capital. The State and Revolution* by Vladimir Lenin. *Why Marx Was Right* by Terry Eagleton. Friedrich Engels's *Socialism: Utopian and Scientific.*

Why would these books be hidden away?

Maybe they were sensitive to the fact that having those titles in the bookcase downstairs might prompt unwelcome political conversations.

But it was not like they were forbidden texts; many undergraduates had these same volumes in the cinder block bookcases of their dorm rooms.

Lisa suspected that the books were there because the couple had something to hide. The volumes were not covered with clothes like items that had been tucked away years ago, and they weren't coated in a patina of dust. She flipped open the copy of *Capital* and found that it was full of yellow highlighting and scribbled notes in the margins. The ballpoint pen ink wasn't faded like it would have been in a volume nostalgically retained from college; it looked fairly recent.

These were objects that were secretly treasured—and returned to often.

She wasn't sure what the books meant, but they made her much more certain that Natalya had been there and had done the killings.

A belief in the ideals of Marxism certainly did not mean that a person was a Russian spy. The recent crop of Russian autocrats still paid qualified lip service to Marx and Lenin, though it was clear that their true allegiances were to nationalism and power. But a person who had been identified as having an interest in Marxist ideology might be viewed by the GRU as someone who might lend a sympathetic hand to an operative in need. In the parlance of the McCarthy era, the Pennebakers might have been considered "fellow travelers" by the GRU.

Lisa speculated that Michelle and Jamie Pennebaker might have been identified as people who could offer Natalya a night or two of food, shelter, and a place to hide while she completed whatever her mission was in the area. They were trusted enough to be allowed to take her in, but not enough to be allowed to live after her stay was done.

And that begged the question—what was the mission that had brought Natalya there?

34

Arkady Orlov was agitated. It seemed to be his natural state lately, ever since CyberCom had summoned him. He probably knew more about the GRU's offensive cyber capabilities than anyone, and yet they were no closer to making a definitive, smoking gun link between the GRU and the cyberattack that was crippling the US.

This was his chance to redeem himself for failing to protect his homeland against the same type of attack, and he was failing all over again.

The trip to Brooklyn that morning had not been a complete waste, but it hadn't brought them any closer to finding NatalyaX either. They had a strong suspicion that they had identified two Russian operatives, or at least sympathizers, in Michelle and Jamie Pennebaker. Further review of the couple's contacts and history might lead to identifying other members of the GRU's network inside the US. The NSA was in the process of combing through the Pennebakers' credit records, social media profiles, and web search histories.

Orlov was in Fort Meade after he and Lisa had managed to catch a ride on an army helicopter back from Brooklyn. It was midafternoon, and he was waiting in a conference room at CyberCom while Special Agent Tanchik briefed her FBI bosses on the progress of the investigation. At least he had a secure computer with internet access and a Tor browser, so he was using the time to visit IRC chat boards frequented by hackers in hopes of stumbling upon some interesting bit of gossip. Hackers loved to brag about their exploits, so it was hard to imagine that everyone was observing radio silence on something as big and damaging as the current series of attacks.

And then he received an email from Lisa on his phone, which had been cleared of malware by CyberCom.

LISA: Where are you?

ORLOV: Right where you left me. Where are you?

LISA: Long story, but I have a lead on NatalyaX. I had to hop an NSA helicopter into DC to follow it up right away. Sorry, didn't have time to come and get you. Meet me at the bar of the Hay-Adams Hotel at 5:30.

ORLOV: That's just an hour away!

LISA: Get on one of the helicopters. Don't take no for an answer. If you come by car you won't make it in time and I'll have to leave without you.

ORLOV: Can you tell me what's going on?

LISA: Yes, when you're here. This isn't secure enough.

ORLOV: Do they have power over there?

LISA: Don't know yet, I'm still on the way. But if they don't have electricity, they'll have candles.

One thing I know is that even in a time of great stress, two things never stop in DC—drinking and dealmaking. Trust me, the bar at the Hay-Adams will be open. But shouldn't you be MOVING?

ORLOV: Okay! Got it! On my way. I hope this is worth it.

CyberCom and NSA were still ferrying cabinet officers, representatives, and senators to and from the Capitol for intelligence briefings. Orlov took the stairs two at a time on the way up to the rooftop helipad.

There was a chopper warming up, with several official-looking passengers already inside waiting for takeoff.

The pilot was the same one who had dropped him and Lisa in Falls Church a couple of days ago. The pilot acquiesced to letting Orlov ride along after only a little pleading.

When the helicopter touched down behind the Capitol Building on its helipad, Orlov had twenty minutes to make it to the Hay-Adams. He ran/power walked the mile to the hotel—and running was not something that Orlov did very often.

The Hay-Adams was one of the most prestigious addresses in a city of prestigious addresses, a stone's throw from the White House. Outside its Italian Renaissance facade, flags snapping in the wind above the porte cochere, Orlov ran a hand through his wild tufts of black hair, plastering them down to his skull with the sweat that seemed to be flowing from every pore and orifice. He'd made it with three minutes to spare.

Orlov stepped through the doors into the hotel's lobby, with its intricate cream-colored plaster ceilings and walnut wainscoting. This place was historically such a waiting room for political influence peddlers that it had led to the coining of the term *lobbyists*.

He scanned the lobby for Lisa, but she wasn't there. Orlov headed for Off the Record, the hotel's bar, which was on the right side of the lobby.

Outside the doorway, he took in the red upholstered banquettes, the pressed tin ceiling, the circular wooden bar in the center of the room lined with political caricatures. The bar's guests were all paired up.

No sign of Lisa.

Orlov felt a shove from behind followed by "I'm so sorry!"

He staggered forward a step and then turned around to see an attractive woman in her late twenties, taller than him at more than six feet, with high cheekbones and jet-black hair cut in a bob.

Maybe it was his exhaustion from running, but he thought she looked familiar.

"Are you okay?" she asked, touching his shoulder solicitously. "I really should watch where I'm going."

He wanted to respond, but he felt a strange light-headedness—and a pain in his lower back that he hadn't noticed before. Orlov reached back to locate the source of his pain, and when he withdrew his hand, his fingertips were smeared with blood.

"Let me help you," the woman said, moving in close to offer support with her left arm and shoulder.

Reflexively, because he felt so suddenly and overwhelmingly tired, he accepted the assistance and leaned into the young woman.

The woman smiled, not unkindly, as she brought her right hand up. The hand gripped a long thin knife, which she plunged three, four, maybe five times into his chest and stomach.

It all happened in no more than eight seconds, but he tried to absorb every detail, because he knew those moments were his last.

Now Orlov was lying prone on the floor of the lobby, on a patterned rug over a beige marble floor. The woman was no longer in view, but he could hear her calling for help, ever so distantly.

He gazed up at the whorls and filigree of the plaster ceiling. On the helicopter ride over, one of his fellow passengers, a representative from Wyoming on the House Armed Services Committee, had asked about his destination. When Orlov had told him that he was going to the Hay-Adams, the politico had launched into a story about how the Hay-Adams was said to be haunted by the ghost of "Clover" Adams, the wife of Henry Adams, the historian and descendant of presidents. She had committed suicide by ingesting potassium cyanide, which had been kept as a home darkroom chemical. The congressman had leaned across the cabin of the helicopter to reveal that Clover was said to walk the hallways of the hotel, trailed by the scent of almonds, which was also the scent of potassium cyanide.

As Orlov's vision blurred and failed, he thought how much he liked the scent of almonds, and how pleasant it would be to stroll the halls of the grand old hotel with Clover Adams. And how strange it would be for his spirit to find its resting place here, so far from his beloved Ukraine.

35

Lisa was in a conference room listening to a CyberCom briefing on Russian malware when Emma Glass's assistant entered and whispered something to her.

Lisa turned sharply to face her. "What?"

"Arkady Orlov is dead."

Lisa felt the breath go out of her.

"You must be mistaken. He's downstairs. I was with him just two hours ago." While she couldn't believe what she was hearing, she also instantly knew it had to be true.

"I'm sorry," the young assistant said helplessly.

"Where is he? What happened?"

The assistant explained that a spoofed email had been sent to Orlov, posing as Lisa, luring him to his death in the lobby of the Hay-Adams.

Lisa had no doubt that NatalyaX had set the trap. Orlov probably hadn't even realized until the final moment what was happening. He had been targeted because the Russians understood just how well their old adversary from Ukraine knew their tactics—and was sharing all that knowledge with CyberCom. The fact that Orlov's death would hurt her was just an added bonus.

She hadn't known Arkady Orlov for very long, but the death of the surly Ukrainian security consultant brought her up short, like a forearm to the chest. She sat down in a chair and tried to catch her breath, gather her thoughts.

When Natalya had attempted to kill Orlov in the lobby of that apartment building in Falls Church, Lisa had on some subconscious level believed it was fate that he had survived. Orlov had seemed destined to exact some measure of retribution for what the Russians had done to Ukraine, and the threats that they had made to his family.

But this was just one more way in which the world had been turned upside down. The good guys could no longer be counted on to prevail.

She knew then only one thing would set the world right again, or at least send it spinning so far off its axis that it would eventually return to its former orientation.

She needed a drink.

Correction: she needed many drinks.

Lisa saw a pair of high heels planted in front of her and looked up to see Emma Glass staring down at her with a concerned expression. Her assistant had retreated to the background.

"Are you okay?" she asked. "I know that you and Orlov had grown close."

"Yes," Lisa said. "I don't think I realized how much until I heard the news."

After a beat, Lisa asked, "Was his phone compromised?"

Glass shook her head. "We don't think so. It was just a spoofed email."

"Have you confirmed that it was NatalyaX? Is there security camera footage of what happened?"

"It might have been NatalyaX, but we don't know that for certain. The security cameras were out. If it was her, she was wearing a black wig."

"I want to see everything we have."

"I think you need to take some time off."

"That won't be necessary."

"I'm afraid I have to insist."

"I'm going to find her."

"*You're* not going to do anything. This is a massive team effort involving multiple agencies, hundreds of law enforcement officers and emergency responders. You were never doing this by yourself."

"Of course I understand that," Lisa said. She wasn't looking for an argument and was ready to say whatever it took to avoid being benched.

Glass sat down next to her. "The attackers are targeting us personally. They did it with me, they did it with Orlov, and they've done it with you. It would be irresponsible of me to put you back in the field right now when you're so clearly vulnerable to the sort of trap that killed Orlov."

"You've always felt threatened by me," Lisa said. "Ever since that classroom at CyberCorps when you sabotaged my team."

Glass placed a thumb and forefinger over her eyes in pained exasperation. "You just don't get it, do you, Lisa? This is not about you, and it's not about us either. Go home before I say something I'll regret. Take the rest of the day off—and then get back here tomorrow. I think you've already said something that *you're* going to regret."

Emma was right about that. She'd regretted the remark as soon as it was out of her mouth. There might have been some truth to it, but it had sounded petty at a time when there were far more important concerns.

A couple of CyberCom officers arrived to escort her home over her protests.

"Don't even think about trying to con these officers into letting you stay," Glass said. "If you aren't on that bird out of here in five minutes, I'm going to deactivate your security badge."

———

Lisa sped across Maryland toward Washington, DC, in a government helicopter. As they drew closer to the city skyline, she noticed there were more lights on than the last time she had been back. Normally, the freeways below would be clogged with rush hour traffic, but they were nearly deserted as citizens continued to shelter in place. She felt as empty as the landscape, the old familiar darkness of depression seeping through her, drawing her in upon herself like a wounded animal.

Jon wasn't home when she arrived, which, to be honest, was a relief to her. He was no longer teaching his class on counterterrorism, but he was still reporting to the academy. He had been conscripted into one of the FBI teams responding to the new threats to critical infrastructure that were being uncovered daily, such as the cyberattacks that had shut down JFK Airport and the ports of Newark and Philadelphia. His academy trainees were being put into service on low-level assignments. It was all-hands-on-deck time.

Lisa went to the pantry and retrieved a bottle of Ketel One vodka that she had tucked away for emergencies and nearly forgotten. She poured a tumbler and fell into the couch.

The vodka was already beginning to illuminate the blackness in her head, allowing her to climb a few rungs up the dark ladder. Not toward the light, really, but toward a less stygian gloom. She knew that pale light would only recede from her the more she drank, but that wouldn't stop her from trying to reach it. The Black Dog was with her now, curled up on the rug at the foot of the couch.

Lisa wanted to go online to check some of her Dark Web haunts to see if she could gather any intelligence on Natalya. Lisa eventually ended up on the BlackHoleSun chat board, where her old source HelenWheels was holding court. Lisa was logged in as ShivaTGOD.

SHIVATGOD: Surviving the apocalypse? What I want to know is when do the zombies arrive?

HELENWHEELS: I know, right? Just send in the fucking zombies and let's get to the endgame here.

SHIVATGOD: Missed me?

HELENWHEELS: Terribly. Good to have you back.

SHIVATGOD: What have I missed?

HELENWHEELS: Everyone's talking about the attack that's supposed to be coming in the next 48 hours.

SHIVATGOD: Any idea what form the attack is going to take?

HELENWHEELS: Nah. Anyway, that would spoil the surprise, wouldn't it?

SHIVATGOD: Anyone we know claiming credit as playing for Team Russia?

HELENWHEELS: Some people say they were involved, and others claim they saw it coming. But nothing credible.

SHIVATGOD: Who says they were involved?

HELENWHEELS: HaloJen.

SHIVATGOD: Oh ok. So I think we can dismiss that one.

HELENWHEELS: Right.

The chat hit a lull. Lisa could imagine HelenWheels with her fingers resting on the keyboard, unsure of what to say next. Then an ellipsis appeared on the screen as HelenWheels resumed typing.

> HELENWHEELS: Shiva?

> SHIVATGOD: Yeah?

> HELENWHEELS: I'd like to change my name.

> SHIVATGOD: Ok. Everyone needs an image refresh now and then. What name will you be using?

> HELENWHEELS: NatalyaX. I've used it before.

Lisa felt like a black sheet of rain had just swept over her. She sat at the keyboard for what might have been a minute or two. She tried to think of how long she had been communicating with HelenWheels online. At least a year and a half.

Could NatalyaX have been catfishing her, observing her, for all that time?

Yes. It was possible.

Lisa had always taken pride in her ability to prowl the darkest corners of the Dark Web unobserved, using a host of online identities. Apparently she had been observed, and she had met a player who was as good as she was.

Maybe better.

> SHIVATGOD: Hi Natalya. It's good to finally speak to you directly.

HELENWHEELS: I thought it was time.

SHIVATGOD: You murdered Arkady.

HELENWHEELS: Third time's the charm. First the poisoned package (which was really intended more for you, but still). Then that shot I took at him in the apartment building. I think we can agree that he was living on borrowed time.

SHIVATGOD: I'm going to find you. Make you pay for what you've done.

HELENWHEELS: I knew Orlov would come running if you called. It was kind of sweet. Also kind of sad.

SHIVATGOD: You're going after us personally. That's not how the game is played.

HELENWHEELS: Cyberwarfare is not some game of tag. Not anymore. And isn't it more fair that the casualties should include people like us, the soldiers in that war?

SHIVATGOD: You make it sound like you're not killing civilians. There have been hundreds of deaths so far.

HELENWHEELS: And more to come.

SHIVATGOD: You've changed the rules of engagement. Now you're going to have to live with the consequences.

HELENWHEELS: Warfare stopped being polite more than a century ago. Now all war is total war. I've heard this attack being compared to Pearl Harbor. But you Americans always assume that after Pearl Harbor comes Midway, Guadalcanal, D-Day, the fall of Berlin. You think that's the way the story goes for your country, that it's your destiny. But what if it isn't?

SHIVATGOD: We both know who you work for. You and the GRU have crossed a line, and you're going to pay. I'm going to see to it.

HELENWHEELS: Did I say I was with the GRU? I said no such thing. Anyway, neither of us makes the rules. We have intelligence agencies and presidents for that.

SHIVATGOD: The difference is we still believe in rules.

HELENWHEELS: Tell yourself that if it makes you feel better.

SHIVATGOD: I'll see you soon.

HELENWHEELS: If you do, you're not going to like what happens. And, once again, I'm so sorry for your loss. [Frowny emoji with tears]

And with that, NatalyaX was gone.

Lisa felt hopeless and outmatched. She emptied her tumbler of vodka and poured another. The Black Dog let out a stertorous sigh and curled up contentedly at the end of the couch, settling in for a long evening.

36

Day Seven

First impressions of the morning: the vodka bottle was empty on the coffee table, and Lisa felt like she had been poleaxed. She had slept on the couch with all her clothes on. It took a moment, but when she recalled the conversation with NatalyaX, she experienced the shock all over again. The emotions that she had tried to kill with alcohol came back full force, diluted only by the throb of her hangover. She felt frustrated, embarrassed at being played, and angry.

On mornings like this, what she experienced was worse than any hangover, because drinking exacerbated her depression. Although it provided a momentary relief when she was bingeing, the crash was always so much worse than the high. Of course, the cure for that was to keep drinking. She wanted to go out and find a store where she could buy a bottle of wine, but she felt a little too queasy for that at the moment.

Jon entered the living room, his hair wet from a shower and hair gel. She had informed him that hair gel had been over since the nineties, but he would not be dissuaded. She wondered when he'd gotten in.

"Have fun last night?" he asked.

"A blast," she said, rubbing the sleep from her eyes.

"There's no more alcohol in the house."

"Yeah, I saw to that. But I'm not going to let this go any further."

"Good."

"I'm just going to lie here quietly for a while and suffer." She rose carefully, as if her head were full of nitroglycerin, and got a Diet Coke from the pantry.

"Are you reporting to CyberCom today?" he asked.

"I think so. A little later this morning, though. After I've puked my guts up," she said, nodding to the red plastic bucket that Jon had placed beside the couch during the night. She couldn't decide if the move was considerate or passive aggressive. If she had to think about it, it was probably passive aggressive.

"Boot and rally, babe," Jon said. "I'll see you later then."

"Jon?"

"Yes?"

"You'd tell me before you reported any of this to the bureau, right?"

"Yes, I would do that."

"Because, as much as I want to keep going right now, I'm going to stop. And it's not because of your veiled—or not so veiled—threats. It's because I have a job to do, and I don't think I've been doing it well enough so far."

"I'm really glad to hear that," he said.

"That I feel like I'm screwing up?"

"That you're stopping."

"I'm going up against someone who's very good at what they do, and if I'm even a step off of my A game, this is not going to end well."

"Your A game is as good as anyone's."

"I like to think that, but I guess we'll see."

Jon gave her a kiss on the forehead as he headed for the door. He was right not to kiss her on the lips. Her mouth was not exactly minty fresh, and her tongue felt like a dead baby seal washed up on a beach.

After he'd gone, Lisa sat in the quiet of the apartment with no television or music to distract her. The silence was interrupted only by the sound of the occasional ambulance or fire engine, and the periodic thwup of helicopters.

She sipped her warm soda and popped aspirin, thinking back on her conversation with NatalyaX. There was something that nagged at her about it, but she couldn't pinpoint it.

Something that Natalya had said had struck a chord in her memory.

Lisa rose and walked around the room. She went to the window, opened the blinds, and gazed down at Q Street and the neighboring apartment buildings.

All that talk about cyberwarfare had made NatalyaX sound like an ideologue, which was not what Lisa had been expecting. It was hard to tell if she sincerely believed those things or was simply reciting talking points.

The references to Pearl Harbor, Midway, Guadalcanal, D-Day, and Berlin also puzzled her. NatalyaX was a millennial. Those World War II allusions were more likely to come from the millennial's middle-aged dad who watched too much History Channel.

Then Lisa remembered where she had heard those references to Pearl Harbor, Midway, Guadalcanal, D-Day, and Berlin before—those exact references.

They were lifted straight from the impromptu speech that General Holsapple had given to the assembled personnel in the CyberCom war room on the first day of the attacks.

Consciously or unconsciously, Natalya had been mocking the director's attempt to inspire the troops. But in order to know what the general had said . . .

The Russians had to have a mole inside CyberCom.

Lisa's stomach lurched. It was someone who had been in that room and heard Holsapple's speech. A mole would help explain the degree to which the Russians had been able to anticipate CyberCom's every move. It would also explain why NatalyaX had left the deadly package at the apartment in Falls Church, knowing that Lisa would be there.

The Russians' intelligence was so good that it had to extend beyond hacking CyberCom and NSA systems.

Lisa recognized that she had no real evidence to support her theory. The attacks were routinely referred to in the media as a "cyber Pearl Harbor." But it was the references to Midway, Guadalcanal, D-Day, and Berlin, in the same precise order that Holsapple had used them, that convinced her.

Even if it might not convince anyone else.

This was little more than a hunch, and no agency, least of all CyberCom, wanted to believe that it had been so extensively infiltrated. Even if the references to World War II battles were accepted as more than a coincidence, NatalyaX could have picked them up from someone at CyberCom who had indiscreetly quoted Holsapple's address on social media. She also didn't understand why that sort of detail would filter down to a field operative like NatalyaX, except maybe to impress her and others like her with the GRU's success in penetrating CyberCom, helping to ensure that they stayed committed to the mission.

Besides, if Lisa obtained credible evidence of a mole, who would she take it to? That was the dilemma faced in any mole hunt. How do you choose a team to conduct the investigation if there was no one that you really trusted?

She could take this hunch to Special Agent in Charge Pam Gilbertson, who was her FBI supervisor and ran the San Francisco field office that was her home base. Gilbertson was removed from CyberCom and, in Lisa's opinion, could be trusted. However, Gilbertson would never take on another federal agency like CyberCom without proof.

At most, Gilbertson would give her the green light to quietly investigate further. She didn't need Gilbertson's authorization to do that, and sharing her suspicions with the SAC would only involve her boss in an interagency knife fight and likely congressional oversight hearings if Lisa's inquiry went south.

Whoever the mole was, he or she was likely responsible, either directly or indirectly, for the murder of Arkady Orlov. The mole would have firsthand knowledge of just how integral Orlov's knowledge of Russian cyber tactics had been to CyberCom's countermeasures. Finding the mole would also provide further support for President Bilton's decision to declare war on Russia.

If she could establish the link between the presumed mole and NatalyaX.

If she could do that, then everything else might fall into place.

Unfortunately, she had no idea who the mole was, and no current leads on the whereabouts of NatalyaX.

Apart from those two minor hurdles, her plan was perfect.

37

Lisa sat in an amphitheater conference room at CyberCom, listening to a briefing of analysts and agents led by Emma Glass on the latest developments in the response to the cyberattacks, her head still throbbing from the hangover. She scanned the tense faces around her, knowing that the mole was most likely in that room.

Apparently, the digital exorcism of the attacker's malware from CyberCom's systems had been successful, but only up to a point. The APT, or advanced persistent threat, had been expunged from CyberCom's network, but had then activated on the White House's systems. The malware had then used the connections between the White House and CyberCom to reintroduce itself into CyberCom's network in a new and more insidious form.

Glass stood at a podium in front of a long whiteboard. "As much as it pains me to say it, we have to assume that the attacker has access to any intelligence or strategy documents in our system. For now, we're going back to the Dark Ages, pen and paper and person-to-person verbal reports. Many of you will be issued new air-gapped laptops that are not connected to the internet or our networks."

"What about sensitive material that we've already saved to the CyberCom network?" Lisa asked.

"For the most recent mission-critical data, print it out and delete it from the system. For documents that are not absolutely current"—Glass looked visibly pained to complete the sentence—"we have to assume that they've already been compromised."

A murmur ran through the room as they realized that all their round-the-clock work over the past six days had accomplished little if it had been exposed to the Russians. For those CyberCom and NSA agents in the room who felt that they were getting closer to striking back at their adversary, the news was crushing. Lisa could practically hear it land like a blow.

Chuck Salem, the red-bearded head of NSA's Tailored Access Operations group, known as TAO, spoke up. "This malware that has infected our systems is particularly nasty. It's called BlackEnergy, and it has more features than a Swiss Army knife. When one gets disabled or countered, another is enabled."

TAO was the NSA's elite team of hackers who developed the sophisticated cyber offensive weapons that penetrated some of the world's most secure, walled-off government systems. While TAO had been folded into other NSA units, the term was still used to encompass a cadre of the agency's most talented cyber operatives.

"What are some of the features?" Lisa asked.

"Well, it doesn't seek to simply exfiltrate sensitive information in large volumes. It's selective. It knows to look for certain types of documents by certain authors, and it will scan directories to search for them. For example, if there's a particular type of analysis that they're looking for, the malware will be waiting for the first instance in which someone uploads a document containing the relevant keywords, and then that one document will be extracted to the command and control center."

"And where is that command and control center?" Lisa asked.

"The first stop is in Thailand, but then it's relayed through a string of proxy servers that we haven't been able to crack."

"I'd like to take a shot at that," Lisa said.

"We've got this, Special Agent Tanchik," Salem said, pushing his wire-rimmed glasses up on his nose. "You'd only slow us down."

"Because clearly you've been doing such a great job so far," Lisa said.

"I understand that the FBI considers you to be hot stuff, but that doesn't mean you're ready to level up and play with NSA and CyberCom."

Before Lisa could fire back, Glass interrupted. "We don't have time for squabbling. Your teams are going to work together, and there will be no holding back or protecting turf. We've got a common mission here, and lives are at stake."

She continued, gripping the sides of the lectern and leaning into the mic, "And that's not the worst of it. We've detected chatter on the IRC boards suggesting that the biggest attack is yet to come."

"Do you have any clue as to the target?" Lisa asked.

"No, just that it's going to be big. And damaging. And it's going to happen in forty-eight"—she checked her watch—"make that forty-six hours."

Glass pressed a key on the laptop on the lectern, and an image was projected behind her.

It was a screen grab of an IRC message board string. One statement by an anonymous user named Wintermute was blown up to stand out. It read:

> The attacks on the US so far are just Phase 1. In 48
> hours, shit's about to get real. Tick tock. Duck and
> cover, bitches.

Lisa had visited the IRC board where the message had been posted, which was a kind of clubhouse for black hat hackers, but she had never encountered a poster named Wintermute.

"Do you have any history on Wintermute?" Lisa asked.

"No, as far as we can tell, that was a new screen name. It doesn't appear in any of our intelligence. How about you? Have you ever run across Wintermute?"

"No. But the name is taken from an AI in William Gibson's novel *Neuromancer*. That AI was all-knowing, and I guess the poster wants us to believe that about him or her."

"Okay. Interesting, but not all that helpful," Glass said.

"How credible is this threat?" Lisa asked.

"As terrorist chatter goes, fairly credible," Salem said. "Based upon the bad actors who were on that board at the time and the way they responded to, and interacted with, this Wintermute, we believe the message has to be taken seriously."

Glass nodded. "We're going to need to concentrate on the types of infrastructure that could create a 9/11-like event—and that haven't already been impacted by the attacks. Airlines are grounded, so they're out. The electrical grid couldn't be hit any harder than it's already been hit. Maybe a nuclear power plant. Maybe the water supply."

Glass pointed around the room. "Look, we're going to need to break up into smaller groups now. There are teams in this room that are going to need to be briefed in more detail about the malware and what we know about its functionality. But I wanted you all to know about the new security protocols that we're implementing. We'll let you know when it's safe to start using our network again. We're adjourned."

As people filed out of the room, Deputy National Security Adviser Geoffrey Tobin, who had gotten her booted out of the president's war council earlier, approached.

"I'm surprised that you're still here at CyberCom," Tobin said.

"Why is that?"

"Because I don't see what value you bring at this point in the process. The FBI has its job, and we have ours."

"Aren't we all ultimately on the same team, Geoff?" She said it with a blithe tone that she knew would infuriate him even more.

"Of course. But we all have our positions to play. And you're out of position right now, Agent Tanchik. Besides, you're no closer to catching

NatalyaX, and you weren't even able to control your partner, Orlov. You let him go and get himself killed."

"I recommend that you watch your tone. Arkady didn't 'get himself killed.' He was murdered by a Russian operative. Those are the kinds of risks that you face when you actually get out from behind a desk and put yourself in harm's way."

Tobin cocked his head and gave her an assessing look. "You two were close, weren't you?"

"Yeah, we got to be. Why?"

"Some new facts came to light recently that he may have collaborated with the Russians in their attacks on Ukraine. Did you know anything about that?"

"No." Lisa knew that if she was completely forthcoming about Orlov's disclosures to her on that subject, her access to CyberCom and NSA resources would probably be revoked, and maybe her FBI credentials too. Someone must have ordered a very deep background check on Orlov when he was read into the CyberCom defense initiative.

She believed that Orlov had been telling the truth when he'd admitted that he had cooperated in order to save his family. She also believed that he had been seeking redemption ever since and had not posed a security threat.

"Would you submit to a polygraph on that?"

"Sure," Lisa said. "Bring it. That would be a really productive use of our time during this crisis."

"I may get back to you on that," Tobin said, turning to leave.

"Oh, and Deputy Director?"

"Yes?"

"Arkady Orlov was a brave man. He didn't have to be here in this country helping us. And if you talk shit about him again, I swear I'm going to break your nose."

Tobin smiled thinly. "Noted, Special Agent Tanchik. And you keep making statements like that, you're going to make this way too easy for me."

After Tobin was gone, Lisa was still boiling as she strode through the long curving hallways of CyberCom. When she cooled down a bit, she returned to the problem at hand, and to the new information that she had learned during the briefing.

Glass had said that the BlackEnergy malware targeted particular documents when it found them on the system, so there must be search criteria.

What would those criteria be?

The Russians would be looking for documents created by certain top-level personnel, cabinet members, and agency directors. They would probably also be targeting references to the GRU, cyberwarfare response scenarios, NatalyaX.

Lisa decided that if there was a mole in CyberCom, she would need to pursue her own investigation, and that meant "hacking back" at the GRU. She'd create a document on the CyberCom network that was so attractive that the BlackEnergy malware would be drawn to it, and then would exfiltrate it back to the GRU's hackers in Moscow, or wherever they were based. And that document would need to contain some malware of its own, something so new and stealthy that the Russians would not immediately detect it.

This was a job for Rawlings at the Quantico computer forensic lab.

She placed the call, and Rawlings picked up on the second ring. She had missed hearing his Georgia drawl.

"I wasn't sure if you'd be there," Lisa said.

"Oh, since the attacks began, I'm always here. I've even got a little cot set up in the corner of the lab. I must admit it has been challenging maintaining my usually impeccable personal hygiene."

"Glad to hear that you're hanging in there."

"And how are you doing among the spooks over at CyberCom? They're a warm and welcoming bunch, aren't they?"

"Oh yeah, they've really rolled out the red carpet. There was a fruit basket for me when I arrived."

"So as pleasant as this is, I have a feeling you didn't reach out just to chitchat."

"No, I need some malware, something special."

"You've come to the right place, Special Agent. Go on."

"I need that thing you were working on last month. It has to be something that I can attach to a Word document, something new that isn't on any blacklist yet, extremely stealthy."

"Stealthy enough to get past the GRU? At least for a while?"

"Exactly."

"What functionality are you looking for?"

"Something that can capture a webcam and send back images to my command and control, give me root-level access to the infected network, and the ability to exfiltrate documents."

"You're not asking for much, are you?"

"What have you got for me?"

"You know that CyberCom and the NSA aren't entirely unskilled. Chuck Salem and his bunch at TAO have malware of their own that's approved for these sorts of uses."

Lisa wanted to give Rawlings some plausible deniability if this operation went south. After a pause, she said, "You understand, Rhett, that I'm asking you for this as part of one of my ongoing FBI investigations. It has nothing to do with my work with CyberCom and NSA."

There was silence on the line for a long moment. "I hear you loud and clear."

"Send the attachment to my FBI email account, and I'll take it from there."

"Will do. I've made some advances in the coding since the last time you saw it. I think you'll be pleased."

"You're the best."

"I know that, but I'm glad that you do too," Rawlings said. "I hope you know this isn't like those times when we've taken a few liberties and annoyed our SAC. You go off the reservation on this one, and you're messing with CyberCom, NSA, even the White House. I assume you must have a very good reason for this."

"I'm afraid I do."

Rawlings seemed to grasp the unspoken—that she wouldn't be doing something like this on her own unless she believed that CyberCom was compromised.

"Then you watch your back, girl."

———

As soon as she finished her call with Rawlings, Lisa sat down at her laptop and began typing up notes on her investigation and pursuit of NatalyaX, using as many red flag phrases as she could come up with. The document did not contain anything that the GRU didn't already know; it was designed purely to be picked up by their malware and exfiltrated.

Lisa thought of it as baiting the hook.

38

Glass appeared in the doorway of Lisa's conference room at CyberCom with a grim expression.

"What is it?" Lisa asked.

"I debated whether I should share this with you, but I figured you needed to know."

"Just tell me."

"A hotel desk clerk came to Orlov's aid while he was dying. NatalyaX had left the scene—and apparently took Orlov's cell phone. Orlov asked the clerk to record a message on his phone. For you. I understand if you'd prefer to hear it later."

"I'd like to hear it now."

"I thought you'd say that." Glass pressed a key on her phone. "There, I just sent you the audio file."

Lisa went directly to her computer and opened the in-box. She heard the door quietly shut behind her as Glass left the room.

The recording began with background sounds of people calling for assistance. A panicked man's voice said, "Somebody help him! Is anyone here a doctor?"

Scraping sounds on the speaker, and the sound of rough, shallow breaths. Then the voice of Arkady Orlov.

ORLOV: *Give this recording to Special Agent Lisa Tanchik at the FBI.* [*A long pause and a wet cough.*] *NatalyaX has dandelion tattoo over her right ankle.* [*A longer pause, and then Orlov's voice returned, more faintly this time.*] *Lisa, you find that bitch. Sorry I won't be there when you do.*

39

Lisa was awakened at three a.m. by an insistent pinging from her laptop. In her partial dream state, she thought it sounded like the tone heard on an airline before it took off.

Please fasten your seat belts, and make sure your seat backs are in a fully upright position.

She rolled over and nearly toppled off the cot in her conference room at CyberCom.

Now she was fully awake.

The ringing was a signal that Rawlings's malware had been uploaded. Apparently the attackers had taken the bait—or at least their BlackEnergy malware had.

She opened up her laptop and examined the malware's dashboard. The first thing she noticed was that she appeared to now have a fix on the attackers—geolocation coordinates somewhere in central Moscow. She needed to have the CyberCom team establish a street address for that pin, which she strongly suspected was going to be a building owned by or associated with the GRU.

Even if she learned nothing else, definitively linking the GRU to the attacks was a major breakthrough in the investigation. CyberCom had been attempting to bait the GRU with similar tactics, but without success. The tailored malware that Rawlings had developed in the FBI's computer forensic lab was living up to its billing.

But that wasn't all.

The malware had successfully activated the webcam of one of the attackers, and Lisa's screen displayed a video feed. She was observing a large open-plan office filled with cubicles on one side. Five figures, three men and two women, were in view, doing the things that all bored office workers do—sharing videos on their phone with one another, drinking coffee, making small talk.

On the other side of the large room were three groupings of devices. Lisa didn't know what she was looking at, but each assemblage included what appeared to be a desktop computer, mechanical switches attached to hoses, and a small tank enclosed in a sealed glass box. While the three contraptions bore similarities, each one featured a slightly different arrangement of components. A laptop sat on a table in front of each of the installations.

It dawned on Lisa what she was looking at—these were models. The GRU was mocking up versions of the systems that they were targeting in the next major wave of the attacks, the one that would be launched in thirty-six hours.

But what were these devices? The models seemed to be three different versions of the same basic process. That would be consistent with an attack on a legacy system that existed in a variety of iterations, requiring several versions of a targeted malware. Each model included some type of fluid stored in a tank, but that could describe a host of manufacturing and industrial processes.

Lisa watched another display in the malware's dashboard, where a string of Cyrillic characters was marching across the screen. This was the malware's other critical feature—a keystroke logger, which was set to transcribe the Cyrillic keyboard that she'd assumed her target would be using.

She couldn't read Russian, but she watched the rhythm of the characters dancing across the display and tried to match them up to the moving fingers of the Russian hacker whom she was observing on the webcam feed. All the input from the hacker's keyboard would be stored for future translation into English.

The workstation that had been infected with the malware seemed to belong to a young man with bleached blond hair, who loomed in the webcam's picture. The hacker stopped typing at his keyboard to take a sip of coffee. At that precise moment, the stream of text paused.

The hacker put down the coffee next to his monitor and resumed typing.

The stream of Cyrillic characters resumed.

Lisa grinned. It was working.

Many hackers placed Post-it notes over their webcam lenses in order to avoid this form of exploit, but Bleach-Blond Boy was apparently too arrogant to take that precaution.

Lisa needed to figure out what the three models were meant to represent. It was a puzzle that had to be solved before the next attacks commenced. And time was running out.

None of the models appeared to be a nuclear power plant—they were far too simple for that. The Russians were clearly targeting three varieties of a type of industrial facility; only legacy systems would utilize the types of basic switches and valves that were included in the models.

Lisa's pulse raced. Actually, they had far less than thirty-six hours, because it was going to be necessary to develop custom software to counteract the malware in each location before the clock ticked down to zero.

Lisa recognized that she could not continue running her own investigation, particularly now that she had uncovered critical information. She could at least take her new intelligence to the highest level possible and hope it didn't become known to the mole at CyberCom, if there was one.

That meant taking it to the executive branch.

To POTUS.

40

Lisa reached out directly to the president's chief of staff to explain what she had discovered. The chief of staff was another member of the executive branch team who had set up a second base of operations at Fort Meade.

"There's been a breakthrough in the investigation," Lisa said. "I have hard evidence linking the GRU to the attacks. I also have some important information about their next target, the attack that's supposed to occur in thirty-three hours."

"That's excellent," said Chief of Staff Adam Felker. "But why are we hearing about this from an FBI agent? Do CyberCom and NSA have this information?"

Felker was in his early thirties, with short black hair, rolled-up shirtsleeves, and dark shadows under sleepless eyes. He looked far too young to be running the Oval Office, but Lisa knew he was regarded as a political prodigy. He had managed President Bilton's campaign and had been widely credited with her brilliant use of Big Data and social media to reach voters. Lisa appreciated that she was speaking with someone who had no difficulty understanding how data, algorithms, and a talented hacker could change the world.

"Not yet."

"And why is that?" Felker asked.

"I wanted to come directly to you because I have reason to believe that CyberCom may have a mole."

"What does that mean—'reason to believe'? Do you have evidence?"

"Not exactly."

"Of course I want to hear you out, but in a time like this we can't afford to devote resources to chasing our tail. Besides, the idea of a mole in CyberCom sounds a little far fetched."

"Is it really? Don't tell me that the CIA has never had agents placed in positions of authority in Russia."

Felker glanced away, a nonreply reply if there ever was one. "If you came to me because you think we can keep this from CyberCom and NSA leadership, you're mistaken."

"No, I get that. But I wanted to start here in hopes that dissemination of this material can be as limited as possible."

"Fine, we'll hear you out, and we'll do what we can to limit disclosure. But we need to involve General Holsapple right away so that NSA and CyberCom can confirm that your intelligence is legit. For all we know this is another trap set by the Russians. They've been one step ahead of us since this thing began. Why should we think that's changed now?"

President Bilton appeared behind Felker in the hallway. "Because we don't trade in that kind of defeatist whining around here, Adam."

Felker looked mortified. "My apologies, Madam President. Of course we're going to turn this thing around."

"I have definitive proof that the Russians are behind the attacks," Lisa said. "No more circumstantial evidence."

"Well then, let's see it," President Bilton said, motioning her into the office that she had emerged from. "It'd be nice to know for certain that I was right in declaring war on them."

The president's makeshift office had an impressive mahogany desk and original paintings on the walls. Clearly some CyberCom senior director had been evicted to make room for the chief executive. Lisa guessed that it would be easy enough to tell whom the office belonged to by examining the framed photos that had all been turned facedown on the bookcase.

"Get Tobin in here," President Bilton said to Felker. "He's going to need to hear this."

Bilton saw the look on Lisa's face. "Is there a problem, Special Agent Tanchik?"

"No, no problem. It's just that I'm not the deputy national security adviser's favorite person."

"Don't worry about it," Bilton said. "I don't think Geoff *has* a favorite person."

When Tobin entered the room a few minutes later, he was clearly surprised to see Lisa in the room with the president and chief of staff.

"Special Agent Tanchik," Tobin said. "What are you doing here?"

"It's nice to see you too," Lisa said.

"She has something that she wants to show us," the president said, raising a hand to preempt any sniping. "Please sit down, and let's see what she's got."

Lisa set up her laptop on a round worktable in the corner, and the other three pulled up chairs. She played the video that she had captured from the GRU hacking operation.

When the video clip was done, President Bilton said, "Okay, tell me what we just saw."

"The people working in that office appear to be command and control for the malware that has infected CyberCom's network and exfiltrated its classified files."

"How do you know that?" Tobin asked.

"Because they stole a document that I created to draw their attention, which was infected with our own malware."

Tobin shook his head dismissively. "That tactic has been attempted before, without success."

"Not with the malware that I used. It's an exploit that the FBI's computer forensic lab recently developed. State-of-the-art stealthy."

"Interesting," Tobin said. "But what if the malware isn't as stealthy as you think? What if the attackers know it's there and are staging this for our benefit so that we waste more valuable time chasing false leads?"

"That's possible, but I don't think so."

"Isn't that sort of call above your pay grade, Special Agent? Which begs the question—why are you here alone, without anyone from CyberCom?"

"There's a reason for that," President Bilton said. "And you'll hear about it later. Right now, I'd like to know how we know that the people in that room are affiliated with the GRU."

"I have geolocation coordinates for that office," Lisa said. "I know it's located in Moscow, but I don't have a street address yet. Your team"—she turned to Tobin—"could help with that."

The president motioned to her chief of staff. "Adam, please get that geolocation data and run it by the NSA immediately. We need a street address, and we need to know who owns the building."

Lisa scribbled the coordinates on a scrap of paper and handed it to Felker, who promptly left the room.

Ten minutes later, Felker was back, with a handful of printouts. He fanned them out on the table.

"This is the place," he said. "It's an office building in central Moscow less than a mile from the Kremlin. It's a known outpost of the GRU."

President Bilton clenched a fist and tapped the table twice. "Combined with the other evidence we've gathered, I think we may finally have what we need for a full counterstrike. No more half measures. But I want to hear that from the entire national security team."

"Shall I call the meeting?" Felker asked.

"Yes. Now."

Lisa moved her chair back, preparing to leave.

"No, you stay for this," President Bilton said. "You can't just come in here, drop the mic, and leave. I think the team is going to have a few questions for you."

———

An hour later, Lisa's video had been played three times on a large projection screen for the assembled National Security Council, which included the president, secretary of defense, the secretary of state, various national security advisers, and General Holsapple, who had been furiously staring at her throughout the entire meeting. He didn't understand why she had been allowed to jump the chain of command, but he was shrewd enough not to ask that question in the middle of the meeting and highlight how out of the loop he had been.

After Lisa had managed to withstand the team's exhaustive interrogation, President Bilton called the question. "How many here think we now have the evidence that we need to support a decision to strike back at the Russians with full force?"

"Just to be clear," Secretary of Defense Richard Stansfield said. "Are you open to considering all offensive options?"

"Yes," the president said. "There have been plenty of incidents in the past where we've sparred with other nations using our cyber capabilities. They hack us, we hack back—tit for tat. But what the Russians have done to our power grid, our nuclear plants, our financial system, even attacking and killing our cyber defense personnel— it's every bit the equivalent of missile strikes on our Eastern Seaboard. The damage and loss of life was as great or greater than a conventional attack. We need to send a message and hit them—hard. Tell me what that would look like."

"We have several scenarios that we've modeled," the secretary of defense said.

"You can show me a full proposal later. Just give me the high points. What can we actually do to them?" President Bilton asked. "Right now."

The secretary of defense nodded. "We have red-button capability to take out the electrical grids in all of their largest cities—Moscow, Saint Petersburg, Novosibirsk, Yekaterinburg. We have implants in their critical networks that have already been tested. It's literally a matter of flipping the switch."

"It's the middle of the Russian winter," President Bilton said. "If we cut off the power, their people are going to freeze to death."

"They did it to us," the secretary of defense said.

"That doesn't necessarily mean we do it to them. I want other options. For example, could we take out the electrical grid in just one city, say Moscow, and then allow them to bring it back up in twenty-four or forty-eight hours?"

"As we've seen with our legacy electrical power systems, once you crash them, it's not always so easy to bring them back online. It's like Humpty Dumpty; it may not be possible to put the pieces back together. Also, we couldn't predict the cascading effect on their other Russian electrical grids if we took down Moscow."

"So you're recommending a strike against Russian power grids?"

"I'm saying that's a mission that we could execute effectively," Holsapple said. "But I also think I know another measure that would get President Vasiliev's attention. We could bring the Russian economy to a standstill by cutting off its banking system, terminating their connection to SWIFT, the international clearinghouse for banking transactions."

Secretary of State Mona Washington interjected, "That may be very satisfying, but you can't lose sight of what that would mean for the EU. The Europeans are dependent upon being able to purchase

Russian oil and gas. You cut off the Russians' ability to engage in international transactions, then there are going to be gas shortages in Europe this winter."

"If we strike any major blow against Russia, there are going to be ripple effects," President Bilton said. "Someone model the consequences for terminating the Russians from SWIFT. We want to avoid civilian casualties, but we need a proportionate response. And given what they did to us, that response has to be significant."

The secretary of state continued, "President Vasiliev wouldn't like it if the millions of rubles that he's stashed in foreign banks were suddenly unavailable and the Russian press received detailed inventories of the financial dealings of Vasiliev and his oligarch pals. We have plenty of evidence of how the president and his cronies have siphoned off the riches of the Russian economy into international accounts. We even have ways of making the money in his foreign accounts just—disappear."

"I like it," the president said with a tight smile. "That's a good start. Can you put together a comprehensive plan for me?"

"Of course," said the secretary of state. "We have a plan of attack that State and CyberCom have been working up. We'll revise it in accordance with your instructions and get it to you."

"Good," President Bilton said. "But our highest-priority task is to stop this impending attack. I thought the Russians had already taken their best shot."

"Apparently not," Lisa said. "Those devices in the video represent some US industrial system that involves a form of toxic liquid or gas—and can somehow do more harm than anything they've done so far."

She could tell from the way several people around the table were looking at her that they didn't think she should be speaking during this meeting. She couldn't care less.

"And, if that message is to be believed, we have about thirty-two hours to figure out the points of attack and disable their malware," President Bilton said. "That sounds like a tall order."

Holsapple nodded. "We're working with Homeland Security to determine what those models might represent. We have some of our best industrial engineers working on it nonstop."

"But with so little time left, we also need to be preparing for the possibility that this will be a disaster relief situation," said the president. "What are we doing on that front?"

Sandra Ochoa, the director of Homeland Security, spoke up. "Our emergency response capabilities are pretty much maxed out at this point addressing the casualties arising from the power grid failures, particularly the fires. And it's hard to ready our teams for an attack when we don't know its location or the nature of the threat. Nevertheless, we have FEMA teams ready to mobilize by helicopter."

"Well, on that positive note." President Bilton rose. "I think the rest of our work can be done in smaller groups, unless someone has something to add."

There was no response from the room.

"Okay then," said the president. "This is one of those moments when Americans have historically risen to the occasion. So let's do that now, okay? I need the best work from each and every one of you. This is where we turn the tide on this thing. Right now."

And then she turned to Lisa. "And I think we all owe Special Agent Tanchik thanks for taking the initiative and uncovering these plans. Otherwise, we'd be going into this blind."

Lisa nodded. She knew there were people in that room who would be after her scalp, but they weren't going to do it in front of POTUS. Her violations of protocol, deploying malware against Russia without agency approval, and then going directly to the White House team and bypassing her supervisors at CyberCom were more than enough to end her career.

In that moment, she was prepared to pay any professional cost as long as she helped bring down NatalyaX and stop the impending deadly attack.

And there were only thirty-two hours left to do it.

41

As expected, General Holsapple found Lisa in her conference room shortly after the meeting with the president and her war council had adjourned.

"What the hell were you thinking, Tanchik, going over my head to POTUS with that information? I'm inclined to take this up with the FBI director right now and get your ticket pulled."

"I believe there's a mole at CyberCom."

Holsapple took a moment to absorb the statement.

"And you thought it was me?"

"I thought that the mole could possibly be one of your closest advisers. I thought telling you meant telling them."

"What makes you think there's a mole?"

Lisa laid out the evidence, which sounded less convincing every time she repeated it. But she still believed she was correct.

Holsapple shook his head. "That's it?"

"That's it."

"You realize how weak that sounds?"

"Yes."

"It would explain a lot, though, wouldn't it? How they've managed to maximize the impact of their attacks, avoid detection, anticipate our moves. But they could do a lot of that by penetrating our network with their malware."

"They'd want to supplement that with human intelligence," Lisa said. "Because they knew we'd eventually find their implants and kick them out of our network once the attacks began."

"True," Holsapple said. "It's what we would do. So assuming for a moment that you're correct, do you have any idea who it might be?"

"No. I suppose it could be anyone."

"That's not very helpful, Agent Tanchik. The president has just tasked me with presenting a plan for escalating our attacks against Russia. And you're saying that I can't trust that a member of my team won't disclose those plans to the enemy."

"That's what I'm saying."

"I want you to help me find this mole—if there is one," Holsapple continued. "Can you do that?"

"I'll do my best," she said.

"You do that," Holsapple said. "And maybe, just *maybe*, I won't have you thrown out of the bureau for your insubordination."

———

Holsapple provided Lisa with an all-clearance pass that permitted her to go and come as she pleased at CyberCom. She used that freedom to return to the war room, and now *everyone* she encountered seemed to be a candidate to be the mole.

Or, perhaps more accurately, *no one* could be ruled out as the infiltrator.

Simply observing CyberCom personnel and speculating was an unproductive exercise, but she didn't know what else to do.

She watched Geoffrey Tobin speaking with a team of engineers who were examining the video footage of the three devices, trying to determine what they were. Tobin was an obnoxious jerk, but that didn't make the deputy national security adviser a spy.

She considered several more members of the CyberCom team, eliminating for the time being those whose lives had been put at risk by GRU measures such as the pacemaker malfunctions. A mole in CyberCom was a valuable and carefully cultivated asset, and she had to assume that the Russians would not take life-threatening risks with such a person.

Lisa decided on two approaches to narrowing down her search. First, she would get Holsapple to grant her access to the personnel files of everyone who was working in the CyberCom war room. She would start by focusing on those who had joined the agency more recently and work backward from there, looking for anomalies in their histories.

At the same time, Lisa would also continue to review every word of the communications that they were gathering from the GRU's team in Moscow. If the hackers were relying directly on intelligence obtained from a source inside CyberCom, then they would almost certainly know the mole's identity.

Everyone working in the war room seemed to be amped up, working at top intensity. She could see it in the taut expressions and red-rimmed eyes. They all knew that this was their 9/11, the event that they would be judged by, and that they would judge themselves by, for the rest of their lives. Many CyberCom team members knew colleagues at NSA who were haunted by the missed opportunities to avert the attack on the World Trade Center.

Lisa understood that sense of guilt. Since the attacks had begun, she had often wondered if she could have changed the course of events if she had managed to track down NatalyaX earlier, before she'd killed John Rosenthal with the strobe attachment. Perhaps Natalya might have cut a deal and turned on her GRU bosses, revealing the impending threat. There was plenty of guilt to go around, and Lisa knew that she would be turning these recriminations over in her head for the rest of her life.

It wasn't so different from the guilt that Orlov had felt.

A flurry of activity among the team of engineers that Tobin was speaking with caught Lisa's eye. High fives were exchanged by a couple of pocket-protector types. She approached the group.

"Good news?" she asked.

A wide-eyed young man in CyberCom fatigues and a buzz cut was clearly anxious to share his discovery, but he glanced over at Tobin first.

The deputy national security adviser nodded somewhat grudgingly. "It's okay. Special Agent Tanchik obtained the video feed that you've been analyzing."

The young man in fatigues said, "Yeah. We think we've identified the type of industrial facility that those devices in Moscow were intended to replicate. Of course, the match is not one hundred percent certain, because the models don't precisely replicate the factories that they're intended to—"

"What are we looking at?" Lisa asked. She didn't have time for all the caveats and disclaimers.

The engineer snapped out of his wonkish digression. "Okay, right. We think they're different types of water purification plants."

"They're going to try to poison the water supply?"

He shook his head. "That tank in the middle of each model? It contains chlorine gas, which is highly toxic. Water purification plants store millions of milligrams of the gas. And if a major explosion occurs in one of those plants, then that deadly gas will be released into the atmosphere."

Lisa didn't know if that was better or worse than infecting the water supply. "What's the potential impact of that sort of attack?"

"Well, the fact that they developed three different models with different mechanisms and configurations indicates that they've developed malware that is tailored to create explosions in several different filtration plants—at least three, probably many more than that since some plants share common designs."

"And how much damage could be done if this sort of event occurs in a single facility?"

"Depends upon the location, of course," the engineer said. "In a densely populated urban area, if you release an enormous cloud of chlorine gas on a population that isn't prepared for it, doesn't have gas masks, then that sort of event could result in thousands of fatalities. Maybe tens of thousands."

"For each plant that's compromised."

"That's right. For each plant."

Tobin had been listening along with Lisa. He was still absorbing the information just as she was.

"Still feel like a high five?" Tobin asked the engineer.

"No, sir."

"Do you have malware to counteract the attacks?" Lisa directed this question to Tobin.

"No, we only just identified the targets. I'm going to go brief Homeland and CyberCom on this now. I'm not sure it will be possible to develop cyber countermeasures in time. We may just have to shut down every water filtration plant that we can get to in the attack zone on the Eastern Seaboard."

"But given the state of telecommunications systems right now, it won't be easy to reach them all."

"I know that."

"And stopping the supply of clean water to the East Coast cities is going to pretty quickly lead to adverse consequences."

"Tell me something that I don't know, Agent Tanchik. I realize that there are no good options."

"First, you'll need to isolate the malware that's embedded in those water filtration plants. It has to be there already, if you know what to look for."

"I'm going to brief our team on this right now," Tobin said. "We'll find that malware, and then start figuring out how to counteract it."

"I'd like to be part of that effort," Lisa said. "And there's a member of the FBI computer forensic lab at Quantico who would be perfect for this assignment." She would put Rawlings up against any forensic expert at CyberCom.

"We'll handle this from here, Tanchik. This is what CyberCom does."

"But my FBI team was the one that developed the malware that slipped past the GRU and provided us with the intelligence that got us here."

"Has anyone ever told you that you're a very special sort of pain in the ass, Special Agent Tanchik?"

She kept a poker face. "So you're saying that you think I'm special?"

"Thank you for your offer, but I'm going to go do my job now. Remember, we're all on the same team here." Tobin crooked a finger at the engineer Lisa had been speaking with, and the two of them strode out of the war room.

42

Since Lisa and her colleagues at the FBI were not permitted to participate in developing a response to the malware targeting water filtration plants, she decided that the next most productive use of her time was to continue to monitor the feed from the GRU's hackers in Moscow. The small conference room that was her temporary office faced out on the bustling CyberCom war room. Through the sheet of soundproof glass, she saw the agents' lips moving but couldn't hear anything other than the clicking of her own fingers on her keyboard.

As far as she could tell, the GRU hadn't detected their malware, which was continuing to capture keystrokes and webcam images of Bleach-Blond Boy, who she'd learned was named Gregor.

Viewing Gregor's email in-box and instant messaging also provided a picture of the other hackers in the office. Gregor communicated most frequently with Petra, a tiny girl with chunky black glasses and a blue streak in her hair who sat two workstations away. Gregor had been involved in combing CyberCom's systems for actionable intelligence for nearly six months. He did not appear to be a member of the team that was targeting the water filtration plants, but he almost certainly knew the identity of the mole inside CyberCom.

The problem was that he never referred to the mole by name. Instead, he used a code name—Bulletproof.

She watched the characters materialize on her screen, automatically translated into English from the Cyrillic keyboards that the hackers were using.

GREGOR: Favorite GOT character?

PETRA: Tyrion, of course.

GREGOR: You're tiny like the Imp.

PETRA: And you?

GREGOR: Sam.

PETRA: I see you as more of a Hodor.

GREGOR: Ouch. Could be worse—at least I'm not a Joffrey, or a Ramsay.

PETRA: You are very difficult to insult, you know that?

GREGOR: Thank you.

PETRA: But I will keep trying.

GREGOR: Look at all of the activity today! CyberCom is freaking out.

PETRA: They know they've been pwned.

GREGOR: Nineteen hours until the attack.

PETRA: And they clearly have no clue who Bulletproof is.

GREGOR: I almost feel sorry for them. Almost.

PETRA: Don't let Dusan hear you talking like that.

GREGOR: I'm not afraid of him.

PETRA: You should be.

GREGOR: Maybe you're right. Let's move this to text.

The stream of characters on Lisa's screen came to an abrupt halt. Gregor and Petra were undoubtedly continuing to trash-talk their supervisor via SMS.

Ten minutes later, the conversation on their workplace IM resumed.

GREGOR: When this is all done, we will be heroes.

PETRA: Just for one day.

GREGOR: Bowie. Ha!

PETRA: I heard we will all get bonuses if the work continues to go as well as it has. What will you do with yours?

GREGOR: Snowboarding vacation. Krasnaya Polyana. It's beautiful in season. You ever been?

Lisa googled it and learned that Krasnaya Polyana was Russia's most famous ski region, located in the city of Sochi in the Western Caucasus. She remembered Sochi as the site of the 2014 Winter Olympics. It was easy to imagine the GRU's hackers as malevolent archvillains, but she should have known that in reality they would turn out to be a bunch of bored and geeky young office drones.

PETRA: No. I wish.

GREGOR: You ski?

PETRA: Not really.

GREGOR: You'd be good at it with your low center of gravity.

PETRA: Shut up.

GREGOR: No, you shut up!

PETRA: Go back to work.

GREGOR: No, you go back to work!

PETRA: I hate you.

GREGOR: Don't make me USE ALL CAPS.

PETRA: You are incredibly annoying.

GREGOR: I'll leave you alone if you give me one smiley emoji.

The characters stopped as Petra played out a long pause.

GREGOR: Come on.

PETRA: [Cursing emoji]

GREGOR: You can do better than that.

PETRA: [Neutral emoji]

GREGOR: Almost there.

PETRA: [Half-smile emoji]

GREGOR: There it is!

PETRA: Can we go back to work now?

GREGOR: Of course. Any new intelligence from Bulletproof?

PETRA: That is a stupid code name for a mole.

GREGOR: You have a better one?

PETRA: I like Demolished.

GREGOR: And you think Bulletproof is stupid? You didn't answer my question.

PETRA: Dusan hasn't provided a briefing report yet today.

GREGOR: I had to ask because you always seem to get the reports before I do.

PETRA: Because Dusan likes me better.

GREGOR: He was hitting on you yesterday.

PETRA: Was not.

Lisa tuned out for a bit as Gregor and Petra continued their small talk. They seemed to be more concerned with interoffice flirting than obtaining actionable intelligence. She would review the full transcript later.

But there was something that didn't seem quite right about the exchange. Petra had tried out a different code name for the GRU's mole—Demolished.

That didn't sound like a word that Petra would use in that context. It didn't jibe with any of the qualities that seemed to appeal to Petra. It wasn't funny, or cute, or cool.

What could it mean—Demolished?

Lisa considered that maybe the Russian-to-English translation software might have made an error.

She hit a key and converted the text back to its original Cyrillic. Lisa couldn't read Russian, but she was able to isolate the word in question.

Razrushennoy.

Lisa rose from her desk, entered the war room, and called out, "Who speaks Russian?"

An analyst in CyberCom fatigues looked up from his monitor. "I do. What have you got?"

Lisa motioned him into her office.

"This word," she said, pointing to *razrushennoy* on her monitor. "Does this mean 'demolished'?"

The analyst leaned and peered at the screen, then shook his head. "Not really, no. I'd say 'shattered' was a better translation. 'Demolished' is *sneseny*."

"Are you sure?"

"Yes, I'm sure. What is this?"

"Thanks. That's very helpful."

The analyst appeared curious, but he left, seeming to sense that he wasn't going to get any more background.

So she had two different code names for the GRU's mole at CyberCom.

Bulletproof.

Shattered.

Perhaps those two descriptors told her something about the person she was pursuing.

What was something that could be bulletproof or shattered?

The answer came surprisingly quickly, like something that had already been just beneath the surface of her subconscious.

Glass.

Bulletproof glass.

Shattered glass.

Emma Glass.

Emma Glass, deputy director of CyberCom, and her old classmate and rival from the CyberCorps program at GWU, was a GRU operative and their mole within the agency.

43

Lisa brought her suspicions to General Holsapple. Glass was one of his chief aides at CyberCom and one of his most trusted advisers. They had worked together for five years.

"Does the FBI not deal in forensic evidence anymore?" he asked. "Is this what passes for an investigation these days? Word games?"

Beneath Holsapple's exasperation, Lisa could tell that he was unnerved by the possibility that someone with such access to top-secret sources and methods might be a Russian spy.

"I know it's not definitive."

"Not definitive? That's an understatement. And don't you and Emma have a history?"

"We were classmates in the CyberCorps program at GWU."

"And there isn't anything personal driving this?"

"I find that question offensive. You've heard what I found. I think this merits further investigation. What do you think?"

Holsapple pressed a button near the door to his office, changing the transparency of his window from opaque to clear. He looked down into the CyberCom war room from a floor above. Lisa couldn't tell, but she suspected that he was trying to pick out Glass from among the swarm of agents.

"I can't believe I'm authorizing this, but yes, we should investigate."

"Good."

"And you should do it. I'd like to involve my people as little as possible. If this amounts to nothing, which I'm hoping will be the case, then I don't want anyone here to know that Emma was ever under suspicion."

"I could reach out to my SAC at FBI, Pam Gilbertson, and we could staff it that way."

"Yes, do that."

Lisa rose to leave but paused in the doorway. "How damaging would it be if Glass was a Russian operative? How much does she know?"

"She knows everything. Nearly as much as I do. If your theory is correct, then this is the most significant US security breach since Aldrich Ames. But it would explain how the GRU knew how to tailor their cyberattacks for maximum damage."

"Does she know that CyberCom has discovered that the next wave of attacks is aimed at water filtration plants, and that we've identified their malware?"

"Yes, she knows."

"Then, if she's a mole, she'll want to alert her handler to that."

"Access to all CyberCom systems is strictly monitored, but I'll make sure that Emma's audit trail is being reviewed in real time. Of course, she knows that and would use another channel."

"Then when she makes contact, we'll be watching."

———

In the flurry of activity at CyberCom, it wasn't difficult for Lisa to track Glass's movements. She spent most of her time in the war room consulting with other agents, or in her office.

Lisa knew that Glass wouldn't communicate by personal cell phone because all wireless transmissions within the CyberCom facilities were subject to monitoring. Glass would need to leave the premises to make contact with her handler, and, with only twenty-five hours until the anticipated attack, she would need to do it soon.

Sure enough, after only an hour of observation, Glass left her office and headed for the security station in the main lobby. Lisa followed from a distance, keeping her within sight down the long hallways.

Lisa dialed her cell phone and connected with the FBI agents who were stationed in the parking lot.

"She's coming out," Lisa said to Special Agents Samir Rafsanjani and Rachel Mills.

"Got it," said Rafsanjani. "That in itself is suspicious, right?" Lisa had once worked a case with Rafsanjani and thought of him as the prototypical "brick agent," the hardworking, nonmanagement case agents that the bureau's reputation was built on.

"Yes, I can't imagine that there's a legitimate reason for her to leave the war room in the middle of a crisis."

"You follow from ahead, and I'll follow from behind," Lisa added. She told Mills to follow behind her for when Lisa needed to turn away from the pursuit to avoid suspicion.

When she emerged into the parking lot on a gray day with low clouds, Glass was already getting into her car about fifty yards away.

Glass pulled out of the parking lot and, a few blocks later, turned her gray Nissan Sentra onto the Baltimore-Washington Parkway, heading southwest. Lisa followed from several car lengths back, barely keeping her in eyesight.

It was a good thing that they had three cars to follow her, because Glass would know how to spot a tail. Even with three cars, it was difficult to avoid detection by an experienced operative. Fortunately, there were a few other cars on the road.

"Glass doesn't seem like the type of girl to drive a Sentra," said Rafsanjani in her earpiece.

"You're right about that," Lisa said. "The car's a loaner that she was given because she wrecked her Mercedes."

"What happened?"

"She said that the GRU hacked her car through its navigation system and caused her to lose control."

"How messed up was the car?"

"Pretty smashed up."

"How about her?"

"Some nasty cuts and scrapes, but now that I think about it, she came through it surprisingly well. They wanted to make sure we wouldn't suspect Glass, and, I have to hand it to them, it worked pretty well."

"Wait. She's got her turn signal on. I'm going to have to double back after she takes the exit. You got the target?"

"I've got her."

Glass's car turned at the exit to downtown Russett. The little town was quiet, so Lisa needed to give her plenty of room, so much that she was afraid she might lose her.

The gray Sentra pulled off into the parking lot of an auto body repair shop. Lisa parked her car on the street in front of a furniture store and used her binoculars.

"You still with her?" Rafsanjani asked.

"Yeah, she's stopped at an auto repair place in about the fifteen hundred block of Russett Green East. You could drive by and take a look. Just don't look like a fed."

"My last name is Rafsanjani, Lisa. No one makes me for FBI until they see the badge. And even then they're not so sure."

Lisa watched as Glass climbed out of her car, her scarf flapping behind her in a brisk wind. She approached a badly damaged vehicle that was parked in the shop's lot. It took a moment to recognize the mangled heap, but it was her Mercedes. This was the place where she was having her car repaired.

Lisa felt a moment of doubt. Maybe this wasn't a dead drop with the GRU. Perhaps she was just retrieving some personal item from her car. But what personal item could be so important that it would cause her to leave the CyberCom war room in the middle of a national emergency?

Glass tried to open the car electronically with her key fob, but it didn't seem to work. The car door was too damaged for that.

She used a physical key on the door and had to apply some effort to get it open enough for her to duck her head inside.

It was at that moment that Rafsanjani drove past. Glass stood up abruptly and shot a suspicious glance in his direction when she heard the car, but he didn't slow down or make a show of taking notice of her.

Once the agent's car had turned the corner and was gone, Glass resumed what she was doing. A minute later, she was done. She shut the door of the Mercedes, giving it a hip bump to get it completely closed. She returned to her Nissan and drove away in the direction from which she had come.

"She's moving," Lisa said.

"Could you tell what she did in the car?" Rafsanjani asked.

"No idea, but I think she's going back to CyberCom. Why don't you stake out the car to make sure the Russians weren't watching her make the drop. If no one approaches the car after fifteen minutes, move in and see what's there."

"What if I find a message?"

"Take it. The GRU can't find out that we've discovered their malware in the water filtration plants. They might be able to take countermeasures."

"Got it."

"Oh, and Samir?"

"Yes?"

"Don't move on the car until you have backup. Mills is down the road in case we lost Glass. She's going to join you now. Just in case you encounter opposition. After you've examined the car, you two need to stay on it and see who turns up, then follow them."

"Will do, boss."

Lisa was tempted to confront Glass on the spot and search her car for evidence of an exchange with the Russians, but that might backfire. It was still possible that she had a legitimate reason for visiting the auto body shop.

When Lisa saw Glass turning into the CyberCom parking lot, she drove on past. There was no need to follow closely now. Glass clearly wasn't running and didn't seem to realize that her cover had been blown.

Lisa returned to her office adjoining the CyberCom war room, and from that vantage point she observed Glass going about her business with her customary efficiency. She wondered how Glass justified her actions, which were nothing less than treason. For a moment, she thought that Glass had noticed her gaze. Glass probably thought nothing of it; she was the sort of woman who just assumed that everyone was looking at her.

Even though they differed in temperament and style, ever since their days together in the CyberCorps program at GWU, Lisa had believed she and Glass were both committed to the same worthy cause—defending the US against cyber threats. Had Glass been embedded by the GRU as a sleeper agent from the very start, or had she been turned later? Had she been a willing participant, or did the GRU have something on her or someone she cared about?

As Lisa watched Glass giving commands and taking a junior agent to task, she was frankly impressed with her duplicity. Lisa wondered how many of the qualities that she thought she had envied in her former classmate were the same qualities that made her a traitor and perhaps a sociopath.

Rafsanjani's surveillance report confirmed her worst suspicions. He and Mills had approached the car about fifteen minutes after Glass had left the scene. They opened the door with a lock-picking kit. Normal procedure would require a warrant, but Lisa was confident that any judge would agree there were exigent circumstances.

Rafsanjani peered inside through the front passenger door. At first, he saw nothing out of the ordinary. Then he'd opened the glove compartment and noticed a pill bottle for Emma Glass. The prescription was for Lorazepam, a.k.a. Xanax.

"So I picked up the bottle and shook it," Samir said. "Empty."

"Not surprising these days."

"But something made me think twice. The car was really neat, no trash, no debris, nothing out of place. It didn't seem like someone that fussy would leave an empty pill bottle lying around."

"So you looked inside?"

"I looked inside. And found this."

He reached into his jacket pocket and removed a plastic baggy, which contained a small scroll of paper with writing on it. Leaning in to examine it, Lisa saw a seemingly random string of numbers, letters, and symbols, all printed in a small, neat hand with a fine-tipped pen.

"A cipher," she said. "Have you showed this to the cryptography team?"

"Next stop."

"We've got her."

"Yes, and it gets better. We watched the car through the rest of the afternoon. Just after nightfall, at seven fifteen p.m., a man parked down the street and walked into the parking lot of the body shop. He had a key to the door. Like Glass, he spent just a minute ducking his head into the front cabin. Then he stood up and looked around, up and down the street, like he was disappointed."

"Did he see you?"

"No."

"What happened next?"

"He left."

"And you followed him, right?"

"Of course we did, boss. And you know where he went, after running a few evasive maneuvers?"

"Don't leave me hanging."

"The Russian embassy."

"Do we know who he is?"

"Maksim Dimitriov, a deputy ambassador who's known to be GRU."

"I think we've found our smoking gun," Lisa said.

Rafsanjani nodded. "Now let's go and turn it on Emma Glass."

"I don't think that metaphor quite works, Special Agent," Lisa said. "But I do appreciate the sentiment."

44

Lisa found Glass in the CyberCom war room. She was studying the massive LED screen that covered the wall, displaying a map of the East Coast that appeared to highlight water filtration plants. If each of those plants was compromised, leading to the release of toxic chlorine gas, then the deadly clouds would blanket every major city from Boston to DC.

Glass was studying the map with a grim and thoughtful expression, as if she were formulating a response to the impending attack. In reality, she was probably admiring her handiwork.

Lisa quietly stepped up next to her. "Emma?"

Glass was startled out of her reverie. "Yes?"

"You left the premises a little while ago. Is everything okay?"

"Yes, fine." Glass turned to look at her.

"Where'd you go?" Lisa said it as blandly as possible.

Glass was a professional, so if she was rattled, she didn't show it. But it was clear from the slight narrowing of her eyes that Lisa now had her full attention. "I don't report to you, Special Agent Tanchik, so I don't think that's any of your business."

"No, Emma, it actually is my business. I saw that you went to the auto body shop. What did you do there?"

"You followed me?" Was it Lisa's imagination, or did she just see a hint of fear? "That is entirely inappropriate! I don't know why I shouldn't report this to your director."

"That's certainly your prerogative. But I'd still like to know—what did you go back to your car for?"

Glass was clearly performing some rapid mental calculations. "Was anyone else with you when you tailed me?"

Lisa knew that Glass was hoping that her exposure was limited to her old frenemy from GWU. If that was the case, then she was most likely calculating whether it was possible to kill Lisa and carry on with her mission.

Just try it, Lisa thought. What she said was: "No. Just me. I thought it seemed odd that you would leave like that in the middle of a crisis."

"I had to go back to the car to get my medications." She reached into her computer bag and removed an amber plastic pill bottle.

She shook the bottle with a self-deprecating smile, which was not her style, and the pills rattled like a maraca. "I have some issues with anxiety. Xanax. I hope you won't share that with anyone."

Lisa smiled back at her. "Don't worry. I take it too."

She had to give Glass credit. She had her excuse ready, and it had the virtue of being in the same zip code as the truth. She had returned to the car about a pill bottle—one that looked very much like the one that she had in her hand, but which contained encrypted state secrets to be shared with her GRU handler. Perhaps the pill bottle she was holding was one that the Russians had used to relay messages to her.

"So you've got my back, just like in the GWU days?" Glass asked.

"No, Emma. Not quite like the old days. Can I see your wrists?"

She watched Glass's expression change.

"This is a joke, right?"

"No joke. We know you're a Russian operative."

Glass looked around quickly and saw that Agent Rafsanjani and members of the CyberCom internal security team flanked her in every direction. There was no escape.

She slowly extended her wrists, and Lisa cuffed her.

Lisa patted Glass down for weapons, then nudged the computer bag out of reach with her foot. Rafsanjani promptly began examining the bag's contents.

"Bag the pill bottle," Lisa said. "If it's been used to exchange intel with the Russians, we may be able to lift fingerprints off it."

The other agents were hanging back, as planned, giving the two former classmates a moment to talk. Lisa was wearing a wire to capture any admission.

"What I want to know, Emma, is if this was the plan from the very beginning, when we were both in CyberCorps together? Did they have you from day one?"

"If I'm the mole, then why was my car hacked? You saw my injuries. I could have been killed."

"And yet those injuries weren't really very serious. If the crash was staged for our benefit, that would be a smart way to avert suspicion."

Glass stared at her impassively. The fact that she didn't vehemently deny it told Lisa enough. "I want to speak with Tom Holsapple."

"It wouldn't help. He gave the order."

Glass absorbed that, and then said, "Well, then I guess I want my lawyer."

"You'll have to take that up with Homeland and NSA."

Glass shrugged, but not persuasively. "Oh, and by the way, I did sabotage your capture the flag team back at CyberCorps."

"Yeah, I was aware. If only that were the worst of your offenses."

"Your view of the world was always so small," Glass said. "That never changed."

"Maybe you're right. But your world is going to be about six by eight feet from here on out." Lisa motioned to the CyberCom security team as she unhooked the mic taped inside her blouse. "Now will someone please show Emma to her new accommodations?"

Two CyberCom agents gripped Glass by the elbows and led her down the hallway to a detention cell. Most prisoners slouched and seemed to retreat into themselves at this point in the process, but Glass walked with her chin up and posture perfect.

As ever, Emma Glass was a Super-Together Lady.

Lisa hated Super-Together Ladies.

45

Day Nine

Lisa had lobbied hard to get Rhett Rawlings from the FBI's computer forensic lab on the CyberCom team that was scrambling to find a fix for the malware that had infected the water filtration plants. While the team believed that they didn't need any assistance, Holsapple had intervened and gotten Rawlings on board. He probably figured that he owed Lisa for the role she had played in uncovering Emma Glass as the mole within his agency.

Now that Glass was in custody, it was more likely that the agency's response plans were secure, but that was still not a certainty. While Rawlings and the CyberCom technical team worked on antimalware, Lisa considered what NatalyaX's next move might be.

NatalyaX's last known location had been in DC—the Hay-Adams, where she had murdered Arkady Orlov. It seemed reasonable to assume that she was still in the District, particularly given the many high-value targets in the nation's capital. There were three water filtration plants in the metropolitan DC area, but the one that was most likely to be a priority for the GRU was the Arlington Water Pollution Control Plant in Crystal City, Virginia, which was near Pentagon City and not far from the Capitol and the White House.

Lisa's next destination was the plant in Crystal City, because it was where she believed she was most likely to find NatalyaX. She'd want to admire the mayhem firsthand.

Lisa would have already been on her way to Crystal City, but she was waiting for the coding team to develop their solution to the malware. It might be necessary for her to physically carry the antimalware to the facility on a flash drive and install it herself. Since the plant's systems were most likely already compromised, and internet connectivity was still spotty, it might not be possible to deliver the solution by email or other means.

Lisa heard a nerdy cheer go up in the room next door, where the coders were frantically working. She couldn't remember the last time she had heard anyone around CyberCom celebrating anything. Wins had been in short supply.

Rawlings appeared in her doorway, looking bleary but triumphant.

"We've got it," he said.

"So you can counteract the malware that has infected the water filtration plants?"

"Yes. Thanks for getting me on the team."

"You can thank me later." She checked the clock on her phone. "We have three hours to roll out the fix."

"CyberCom is on it. They're already mobilizing everyone available to get the solution to every water filtration plant on the East Coast."

"How about the one in Crystal City? Arlington?"

"I know that one's a priority, but we haven't been able to make contact yet."

"I'll go."

"Go talk to Holsapple then," Rawlings said. "He's the one making the assignments."

She knew the reservoir of gratitude that she had with General Holsapple was not unlimited, but she figured she was entitled to at least one more favor.

She was headed for Crystal City to prevent a chlorine gas attack—and hopefully come face to face with NatalyaX. Lisa finally deactivated the GPS on her phone, which had been an open invitation to Natalya to come and find her.

When Natalya saw that she had turned off her GPS, she would probably assume that it was because Lisa was coming for her.

46

Natalya was sitting in the lobby of the Georgetown Ritz-Carlton, where she had managed to locate a functioning Wi-Fi connection. The hotel was a striking modernization of an old firehouse, all redbrick and fire-engine-red furnishings. Natalya thought it resembled a local branch office of hell. She felt right at home.

She watched in amusement as angry people with reservations confronted an embattled front desk clerk. Since the cyberattack had commenced, travelers had been stranded in whatever hotel room they were staying in. The current guests would not leave until the crisis was resolved, and the hotel could not evict them. In the meantime, people continued to show up at the hotel with reservations that the Ritz was not prepared to honor.

Anger and hilarity ensued.

When the desk clerk, a young man in his early twenties developing a nervous eye twitch, suggested that a couple accept an alternative room in one of their sister properties—one without electricity—the woman squirted him with a water bottle and then threw the empty bottle at his head, which bounced off with a hollow thunk.

When the melee concluded and the couple was ushered out of the lobby to their cold, dark, alternative arrangements, Natalya returned her attention to her laptop. She visited the agreed-upon IRC chat room and was instructed by Kazimir, in a coded conversation, that she was to remain in the DC area until the water filtration plant attacks were launched. She—using the screen name Salma—asked Kazimir—using ThirstyBear—what her assignment would be after the chlorine gas clouds had been released.

THIRSTYBEAR: Don't know. Maybe then it's time to talk about your retirement.

SALMA: Can I come home then?

THIRSTYBEAR: Do you really think of this as your home?

SALMA: It's as close as I've got. And I don't think I can stay here when this is done. Will you take me in?

THIRSTYBEAR: Of course. When the assignment is completed we'll provide the exfil plan.

SALMA: Do you like it there?

THIRSTYBEAR: It's like anyplace else. Depends on your situation. But your situation, my darling, will be glorious. You will be honored as a hero of the people.

SALMA: What do you like about it there?

THIRSTYBEAR: Your parents were from here, right?

SALMA: That's right.

THIRSTYBEAR: But they're not with us anymore, right?

SALMA: Right.

THIRSTYBEAR: I'm sorry to hear that. It's hard to explain, but this place is in your blood, and you probably don't even know it yet. The first time you see the Volga, or snow on the spires of St. Basil's, you'll know it was there all along.

SALMA: I'll bet you say that to all the girls.

THIRSTYBEAR: Doesn't mean it's not true, though.

Natalya's next, and probably final, assignment was to visit the Arlington Water Pollution Control Plant in Crystal City on a sluggish inlet that emptied into the Potomac River. It wasn't far from Georgetown, and it was one of the most important objectives in the next wave of attacks.

When the malware was activated, the toxic chlorine cloud from the plant would blanket the Pentagon, the Capitol, and the White House. While the Pentagon staffers would probably have access to gas masks to limit the fatalities, many would not. Natalya figured that many seats in the House and Senate, and maybe even the Supreme Court, would be left suddenly vacant in the wake of the attack. Moscow would delight in the political turmoil and conflict that would arise from attempting to fill so many political offices in a time of such intense division and political tribalism.

Her mission was to observe the plant to ensure that the malware activated properly. One of her fellow operatives had deposited flash drives in the parking lot of the Crystal City plant as she had done at the Hoboken water treatment facility, but it was uncertain whether the malware had been effectively implanted by an employee; GRU command and control hadn't been receiving its signals. If the malware didn't activate, she was to enter the facility and install it herself, just as she had done at the New Jersey power plant in a similar situation.

She went to a hardware store and purchased an extra respirator mask with a carbon filter that would protect her from the chlorine gas; it never hurt to have a spare. In about three hours, nearly everyone within a two-hundred-mile radius would be desperately in search of one of these beauties, but the few available masks would be gone within an hour.

"Doing some painting?" the hardware store clerk asked as he placed the mask in a brown paper bag.

"Exactly," Natalya said. "Paint fumes give me migraines."

She eyed the security camera in the corner of the ceiling above the register. After the fact, US defense agencies would be searching for everyone who purchased respirator masks in the hours before the attacks. She didn't care. They already knew what she looked like, so she directed a coquettish wink at the camera, knowing that Special Agent Tanchik, if she survived, would eventually see the footage.

But by then it would be too late.

———

The Arlington Water Pollution Control Plant in Crystal City doesn't look like a chemical weapon waiting to be detonated, Lisa thought, *but that's what it is.* The facility sat behind a fence next to a turbid inlet to the Potomac. There were low redbrick buildings that sat next to open tanks, where the initial screening of particulate matter occurred. Later in the process, chlorine was fed into the water to kill pathogenic bacteria and reduce odor. Along with other members of the CyberCom response team, Lisa had been briefed on the process. Some municipalities had begun manufacturing chlorine solution on-site in order to avoid transporting and storing large amounts of the gas, but Arlington was not one of those plants. The chlorine gas was contained in large tanks at the rear of the facility, away from the inlet.

The director of the plant had been called and was waiting for Lisa when she arrived. He was a squat man with a ruddy face in a short-sleeve dress shirt.

"You cut it close," he said. "You have the flash drive?"

Lisa pulled it from her pocket. "Where can I install this? Any computer connected to your network will do."

"Follow me."

He led Lisa to a small control room with a console measuring the flow of wastewater and the percentage of particulate matter at each stage of the purification process. He pointed her to one of the desktop computers.

"All you need is a USB port, right?"

"That's right." Lisa sat down and plugged in the flash drive.

They looked at one another.

"Kinda anticlimactic," the director said. "How do we know it worked?"

Lisa checked her watch. "We'll know in twenty-five minutes when toxic chlorine gas doesn't start pouring out of your plant."

"You don't have some sort of diagnostic you can run?"

"We barely had time to create the software fix. But it's been tested, and it should work."

"That doesn't give me as much comfort as I'd like."

"I'm afraid that's the best I can do."

Lisa turned to leave.

"Wait, Special Agent Tanchik, where are you going?"

"I need to go look for someone."

"Can't you wait twenty-three more minutes?"

"No. Once she sees that the malware isn't working, she'll be on the move."

"On the move where?"

"To come here and reinstall the malware by hand. You have a gas mask?"

"Oh yes."

"Good. Do you have one for me?"

"Uh, no. Sorry. I can give you a towel. A wet towel over the mouth and nose helps."

"I'd really better go," Lisa said, hurrying out of the control room.

———

Lisa entered the plant's parking lot and turned in a circle, scanning for a vantage point that NatalyaX might use to observe her handiwork. The approach had worked when she was searching for NatalyaX in Falls Church after nearly being poisoned with Novichok.

She would want to have a clear view of the tanks where the chlorine gas was stored. There was a small parking lot near a bike path, but it would not afford a view of the tanks. Across the inlet, there was a small strip mall with a convenience store, a shoe repair place, and a dry cleaner. It was on slightly higher ground and seemed the most likely observation point, particularly since a lone person would not stand out in that trafficked area.

Lisa crossed a narrow pedestrian bridge over the inlet. She climbed a rise to the strip mall parking lot. There was no sign of NatalyaX, so Lisa began to examine the half a dozen cars in the parking lot.

In the third car, a BMW, she examined the front and back seats and saw nothing of interest. But before moving on to the next, she noticed an object on the floor behind the driver seat.

She had to stare at it for a while before she could make out that it was—a gas mask.

47

Natalya exited the car and walked over to a bench on a hillside above a bike path that ran beside the inlet. It was a frigid, breezy day, and the wind was blowing north across the Potomac toward the nation's capital.

She checked her watch. Just three minutes until the malware would activate, causing an electrical fire in the control panel that regulated the intake of chlorine gas into the plant's storage tanks, igniting a powerful explosion within the container that would release the deadly gas.

There were no bikes or pedestrians on the path. No one had time for exercise or recreation in the middle of a national emergency. One middle-aged man rode past on a bike with pink ribbons and a banana seat. The pink wicker basket between the handlebars was heavily loaded with scavenged canned goods. His breathing was labored, and he didn't look up to notice Natalya.

She figured that this vantage point was better than watching the attack unfold from the strip mall parking lot, where she would be more noticeable.

One minute until activation.

She watched the second hand of her watch tick through its final rotation.

Three thirty.

Natalya stared intently at the storage tanks. Would she be able to see the fire from the explosion? Would the gas have any color as it was expelled into the atmosphere?

Surely there would be some indication that the malware had worked, even if it was only the sound of a distant factory alarm.

Nothing.

She waited another minute, then two, then three.

Clearly, the malware had failed somehow. She smacked her fist into the wooden bench in frustration.

Other explosions were scheduled to detonate at the same time in the DC area. Natalya couldn't see the DC skyline from her location, so it wasn't possible to tell whether this failure was localized. In any event, she needed to remain focused on her mission.

Natalya had hoped it wouldn't come to this, but it was going to be necessary to execute the backup plan. She would need to access the plant and personally connect a flash drive with the malware to the facility's network.

A stream of workers began to hurry from the plant's main entrance into the parking lot. They had clearly been put on alert, but none of them appeared to be gasping or choking. The turmoil would make it easier to enter the plant, just as she had at the power station in Newark. But the difference was that this facility was on alert. CyberCom seemed to have figured out that her bosses were targeting water purification facilities.

That would make her task more difficult, but not impossible.

She would need to have a gas mask to enter the plant. She glanced back at the strip mall lot where her car was parked.

And that was when she saw Special Agent Lisa Tanchik peering in the rear window of her car.

Natalya's pulse raced like a hunted animal, and she immediately scanned her surroundings to make sure other agents weren't closing in. No other figures were in sight. Maybe Tanchik was acting alone.

She stood up slowly from the bench, putting an oak tree between her and the FBI agent. She touched the automatic pistol in her purse.

No, this was not the time to move in. Tanchik was armed—and probably knew she was nearby. If she didn't have backup, it could very well be on the way. It wasn't worth the risk.

Natalya decided that with Tanchik on the scene, she would have to abandon her plan to enter the plant and manually download the malware. Kazimir had told her that she was too valuable an asset to take unnecessary risks. He'd referred to DC as a "target-rich environment."

She needed to return to DC to await her next set of instructions, which would involve assisting in the hack of the electronic medical record system of Washington Medical Center. With a slight corruption of the EMR data, routine transfusions conducted at the hospital would become potentially life-threatening events involving mismatched blood types.

But in order to carry out her next mission, she had to escape and put some distance between herself and Agent Tanchik. And she couldn't even retrieve her car now. If the chlorine gas was released, she would be without a ventilator mask. Both of her masks were in her car.

Natalya headed away from the strip mall, out of view of the FBI agent.

She walked over a green hill to a two-lane road that followed the inlet and crouched behind a berm to wait for the next car to pass.

Natalya didn't have long to wait. A blue Prius hummed toward her with a young man behind the wheel.

She stood up, walked to the road's center stripe, and aimed her gun at the windshield.

The Prius slowed, then stopped.

Natalya advanced on the car, never lowering her aim from the petrified twentysomething behind the wheel.

As she reached the driver's-side door, she heard the locks click.

"I just want the car," Natalya said.

"Please, don't!" the man shouted.

"Locking the doors doesn't help," she said. "Unless this is bullet-proof glass. Is this bulletproof glass?"

"No."

"Then you'd better open the door."

The locks clicked again, and the young man stepped out of the car.

"Good decision," she said. "Now step away, and leave the keys in the ignition."

He did as he was told.

"You don't have to do this," he said. "I would have given you a ride. We all have to help each other in an emergency like this."

"You don't understand," Natalya said. "*I am* the emergency."

48

Lisa knew that NatalyaX must be somewhere nearby. She wouldn't have left her gas mask behind if she had already entered the water treatment plant.

She ducked down beside the car in case Natalya was observing her or aiming to take a shot. She surveyed the surrounding area—the strip mall shops, the bike path, the park benches.

There was no sign of NatalyaX.

If she were NatalyaX, where would she go to get the best scenic view of the coming devastation? Lisa started by moving toward the benches that overlooked the bike path, which were on a green hillside that would afford a better perspective for viewing the plant's chlorine gas tanks.

She checked her watch.

Three thirty-five.

Long enough for NatalyaX to conclude that the attack had failed and move on from her viewing spot.

But if NatalyaX had decided to enter the plant after realizing that the malware had been thwarted, then she would have made that decision only minutes ago. And if that was her course of action, then Lisa should be able to see her walking down the hill, crossing the narrow concrete bridge over the inlet, and entering the plant's parking lot.

But NatalyaX was not to be seen, so she must have taken a different path.

Lisa passed the benches. She kept walking to get a view of the other side of the low hill.

She topped the crest just in time to see NatalyaX hold up the driver of a Prius at gunpoint.

Before NatalyaX climbed into the driver seat of the Prius, she took a look around to see if anyone was watching.

Her eyes met Lisa's.

Lisa considered firing her service weapon, but the distance was too great for accuracy. NatalyaX was undoubtedly performing the same mental calculation and reaching the same conclusion.

Then NatalyaX slowly raised her gun and leveled it at the owner of the Prius. The young man, who had been standing on the road's gravel shoulder, dropped to his knees. At that distance, Lisa couldn't hear what he was saying, but his hand gestures told her that he was desperately pleading for his life.

"Don't!" Lisa shouted.

NatalyaX looked up at her for an endless moment. The Russian operative wasn't smiling, wasn't agitated. She was impassive, as if aiming the gun at the innocent bystander was an experiment, and she was recording the reactions.

Finally, she lowered her gun. Then she tipped the muzzle to her forehead and gave Lisa a sort of mock salute.

NatalyaX drove away, leaving Lisa to run for her car to continue the pursuit.

———

Natalya was slightly insulted when Agent Tanchik shouted from the hillside, urging her not to take the life of Prius Guy. By now, Tanchik should know that she was not some murderous psychopath. When had she taken any action that was not entirely within the scope of her mission? And if Agent Tanchik took Orlov's death personally, then that just reflected a lack of professionalism on her part.

Natalya drove as quickly as she could on Route 1 north toward DC. She needed to be in the city so that she could participate in the Washington Medical Center hack. She also wanted to observe the turmoil firsthand. She wished that she had one of her gas masks with her, but at least she knew how to create a makeshift device.

She checked the rearview mirror for any sign of Tanchik trailing her, but she saw no one. Natalya had a considerable lead on the FBI agent, even if she did guess where Natalya was heading.

Natalya switched on the radio. Because every chase scene needed a soundtrack. To her disappointment, the only music station was playing "Looks Like We Made It," by Barry Manilow. She scanned the channels for something more appropriate but found only news reports on the cyberattack.

Under normal circumstances, it would have been a fifteen-minute drive into DC, but circumstances were far from normal. She had to slow to a crawl and drive slowly on curbs and medians in order to bypass stalled and abandoned cars that clogged the freeway.

Natalya knew that she didn't have long to find cover. She could see an Audi a half mile or so behind her, crazily navigating the tangle of traffic at maximum speed. That had to be Tanchik.

And the FBI agent was probably on the phone to her colleagues in DC, requesting backup to intercept Natalya as she made her way into the city. The fact that the entire metropolitan area was in a state of emergency provided some cover, but she couldn't be sure how much. Every law enforcement agency was probably consumed with responding to the impending chemical disaster. Nevertheless, she needed to get off the freeway as soon as possible.

As she drove over the Potomac, her anxiety level steadily rose. Tanchik's car was closer now in her rearview. And if law enforcement managed to block her while she was on the bridge, there would be no escape route other than a plunge into the frigid waters below.

A light snow began to fall, like debris from the exploded gray January sky.

The bridge seemed endless, but she was almost there.

On her left, the Jefferson Memorial and the Tidal Basin flashed past.

One last short bridge over the Washington Channel, and she was in the city proper, speeding through L'Enfant Plaza.

Now she was in the belly of the beast, the beating heart of the nation that she and her partners in Moscow had brought to its knees. Ahead on her left she could see the Washington Monument. On her right, she would soon be approaching the National Mall, the Smithsonian, and the Capitol.

And then she saw that her way was blocked by a checkpoint manned by two DC police officers, with two cruisers angled nose to nose in the middle of the street as a blockade. The officers had both raised their hands, signaling for her to stop.

But neither cop had drawn his weapon. Perhaps they hadn't yet received word that they needed to be on alert for a woman driving a blue Prius. But she couldn't take that chance.

She also couldn't veer off onto a side street, because there wasn't one between her and the blockade.

Natalya could stop the car and attempt to turn around and go back the way she had come, but by the time she had executed that maneuver, the police would be upon her.

As far as she was concerned, there was really only one move, and so she made it.

Natalya pressed her foot to the accelerator and drove full speed at the two cops and their cruisers. She saw their eyes widen when they realized what she was doing.

One officer grabbed for his gun, and the other dived out of the way.

But it was too late for both of them.

Natalya gripped the steering wheel tightly, bracing for impact. She felt the car collide with the first police officer with a crunching thud and then a much harder impact as her car drove into the parked cruisers.

The airbag deployed, and milliseconds later her face plunged into it rather than the steering wheel. Natalya felt the warmth on her face from the sodium azide chemical reaction inside the airbag.

It took her a moment to come to her senses after the jarring impact. As the airbag deflated, she noticed that she was covered in shattered windshield glass. Natalya tried to move her toes and then her legs. She had survived and seemed to be in one piece. The front end of the Prius was crushed and the hood buckled upward, steam hissing from the radiator.

The body of one of the policemen was pinned into the grill of the police cruiser by the Prius. He was still upright between the two cars, but he was also clearly dead.

She looked for the other policeman and found him a few yards away, facedown but beginning to move. Her car appeared to have struck him a glancing blow, hurling him to the pavement. He was reaching for his holstered gun with slow, pained movements.

Where was her gun?

WHERE WAS HER GUN?

It was in her purse. She ran her hand over the passenger-side seat, where it had been, but found only shards of broken glass.

She glanced into the back seat and felt a sharp pain in her neck as she turned. The purse had been hurled there. She grasped for the bag, dragging it into the front seat. She zipped it open, removed her pistol.

The driver's-side door was wedged shut, so, with some difficulty, she slid into the passenger seat and climbed out of the car.

The downed policeman was still trying to get at his service weapon. His right arm appeared to have been injured in the crash.

Natalya stepped close to him and put a bullet in the back of his head. The man's hand stopped fumbling for the gun. A smattering of snowflakes fell on the back of the officer's jacket and melted on contact.

The gunshot was loud and reverberated off the nearby buildings with a metallic echo that she felt in her chest. Because there were so many national landmarks and government offices nearby, this had to be a high-security area. There had to be more law enforcement agents in the vicinity, and they would be drawn to the sound of the gunshot.

Natalya walked toward the National Mall without slowing a step. She needed to get off the street, find a place where she could hide for a while as things cooled down. Or heated up, depending on your point of view.

In the distance, she saw the sprawling complex of the Smithsonian Institute, and she picked up her pace, her breath clouding ahead of her.

49

Lisa was seething that she had not managed to catch up with and intercept NatalyaX as she drove from Crystal City to DC. There were too many obstructions in the road to make up the distance between them. Nevertheless, she had managed to keep the stolen Prius in sight for most of the way.

When she saw the Prius smashed into the two police cruisers near the National Mall, Lisa was hopeful for a moment that NatalyaX had been stopped in a hail of bullets. But as she drew closer, she felt a numbing dread.

She saw no movement, no sign of police manning the barricade.

Her worst fears were confirmed when she saw the two dead police officers, one crushed between the Prius and the patrol cars, the other sprawled facedown on the pavement with an oozing bullet hole in the back of his skull.

She examined the interior of the Prius, but NatalyaX's body wasn't there. There wasn't even any blood on the dashboard, the steering wheel, or the driver's seat.

Just the deflated airbag, which had apparently saved NatalyaX's life.

Lisa felt a wave of nausea and placed her hand on the hood of the Prius to steady herself.

It was still warm, a reminder that NatalyaX was close at hand.

Lisa checked both officers' bodies for a pulse, but they were gone. As distressed as she was by the scene, she knew she needed to keep moving if she was going to catch NatalyaX.

The most likely escape route was forward past the barricade into the National Mall. Lisa drew her gun and walked out into the grassy park. Off in the distance was the Washington Monument, and at the nearer end of the mall, the Capitol. She felt exposed in the open space.

The Mall was usually crowded with throngs of tourists, school groups, and joggers, but today it was eerily empty. The only sound was an insistent emergency alert siren. The public had apparently been warned of the impending chemical release and told to stay indoors.

It should have been easy to spot NatalyaX if she was still fleeing out in the open. She must have entered one of the nearby buildings to hide from the manhunt that would be launched to find the person who had murdered the two officers. The closest structure was the Smithsonian National Museum of American History, an imposing white stone edifice fronted by an abstract sculpture that resembled a stainless steel ribbon suspended over a granite tower.

Lisa crossed the street and strode quickly past the sculpture to the museum's entrance. She tried the door, and it opened.

She didn't get the sense that looters had invaded the museum. More likely the staff had fled without properly securing the facility after the warning of the deadly gas attack. No security guard stopped her once she was inside. The place was strangely vacant; it was as if the attack had already occurred, and the bodies had mysteriously vaporized.

Though the power was out and the museum was dark, Lisa could see well enough in the lobby by the dim light that emanated from the entrance doorway. She removed a flashlight from her backpack and advanced into the museum.

The museum's first floor was devoted to transportation and technology. She passed the John Bull locomotive, an antiquated behemoth of wood and steel, the mechanical equivalent of the Natural History

Museum's woolly mammoth. The engine was a relic of a technology far removed from the ones that had crippled her country and brought her to this place.

She paused to listen for footfalls, aware NatalyaX could be lying in wait for her around any corner.

Lisa swept the flashlight beam back and forth. With every arc another marker of American history was illuminated. She was apparently entering a wing of the museum devoted to American food.

One swing of the flashlight revealed the first microwave oven available for home use.

A few yards farther in was a display devoted to Berkeley's Gourmet Ghetto neighborhood and Alice Waters's Chez Panisse. It reminded Lisa of the home that she missed in the Bay Area.

A bit farther on, she encountered a replica of Julia Child's kitchen. Lisa cast her flashlight beam over the room, with its blue-green cabinetry and glinting brass pots hung on pegs.

No sign of NatalyaX.

Every step she made seemed to produce some sort of small squeak or scrape. When the power went out, you suddenly realized that even in the quietest-seeming moments, you were enveloped in the buzz and hum of ventilation, fluorescent light fixtures, and elevators.

Now that the white noise had been taken away, Lisa noticed her every inhalation and exhalation, the friction of her shoes on the tile floor. She could even hear the faint groan of the museum itself, responding to the wind outside, settling on its foundation.

She probed the gloom of the corridor ahead of her with the flashlight beam. She began to think that maybe NatalyaX hadn't come in here and this was a futile exercise.

Then she noticed a reflection in a glass case that showed her a glimpse of what was around the corner.

A woman's legs in a knee-length skirt.

They were so still that Lisa thought it might be a mannequin from one of the exhibits.

Then she saw a dandelion tattoo over the right ankle.

The detail that Arkady Orlov had noticed just before he'd died.

NatalyaX.

Lisa spun toward where Natalya must be standing, the beam of the flashlight in one hand, tracking the aim of her pistol in the other.

But it was already too late.

A gunshot erupted in the enclosed space.

A moment later Lisa was down, but not before squeezing off a shot.

Pain seared in her left shoulder.

Her flashlight clattered to the floor, the beam briefly illuminating a female figure disappearing into the darkness.

50

"Ooh, that must really hurt," NatalyaX said from somewhere up ahead in the darkness of the museum corridor.

Lisa realized that it was the first time that she'd heard NatalyaX's voice. There was no Russian accent, which made sense because she had grown up in the US. It was pitched at a medium-to-low register but still managed to sound girlish.

"And I'll bet you're losing a *lot* of blood," NatalyaX added.

That was true. Lisa's left arm and shoulder were slick with blood. She crawled into the Julia Child kitchen exhibit and used one of the dish towels as a compress on the wound.

It wasn't easy attempting to stanch the flow of blood while keeping her gun within reach and her eyes on the darkness ahead of her. She knew that NatalyaX might return at any moment.

Lisa pulled out her cell phone and dialed an FBI emergency number. "This is Special Agent Lisa Tanchik. I've been shot, and I'm at the Smithsonian American History Museum in DC. Suspect is still present."

"We'll get to you as soon as possible," said a voice on the phone. She didn't hear the rest because she put the phone back in her pocket, still on to permit GPS tracking.

Maybe NatalyaX was just going to wait for her to bleed out. That was probably a sound strategy, because Lisa was already feeling seriously light headed.

Or perhaps Lisa's wild shot had gotten lucky and found its target. Could NatalyaX be out there in the darkness, as badly injured as she was? While she sounded pretty breezy with her taunts, that could be an act.

The voice returned. "If I were you, I'd want to just lie down and close my eyes."

Lisa tried to gauge from the sound of the voice where she was. She guessed NatalyaX was about twenty yards ahead of her, but it was hard to say in the echoing tiled corridor.

She resisted the temptation to respond to the goading, because that's what NatalyaX wanted her to do. If Lisa shouted a retort, NatalyaX would have a sense of her condition and position—and would know that she hadn't yet passed out from the pain and blood loss.

Better to keep her guessing and hope she made a mistake.

A few minutes went by.

NatalyaX had to figure that time was not on her side. She had certainly heard Lisa place her call for emergency help to the FBI line. For all she knew, Lisa had called for backup before she'd entered the museum. And it wouldn't be long before a search for the killer of the two DC police officers would lead to the museum.

If Lisa stayed quiet, NatalyaX would probably have to come to her. She crawled to the wall of the exhibit so that she could fire around the corner into the hallway.

"Lisa?" NatalyaX's voice sounded more tentative this time. As though she really wasn't sure if Lisa was dead or alive. "I can help you get treatment for that wound. Let me help you. I respect your skills—as a fellow professional. I have no interest in seeing you die."

Lisa remained quiet and still, her Glock 27 aimed into the dark corridor.

Another few minutes passed.

Then she heard slow, careful footsteps in the darkness, approaching.

Wait for it.

Wait for it. You may not get another chance.

The gun felt unnaturally heavy in her hand, and she had to keep readjusting her aim upward. Black and green shapes strobed in her vision. She was crossing over into unconsciousness.

A shape began to define itself in the gloom. NatalyaX paused for a moment because there was a shaft of light from a skylight that would reveal her if she advanced any farther.

NatalyaX took the chance, venturing a half step forward.

At that moment, she saw Lisa aiming from around the corner of the exhibit. They both began firing simultaneously.

The corridor exploded around them, intermittently lit by muzzle flashes. The wall that Lisa was crouching behind erupted, the gunshots sending plaster dust into her eyes.

Even though she could barely see, she emptied her chamber into the space where NatalyaX had been standing. She kept pulling the trigger until the empty chamber clicked.

While it seemed like a long time, the volley of gunshots didn't last more than a minute, and then the quiet descended again like the fine dust that coated her hair and face.

Had NatalyaX fired all her rounds?

Was she dead?

The second question was answered a moment later. "Lisa? Are you still there?" NatalyaX was closer now, but her voice somehow seemed more distant than before.

NatalyaX emerged unsteadily from behind an exhibit, placing one hand on the Plexiglas cube for support. With the other hand she pointed her gun at Lisa.

There was a large bloodstain on the right side of her blouse just above the hip. One of Lisa's wild shots had apparently found its mark.

NatalyaX saw Lisa's eyes on the bloodstain.

"Oh, this?" she said. "That's nothing."

"I don't know," Lisa said. "That looks like a lot of blood."

NatalyaX stepped closer, her gun aimed at the center of Lisa's forehead.

Lisa was still weakly pointing her pistol at NatalyaX, who did not seem particularly concerned.

"Sounded like your chamber is empty," NatalyaX said. "And you didn't have time to reload."

Lisa shrugged in acknowledgment and lowered her weapon.

NatalyaX shifted her feet to brace before pulling the trigger.

Lisa gritted her teeth, exhaled roughly, and glared at her with all the rage that she could muster in her weakened state.

NatalyaX's finger tightened on the trigger.

Click.

Lisa slumped back against the wall, exhausted by severe blood loss and preparing for her imminent death.

"Damn," NatalyaX said.

She spent a moment studying Lisa bleeding out on the museum floor, considering how best to proceed.

Then NatalyaX slowly lowered herself to her knees, her hand reflexively moving to the wound in her side as she did so. She swayed above Lisa.

Then she reached out with her long pale hands. Grasping for Lisa's throat.

Oddly, Lisa's first reaction was surprise, then offense at the intimacy of the gesture. Then she took her empty pistol in her fist and punched NatalyaX in the temple with her remaining strength.

The gun's muzzle cut a red gash in NatalyaX's cheek and knocked her back into a sitting position. After taking a moment to touch her face and assess the wound, she sat up on her knees again and advanced on Lisa, this time a little more cautiously.

Lisa realized that this encounter might be decided by who bled out first.

NatalyaX drew close with a somewhat glazed look in her eyes and then threw herself at Lisa, once again going for her throat.

Lisa punched NatalyaX in the ribs twice but couldn't manage to get much heft into the blows. NatalyaX was on top of her, thumbs digging into Lisa's windpipe. She was so near that Lisa could tell that she was wearing a fragrance.

Lisa felt herself fading away. Red explosions behind her eyelids, like an incongruous fireworks send-off for her too-short life.

Then she blacked out, but not before sensing the grip on her throat loosening.

Perhaps that meant she was already dead, Lisa thought as empty blackness descended.

———

It was hard to tell how much time had elapsed before Lisa regained consciousness. NatalyaX was still lying atop her.

As Lisa's brain rebooted after the force quit of blood loss, she performed a quick recap of recent events, like the prelude to a television episode.

1. She had been shot in the shoulder.

2. She was bleeding to death.

3. NatalyaX might try again to kill her, but that didn't seem likely given her apparent condition.

4. She needed to get out from under NatalyaX's limp, and surprisingly heavy, body.

NatalyaX was still alive judging by the slow throb in her carotid, though barely. Lisa wasn't doing much better and felt as if she could slip back into darkness at any moment.

She managed to shove NatalyaX off her so that they both had their backs to the wall just outside the Julia Child kitchen exhibit. The tile floor around them was smeared red with their blood.

NatalyaX's eyelids flickered, and she roused when her head struck the wall. She was quiet for a few moments, groggily inventorying her predicament, a process Lisa had just completed.

"That was a lucky shot," NatalyaX finally said.

"If you say so. Looks like it might have hit a kidney."

"Too bad it took this long for us to meet in person."

"I didn't really feel the need to meet you," Lisa said. "Just arrest you."

NatalyaX sat up a bit and winced at the effort. "Can't we just appreciate each other?"

Lisa thought of Orlov dying in the lobby of the Hay-Adams, and she wanted to see if she was still capable of strangling NatalyaX. But she nearly blacked out at the mere attempt to push herself away from the wall that was propping her up.

"Is this the part where you tell me that we're really not so different?" Lisa croaked.

"Basically. Yes."

"What you and your friends at the GRU have done is not just a matter of tradecraft. You killed innocent civilians. Arkady Orlov was my friend."

"He knew we would come after him when he decided to help you. And your government knew what they were doing when they launched cyberattacks on Russia, on that nuclear facility."

"I don't know what the US has done to Russia, but I know it couldn't be anything close to what happened here in the past week.

There have to be some rules of engagement. It's the only thing that keeps us human."

They fell silent for a while. Lisa wasn't sure if NatalyaX had blacked out.

"You still there?" Lisa asked.

"Still here. Feeling a bit woozy, though."

"You going to try to kill me again?"

"I think that moment has passed."

Lisa wanted to keep NatalyaX talking. Maybe she would learn something useful. And it helped her retain her tenuous grasp on consciousness. "I have to give you credit for that HelenWheels character. You had me there."

"Thank you." A small smile. "I knew I needed to bring my A game with you."

"The details seemed so true about life in a wheelchair. You must have known someone like that."

NatalyaX shook her head. "Stop working me. If we live through this, you want to find someone who can tell you more about me."

"I won't deny it."

NatalyaX's head drooped and then righted itself. She was close to blacking out.

"Someone's going to find us soon," Lisa said. "You killed two cops less than a half mile from here. They're going to come for us. And I've called for assistance."

"How do you know that I don't have people who will find us first?"

Lisa felt herself going.

"You can't win," she murmured.

"I already have."

Lisa's eyelids dropped like a curtain coming down. Or maybe her vision had simply gone to black.

She thought of the scene that she and NatalyaX would present to those who found the bodies. Slumped in front of Julia Child's kitchen in a pool of blood.

Bon appétit.

Lisa heard footsteps approaching. Heavy, echoing footsteps.

Or maybe it was all in her head, the hollow, vacant sound of a system shutting down.

51

Day Twelve

Lisa awoke in a hospital bed. When she found herself staring at the drip of the IV like it was the most fascinating thing ever, she knew that the pain meds were on point.

Then she noticed that Jon was sitting in a chair across from her bed, dozing with a paperback open and facedown on his knee. He must have heard her shift in the bed, because his eyes opened.

"You're awake," he said.

"Am I?"

Jon laughed uncertainly. "It was touch and go there for a while. You lost a lot of blood. How are you feeling?"

"Fantastic," she said with a slow, loopy smile. "I don't know what's in that thing, but tell my doctor to keep it coming. And a round for the house."

Jon looked down at his shoes. This remark sounded a little too much like the old substance-abusing Lisa for his comfort.

She changed the subject. "Where am I?"

"George Washington University Hospital."

"How long?"

"Three days."

"Did NatalyaX live?"

"Yeah, she survived, but just barely."

"Where is she?"

"She's in another wing of the hospital under heavy security."

"Is she talking?"

"I don't know. That sort of information is way above my pay grade. But I hear that she thinks we'll trade her to the Russians, so she's probably keeping her mouth shut for now."

"You think that's likely to happen? A trade?"

"No way. Not with what she's done."

"I hope you're right," Lisa said. "But it seems like there are some folks in DC who will forgive the Russians almost anything."

"I think that changed when President Bilton was elected."

"How are things out there?"

Jon knew she was referring to the cyberwarfare campaign. "Better. The tide seems to be turning. Power's back for most of the East Coast. And we're striking back at Russia. Moscow and Saint Petersburg are in the dark right now. President Bilton has cut off the Russians' ability to do international banking transfers, which has thrown their economy into turmoil. We've also released copies of President Vasiliev's Swiss banking records, which show how he's been plundering state funds. His opposition is having a field day."

"What about the chemical attack? The water filtration plants."

"The government has issued an all clear to the public."

Lisa had been leaning forward a bit for the conversation, but now she collapsed back into her pillows. Maybe it was the pain meds, but the world seemed to be returning to some semblance of order.

"Look, you've said enough," Jon said. "You should rest. Don't want you telling me something you learned at CyberCom that I'm not supposed to know."

"Okay."

He reached over and touched her arm. This was the point where the boyfriend was supposed to say "Love you" or some other such endearment, but Jon didn't do that.

Maybe it was the shock of a near-death experience, maybe it was seeing Jon after some time apart, or maybe it was just the glorious IV drip, but she felt acute and empathic. Gazing at Jon through her half-mast eyelids, Lisa suddenly felt that she knew exactly how he saw her.

Jon cared for her, but even he wasn't sure if he loved her. Some varieties of love struck like the proverbial lightning bolt, but a different sort of love accrued slowly and quietly over time like a snowfall, deepening with each shared experience and memory. If Jon was going to love her, it would be that latter kind of love.

Over the past few months, he had seen what life with Lisa was going to be like, and it was not for the faint of heart.

As she had so often told him, her depression was not something that was going to be cured or medicated into submission. It was a blue flame that flickered around her constantly at a low level like the burner of a stove that was barely on. And sometimes that flame flared and consumed her.

But that wasn't all that she was. Lisa's true nature was expressed as a duality. She was ultracompetent, and she was helpless. She was loving, and she was hurtful. She was at home in the world, and an alien. Lisa needed someone who was willing to see and accept all of her, even the parts that neither of them liked.

She wanted someone whose love was unconditional, but it took time to build that sort of relationship. Who would make that leap with her when they figured out who she was and what she would put them through?

She was a lot. And she knew that.

In the cool, tender gaze that Jon was focusing on her, thinking that she was half-asleep, Lisa believed she could read his thoughts like they were scrolling on a teleprompter. She could see that he was struggling to understand her, weighing whether she was worth it. There were probably a number of people that he would encounter in his life that he would be capable of loving. Sure, the heart wants what it wants, but people also make choices.

Jon could see that a life with Lisa would involve stratospheric highs and subterranean lows. You hoped that the balance would be at least fifty fifty, but it could skew much lower.

There would be vacations that would go south, with Lisa ordering room service martinis and unable to leave the room.

There would be times when she would embarrass him, and he would have to steady her as they did one of those tandem potato-sack-race walks out of the dining room, or the hotel lobby, or the bar.

There would be days when he'd wonder if she was jeopardizing her career, and whether he was jeopardizing his own by staying home from work to try to help her.

There would be times when he'd wonder if he should report the full extent of her condition to their boss. Because if Jon failed to report it, he feared that she might endanger herself in the field, get herself killed. Or get someone else killed who didn't deserve it. And, though she gave him credit for making his job the lesser consideration, he'd always worry that not reporting Lisa's condition could get him dropped from the bureau.

She had argued with Jon about her drinking countless times, and she had always defended her outlook on the situation with logic, anger, manipulation, and all the considerable rhetorical tools at her disposal. But in this drug-hazy moment of extreme empathy, she saw Jon's perspective with complete and horrifying clarity.

Lisa closed her eyes.

He didn't know it yet, but she was letting him go.

But she was going to adopt the dog.

52

The next time Lisa awoke, General Holsapple was standing beside her hospital bed.

"How are you feeling?"

She grimaced. "How does it look like I'm feeling?"

"We all owe you a big debt. If not for you, we might not be turning the corner in this conflict."

"Thank you."

"Even President Bilton has mentioned you by name on several occasions. She is very aware of what you've done."

Lisa clicked the button on the railing of her bed and elevated herself with a whir so that she could look Holsapple in the eye.

"Thanks, but I've got a feeling you didn't come here to deliver get-well wishes."

"Yes. NatalyaX is still here in the hospital, recovering."

"I heard."

"We'd like you to visit her, see if she'll say something to you that she wouldn't say to anyone else."

"So she's not talking?"

"No, she still thinks that Russia will make a trade for her, particularly if they think she hasn't told us everything."

"And will they?"

"The Russians might be willing, but we won't do it. She's killed too many of our people, been too instrumental in their attacks. We'll trade other operatives with them, but not her."

"If you can't make her see that, I don't know how I can. What happens if she doesn't cooperate?"

"Then we'll probably be transporting her from here to a black site. But we'd rather not go that route—the results tend to be more reliable if they cooperate willingly."

"Why choose me for this assignment?"

"Frankly, we've tried nearly everything else. And you two seem to have some sort of—affinity."

"That's not the term I would use. But okay. Sure."

———

Lisa still felt woozy as she was helped into a wheelchair by Alan Yang, a young NSA agent wearing a stem microphone headset. As he wheeled her out, the hospital corridor seemed vertiginously long.

"Who have you got on that headset?" Lisa asked.

"Holsapple, and a bunch of top officers from CyberCom and NSA."

"And where are they?"

"They're set up near NatalyaX's room. Just down the hall."

Agent Yang rolled her through a few corridors and up in an elevator into another wing, until they finally came to a stop in front of a patient room with two armed agents in dark suits parked outside on folding chairs. The guards and her escort exchanged nods.

"Let me check," Yang said to whoever was on the other end of the headset, removing the recorder from the pocket of Lisa's gown to make sure the green light was on and the volume was adjusted properly.

Once the recorder was back in her pocket, he asked, "How's that?"

After a pause, he added, "Okay, I guess we're good to go."

The NSA agent handed over Lisa's wheelchair to a nurse in light-blue scrubs, who rolled her into NatalyaX's room.

"Good luck, Special Agent Tanchik," Yang said as he walked away, probably to join the team that would be listening to her conversation.

The nurse rolled her into the room, where NatalyaX was sitting up in bed, eating vanilla ice cream from a cardboard cup with a flat wooden spoon. She was hooked to an IV but seemed much improved.

The nurse placed her chair beside NatalyaX's bed and then left the room. She was about to close the door behind her, but one of the armed agents reached out an arm to stop her.

"Please leave the door open," he said.

When she saw Lisa, NatalyaX smiled and swallowed a big spoonful of ice cream. Then she touched her finger to the middle of her forehead.

"Ouch. Brain freeze." She raised a hand to pause the conversation, then stared off into space for a moment with her brow furrowed. "You ever had one of those?" she asked.

"Yeah, I hate that. But not as much as getting shot."

NatalyaX nodded and shrugged. "So," she said. "It's good to see you looking so well."

"That's kinda funny coming from someone who just a couple of days ago tried to strangle me."

"That was just business. I hope we can move past it. How's your depression?"

"I'm managing," Lisa said.

"I have to admit I don't understand why you can't just suck it up."

"That's really not how depression works."

"I'm a little envious of you, you know. No matter how complicated and difficult you think your life has been, it's nothing compared to mine."

"You were forced to become a sleeper agent, weren't you?"

"No, I chose it," NatalyaX said. "But it was the only choice I had. If I'd had your life—your simple, uncomplicated American life—I wouldn't have screwed it up."

"Now I'm kinda sorry that I confided in you as Helen. She seemed a lot more empathetic."

"She was good company, wasn't she? That was me, you know. Or a part of me."

"Yeah, the part that's not a sociopath."

NatalyaX pursed her lips and shook her head. "You're a depressive. I'm a sociopath. We're a couple of suitable cases for treatment, aren't we?"

"Fair enough, Natalya. Do you mind me calling you Natalya?"

"Not at all. It was the name I chose." She cleared her throat. "I assume that you're recording this conversation."

Lisa lifted the recorder from the pocket of her gown. "Official visit."

"Of course. Everyone here wants me to talk."

"Yes."

"What would you like to talk about? Clothes? Boys? Malware?"

"Maybe that last one. I'd like to know about your relationship with the GRU."

"And your bosses thought that I would tell you something that I wouldn't tell them?"

"That was the thinking, yes."

"And did you think that was going to work?"

"I wasn't particularly optimistic, no. But I'm a team player."

"Me too, Lisa. Me too. And my team wouldn't want me talking to your team."

"We're not going to trade you to the Russians for one of our agents. That's what they're telling me, and I believe them. Not after what you've done."

Irritated, Natalya pushed away her largely uneaten tray of hospital food. "What, you think that there was some line that I crossed?"

Natalya said. "But you just don't get it, do you? Maybe it's because you're law enforcement, not clandestine services."

"What is it that I don't get?"

"There *are* no lines. Your people kill our people. You hack us; we hack back. All the time. It's a war that is waged every day now. And it's never, ever going to end."

"I think even you would agree that what your country did was at another level. Hundreds of innocent citizens died, and it would have been thousands, or hundreds of thousands, if we hadn't stopped you."

"Sometimes in war you have to strike preemptively. I think your people call it 'defending forward.' That's what your bosses did when they hit Iran's nuclear centrifuges. When things escalated in Syria, they took similar measures against Russia."

"I know I probably can't convince you of this, but the two sides are not morally equivalent here. This country still stands for something. Something good."

"You still say that after everything that's happened here in the past few years?"

Lisa nodded. "I'll admit that I have questioned some things lately that I never thought I'd be questioning. But yes. Still."

Natalya shrugged. "Okay. Agree to disagree, I guess."

"Have you heard of the term *spent bullet*?" Lisa asked.

"No."

"It's a term that the SVR applies to a low-grade hired assassin that they pay to murder a so-called enemy of the state. Often they're not even trained professionals, just regular citizens who get paid with a new car or some other cheap inducement in exchange for a hit. And when they have performed their mission and land in prison, the Russian government just leaves them to rot."

"And you think that's what I am?" Natalya asked. "A spent bullet?"

"What do you think?"

Outside in the hallway, a plastic tray clattered loudly to the tile floor.

Then the sound was repeated.

Natalya and Lisa both turned to look. The back and right arm of one of the agents guarding Natalya was visible in the doorframe. The agent was slumped against the wall, and he wasn't reaching to pick up the fallen tray. The room was quiet except for the faint sound of a monitor from across the hall, which was insistently plinking a single note like a minimalist horror movie score.

The fingers of the agent's right hand began twitching violently.

Lisa felt a rising panic.

She turned to Natalya, who was also observing the agent.

"I recognize those symptoms," Natalya said.

"Novichok?"

She smiled. "Novichok. They're coming to get me out of here."

Lisa felt helpless in her wheelchair. She wasn't even sure if she was capable of standing up without passing out.

She spoke quickly. She needed Natalya as an ally if she was going to stop the assassin who was coming.

She spoke quickly. "Listen, Natalya. You're not getting out of here. There are NSA, CyberCom, and FBI agents all over this floor. It's impossible."

Lisa paused to let it sink in. "They're not here to get you out. They're here to make sure you never talk."

She watched Natalya's eyes as she worked it out for herself.

Then Natalya nodded, ripping out her IV.

Lisa locked the wheels of her wheelchair so that she could brace herself on it and stand. She gasped at the sharp pain in her shoulder where the stitches were. Lisa took a few unsteady steps to the tiny bathroom that was to the left of the door. She shoved her wheelchair forward so that it blocked the narrow entranceway to the room, and locked the wheels. Lisa entered the bathroom that was to the left of the door to the hallway.

In the bathroom, she threw open the toiletry cabinet above the sink, looking for a weapon, but there was only a tube of toothpaste and a toothbrush. Nothing useful.

She picked up the ceramic top of the toilet tank, causing another bolt of pain to shoot through her shoulder and up her spine. She smashed the ceramic into the bathroom mirror, sending shards into the sink.

She used a washcloth to grip a large jagged fragment of mirror.

A male nurse appeared in the doorway to the room. "Everyone okay in here?" he asked. "We have an emergency situation, and we need to get you out of here right now."

At first, Lisa wasn't certain about the man. He was tall with longish brown hair and black glasses, and his look of concern seemed genuine. Lisa could see him, but the man hadn't yet noticed Lisa as she crouched inside the bathroom.

But then he saw NatalyaX in bed and smiled—a smile intended to reassure, to make her feel safe. It was a smile that would never appear on the face of a nurse who was standing next to two federal agents who were dying horribly from exposure to a nerve agent.

Lisa gripped the mirror shard more tightly, so tightly that the part that wasn't covered by the washcloth sliced her palm.

And when the nurse, standing in front of the bathroom door, drew his silencer-equipped pistol and aimed it at NatalyaX, she struck.

She slashed at the assassin, making a deep and bloody cut on the bare arm that was holding the gun.

The man cried out and tried to retreat, but Lisa had dropped her weapon and now used both hands to grip his arm.

For what seemed like a very long time, she and the man engaged in an awkward tug-of-war. She used all her strength to pull him forward into the room, bending him over the backrest of the wheelchair, slamming his hand into its armrests, trying to get him to release the pistol.

A couple of shots fired wildly, one into the floor and another into the room.

Lisa heard something that sounded like shattering glass coming from the direction of Natalya's bed.

The man was starting to win the struggle. He was too strong, Lisa was too injured, and her leverage was poor. He had nearly gotten his arm free so that he could take proper aim at them.

Just before he could pull away, Natalya joined the fray, a white blur of hospital gown.

Lisa heard two hard, moist smacks, and then the assassin's resistance lessened. She was able to pull him forward over the back of the wheelchair.

Then his grip on the gun loosened, and it clattered to the floor.

Lisa drew back for a moment and could now see what had happened. Natalya was standing in front of her, holding a broken water glass by its base. The top of the glass had been shattered and turned into a jagged weapon, which was now smeared with blood.

Natalya's hospital gown was covered in bright-red arterial spray, which was still spurting from the assassin's neck.

Natalya shoved the man so that he fell backward into the corridor, and then she sat down in the wheelchair, looking pale and weak.

Lisa heard cries in the hallway as quick footsteps approached to aid the two poisoned agents and the dying assassin.

Lisa and Natalya just stared silently at each other for a long moment, both recovering their breath, coming down from the spike of fear and adrenaline.

Finally, Lisa asked, "Maybe you'd like to have that talk now?"

Natalya nodded as they heard the sound of federal agents swarming the hallway. She wiped a droplet of blood from her cheek with a thumb, then examined it. "You know, Lisa, I am starting to feel a bit chatty."

ACKNOWLEDGMENTS

My heartfelt thanks and appreciation to the people listed below, who helped shepherd this book into print. I have thanked most of these people on previous occasions because they've been supporting and assisting me, each in his or her own uniquely stellar way, for quite a few years. Therefore, another listing on the book's acknowledgments page seems somehow inadequate. So please imagine that I am shouting out the names of this all-star team over a stadium sound system as they emerge from the tunnel to cheers and high fives, their faces ten feet tall on the jumbotron:

- David Hale Smith, my friend and the überest of agents.
- My excellent and simpatico editor Megha Parekh, who is a joy to work with.
- My developmental editor, Caitlin Alexander, who is relentless in the best possible way and made this book better line by line.
- The entire team at Thomas & Mercer and Amazon Publishing, especially Grace Doyle, Sarah Shaw, Brittany Russell, and Laura Barrett. I'm enormously grateful for T&M's support for my writing over the course of four books (with number five on the way). I couldn't imagine a more book-loving, forward-thinking, author-friendly place to be.

- Sarah Burningham and Claire McLaughlin of Little Bird Publicity, who rang the bell, banged the gong, and showed me that there was a thing called #bookstagram.
- Erin Mitchell, who is the best advocate that any book can have.
- My wife, Kathy, who makes everything possible, every day of my life.

I also owe a debt to several books and articles on cyberwarfare, most notably *The Perfect Weapon: War, Sabotage, and Fear in the Cyber Age*, by David E. Sanger, and *Dark Territory: The Secret History of Cyber War*, by Fred Kaplan.

ABOUT THE AUTHOR

Photo © by Elisa Cicinelli

Reece Hirsch is the author of six thrillers that draw upon his background as a privacy attorney. His first book, *The Insider*, was a finalist for the International Thriller Writers Award for Best First Novel. His other works include *Black Nowhere*, the first book featuring FBI special agent Lisa Tanchik, and three books, *The Adversary*, *Intrusion*, and *Surveillance*, featuring former Department of Justice cybercrimes prosecutor Chris Bruen. Hirsch is a partner at the San Francisco office of an international law firm and cochair of its privacy and cybersecurity practice. He is also a member of the board of directors of the Valentino Achak Deng Foundation (www.vadfoundation.org). Hirsch lives in the Bay Area with his wife. Find out more at www.reecehirsch.com.